### Jess

"[Jess'] perspective on being a girl and woman while having memories of being a man offers an understanding I'd never thought of. Really interesting book." Poolays, LibraryThing

### Gender Fraud: a fiction

"A gripping read ...." Katya, Goodreads

### Impact

"Edgy, insightful, terrific writing, propelled by rage against rape. Tittle writes in a fast-paced, dialogue-driven style that hurtles the reader from one confrontation to the next. Chock full of painful social observations ...." Hank Pellissier, Director of Humanist Global Charity

" ... The idea of pinning down the inflictors of this terror is quite appealing ...." Alison Lashinsky

### It Wasn't Enough

"Unlike far too many novels, this one will make you think, make you uncomfortable, and then make you reread it ...." C. Osborne, moonspeaker.ca

"... a powerful and introspective dystopia .... It is a book I truly recommend for a book club as the discussions could be endless ...." Mesca Elin, Goodreads

"Tittle's book hits you hard ...." D. Sohi, Goodreads

"*It Wasn't Enough* punches well above its weight and straight in the gut ...." Shefali Sequeira, 4w

### Exile

"Thought-provoking stuff, as usual from Peg Tittle." James M. Fisher, Goodreads

### What Happened to Tom

"This powerful book plays with the gender gap to throw into high relief the infuriating havoc unwanted pregnancy can wreak on a woman's life. Once you've read *What Happened to Tom*, you'll never forget it." Elizabeth Greene, *Understories* and *Moving*

"I read this in one sitting, less than two hours, couldn't put it down. Fantastic allegorical examination of the gendered aspects of unwanted pregnancy. A must-read for everyone, IMO." Jessica, Goodreads

"Peg Tittle's *What Happened to Tom* takes a four-decades-old thought experiment and develops it into a philosophical novella of extraordinary depth and imagination …. Part allegory, part suspense (perhaps horror) novel, part defense of bodily autonomy rights (especially women's), Tittle's book will give philosophers and the philosophically minded much to discuss." Ron Cooper, *Hume's Fork*

## *Just Think about It!*

"An excellent collection of thought-provoking essays and short pieces. *Just Think about It!* (2nd edn) covers an amazingly wide range of topics that really made me think …." Karen Siddall, Amazon

## *Sexist Shit that Pisses Me Off*

"Woh. This book is freaking awesome and I demand a sequel." Anonymous, barnesandnoble.com

"I recommend this book to both women and men. It will open your eyes to a lot of sexist—and archaic—behaviors." Seregon, Goodreads

"Honestly, selling this in today's climate is a daunting challenge—older women have grown weary, younger women don't seem to care, or at least don't really identify as feminists, men—forget that. All in all a sad state of affairs—sorry." rejection letter from agent

## *Shit that Pisses Me Off*

"I find Peg Tittle to be a passionate, stylistically-engaging writer with a sharp eye for the hypocritical aspects of our society." George, Amazon

"Peg raises provocative questions: should people need some kind of license to have children? Should the court system use professional jurors? Many of her essays address the imbalance of power between men and women; some tackle business, sports, war, and the weather. She even explains why you're not likely to see Peg Tittle at Canada's version of an Occupy Wall Street demonstration. It's all thought-provoking, and whether or not you'll end up agreeing with her conclusions, her essays make for fascinating reading." Erin O'Riordan

"This was funny and almost painfully accurate, pointing out so many things that most of us try NOT to notice, or wish we didn't. Well written and amusing, I enjoyed this book immensely." Melody Hewson

" … a pissed off kindred spirit who writes radioactive prose with a hint of sardonic wit …. Peg sets her sights on a subject with laser sharp accuracy then hurls words like missiles in her collection of 25 cogent essays on the foibles and hypocrisies of life …. Whether you agree or disagree with Peg's position on the issues, *Shit that Pisses Me Off* will stick to your brain long after you've ingested every word—no thought evacuations here. Her writing is adept and titillating … her razor sharp words will slice and dice the cerebral jugular. If you enjoy reading smart, witty essays that challenge the intellect, download a copy …." Laura Salkin, thinkspin.com

"Not very long, but a really good read. The author is intelligent, and points out some great inconsistencies in common thinking and action …. may have been channeling some George Carlin in a few areas." Briana Blair, Goodreads

" … thought-provoking, and at times, hilarious. I particularly loved 'Bambi's cousin is going to tear you apart.' Definitely worth a read!" Nichole, Goodreads

"What she said!!! Pisses me off also! Funny, enjoyable and so right on!!!! Highly recommended." Vic, indigo.ca

## *Critical Thinking: An Appeal to Reason*

"This book is worth its weight in gold." Daniel Millsap

"One of the books everyone should read. A lot of practical examples, clear and detailed sections, and tons of all kinds of logical fallacies analyzed under microscope that will give you a completely different way of looking to the everyday manipulations and will help you to avoid falling into the common traps. Highly recommended!" Alexander Antukh

"One of the best CT books I've read." G. Baruch, Goodreads

"This is an excellent critical thinking text written by a clever and creative critical thinker. Her anthology *What If* is excellent too: the short readings are perfect for engaging philosophical issues in and out of the classroom." Ernst Borgnorg

"Peg Tittle's *Critical Thinking* is a welcome addition to a crowded field. Her presentations of the material are engaging, often presented in a conversational discussion with the reader or student. The text's coverage of the material is wide-ranging. Newspaper items, snippets from *The Far Side*, personal anecdotes, emerging social and political debates, as well as LSAT sample questions are among the many tools Tittle employs to educate students on the elemental aspects of logic and critical thinking." Alexander E. Hooke, Professor of Philosophy, Stevenson University

## *What If?... Collected Thought Experiments in Philosophy*

"Of all the collections of philosophical thought experiments I've read, this is by far the best. It is accessible, uses text from primary sources, and is very well edited. The final entry in the book— which I won't spoil for you—was an instant favorite of mine." Dominick Cancilla

"This is a really neat little book. It would be great to use in discussion-based philosophy courses, since the readings would be nice and short and to the point. This would probably work much better than the standard anthology of readings that are, for most students, incomprehensible." Nathan Nobis, Morehouse College

## *Should Parents be Licensed? Debating the Issues*

"This book has some provocative articles and asks some very uncomfortable questions ...." Jasmine Guha, Amazon

"This book was a great collection of essays from several viewpoints on the topic and gave me a lot of profound over-the-(TV-)dinner-(tray-)table conversations with my husband." Lauren Cocilova, Goodreads

"You need a licence to drive a car, own a gun, or fish for trout. You don't need a licence to raise a child. But maybe you should ... [This book] contains about two dozen essays by various experts, including psychologists, lawyers and sociologists ...." Ian Gillespie, *London Free Press*

"... But the reformers are right. Completely. Ethically. I agree with Joseph Fletcher, who notes, "It is depressing ... to realize that most people are accidents," and with George Schedler, who states, "Society has a duty to ensure that infants are born free of avoidable defects. ... Traditionalists regard pregnancy and parenting as a natural right that should never be curtailed. But what's the result of this laissez-faire attitude? Catastrophic suffering. Millions of children born disadvantaged, crippled in childhood, destroyed in adolescence. Procreation cannot be classified as a self-indulgent privilege—it needs to be viewed as a life-and-death responsibility ...." Abhimanyu Singh Rajput, Social Tikka

## *Ethical Issues in Business: Inquiries, Cases, and Readings*

"*Ethical Issues in Business* is clear and user-friendly yet still rigorous through-out. It offers excellent coverage of basic ethical theory, critical thinking, and many contemporary issues such as whistleblowing, corporate social responsibility, and climate change. Tittle's approach is not to tell students what to think but rather to get them to think—and to give them the tools to do so. This is the text I would pick for a business ethics course." Kent Peacock, University of Lethbridge

"This text breathes fresh air into the study of business ethics; Tittle's breezy, use-friendly style puts the lie to the impression that a business ethics text has to be boring." Paul Viminitz, University of Lethbridge

"A superb introduction to ethics in business." Steve Deery, *The Philosophers' Magazine*

"Peg Tittle wants to make business students think about ethics. So she has published an extraordinarily useful book that teaches people to question and analyze key concepts .... Take profit, for example .... She also analyzes whistleblowing, advertising, product safety, employee rights, discrimination, management and union matters, business and the environment, the medical business, and ethical investing ...." Ellen Roseman, *The Toronto Star*

more at
pegtittle.com

◆

# Writing as Jass Richards

### *The ReGender App*

"This book is brilliant. ... The scene at the airport had me laughing out loud. ...." Katya, Goodreads

"A book I really recommend to any book club and to people who are interested in gender differences and gender discrimination." Mesca Elin, Psychromatic Redemption

### *License to Do That*

"I'm very much intrigued by the issues raised in this narrative. I also enjoy the author's voice, which is unapologetically combative but also funny and engaging." A.S.

"I love Froot Loup! You make me laugh out loud all the time!" Celeste M.

"A thought-provoking premise and a wonderful cast of characters." rejection letter from publisher

### The Blasphemy Tour

"With plenty of humor and things to think about throughout, *The Blasphemy Tour* is a choice pick …." *Midwest Book Review*

"Jass Richards has done it again. As I tell anyone who wants to listen, Jass is a comedy genius, she writes the funniest books and always writes the most believable unbelievable characters and scenes. … I knew this book was a winner when … a K9 unit dog kind of eats their special brownies … and dances Thriller. … Rev and Dylan are not your ordinary guy and girl protagonists with sexual tension and a romantic interest, at all. They both defy gender roles, and they are so smart and opinionated, it's both funny and made me think at the same time. … They tour around the USA, in their lime green bus that says 'There are no gods. Deal with it.' Overall, I highly recommend anything by Jass, especially this one book, which is full of comedy gold and food for thought." May Arend, Brazilian Book Worm

"If I were Siskel and Ebert I would give this book Two Thumbs Way Up. … Yes, it is blasphemy toward organized religion but it gives you tons of Bible verses to back up its premises. And besides, it's pure entertainment. There's a prequel which I recommend you read first. *The Road Trip Dialogues*. … I only hope there will be a third book." L.K. Killian

### The Road Trip Dialogues

"I am impressed by the range from stoned silliness to philosophical perspicuity, and I love your comic rhythm." L. S.

"This is engaging, warm, funny work, and I enjoyed what I read. …" rejection letter from publisher

"Just thought I'd let you know I'm on the Fish'n'Chips scene and laughing my ass off." Ellie Burmeister

"These two need stable jobs. Oh wait, no. Then we wouldn't get any more road trips. Fantastic book which expands the mind in a laid back sort of way. Highly recommended." lindainalabama

### Dogs Just Wanna Have Fun

"Funny and entertaining! I looked forward to picking up this book at the end of a long day." Mary Baluta

"… terrifically funny and ingeniously acerbic …." Dr. Patricia Bloom, My Magic Dog

"… laugh-out-loud funny." M.W., Librarything

## *This Will Not Look Good on My Resume*

"Ya made me snort root beer out my nose!" Moriah Jovan, *The Proviso*

"Darkly humorous." Jennifer Colt, *The Hellraiser of the Hollywood Hills*

"HYSTERICAL! … There are really no words to describe how funny this book is. … Really excellent book." Alison, Goodreads

"This book is like a roller coaster ride on a stream of consciousness. … Altogether, a funny, quirky read …." Grace Krispy, Motherlode; Book Reviews and Original Photography

"Brett has trouble holding down a job. Mainly because she's an outspoken misanthrope who is prone to turn a dead-end job into a social engineering experiment. Sometimes with comically disastrous results, sometimes with comically successful results. (Like pairing up a compulsive shopper with a kleptomaniac for an outing at the mall.) I don't agree with everything she says, but I will defend her right to say it — because she's hilarious!

"My favorite part was when she taught a high school girls' sex ed class that 70% of boys will lie to get sex, 80% won't use a condom, yet 90% are pro-life. She was reprimanded, of course. I think she should have gotten a medal.

"You will likely be offended at one point or another, but if you are secure enough to laugh at your own sacred cows instead of just everyone else's, this is a must read." weikelm, Librarything

"Wonderful read, funny, sarcastic. Loved it!" Charlie, Smashwords

"I just loved this book. It was a quick read, and left me in stitches. …" Robin McCoy-Ramirez

"First, let me just say I was glad I was not drinking anything while reading this. I refrained from that. My husband said he never heard me laugh so much from reading a book. At one point, I was literally in tears. Jass Richards is brilliant with the snappy comebacks and the unending fountain of information she can spout forth. … The quick wit, the sharp tongue, the acid words and sarcasm that literally oozes from her pores … beautiful." M. Snow, My Chaotic Ramblings

## *A Philosopher, a Psychologist, and an Extraterrestrial Walk into a Chocolate Bar*

"Jass Richards is back with another great book that entertains and informs as she mixes feminism, critical thinking, and current social issues with humour .... The wedding intervention was hilarious. ..." James M. Fisher, *The Miramichi Reader*

"I found myself caught between wanting to sit and read [*A Philosopher, a Psychologist, and an Extraterrestrial Walk into a Chocolate Bar*] all in one go and wanting to spread it out. I haven't laughed that hard and gotten to spend time with such unflinchingly tough ideas at the same time. ... [And] the brilliance of the Alices! ... I can now pull out your book every time somebody tries to claim that novels can't have meaningful footnotes and references. [Thanks too] for pointing me to the brilliant essay series 'Dudes are Doomed.' I am eagerly watching for *The ReGender App* ...." C. Osborne

## *TurboJetslams: Proof #29 of the Non-Existence of God*

"Extraordinarily well written with wit, wisdom, and laugh-out-loud ironic recognition, *TurboJetslams: Proof #29 of the Non-Existence of God* is a highly entertaining and a riveting read that will linger on in the mind and memory long after the little book itself has been finished and set back upon the shelf (or shoved into the hands of friends with an insistence that they drop everything else and read it!). Highly recommended for community library collections, it should be noted for personal reading lists." *Midwest Book Review*

"We all very much enjoyed it—it's funny and angry and heartfelt and told truly ...." McSweeney's

"If you're looking for a reading snack that has zero saccharine but is loaded with just the right combination of snark, sarcasm, and humor, you've found it." Ricki Wilson, Amazon

"What Richards has done is brilliant. At first, I began getting irritated as I read about a familiar character, or a familiar scenario from our time living on the lake. Then, as the main character amps up her game, I see the thrill in the planning and the retribution she undertakes for pay back." mymuskoka.blog spot.ca/2016/07/book-review-turbojetslams.html

## *Substitute Teacher from Hell*

"I enjoyed reading "Supply Teacher from Hell" immensely and found myself bursting out laughing many, many times. It is extremely well-written, clever, and very intelligent in its observations." Iris Turcott, dramaturge

more at
jassrichards.com

◆

# Writing as chris wind

### *This is what happens*

"An interesting mix of a memoir and a philosophical work, together with some amazing poetry. … *This is what happens* won't only be the book of the year for me, but it ranks high, top 5 on the best books ever read." Mesca Elin, mescalime.wordpress.com

"*This is what happens* relates how women are hamstrung by patriarchy … the sexism both insidious and glaring that profoundly shaped Kris's life from its beginnings … An incisive reflection on how social forces constrain women's lives. … Great for fans of Sylvia Plath, Doris Lessing's *The Golden Notebook*." *Booklife*

### *Thus Saith Eve*

"Short, but definitely entertaining … and serious between the lines." Lee Harmon, A Dubious Disciple Book Review

" … a truly wonderful source of feminist fiction. In addition to being an extremely enjoyable and thought-provoking read, the monologues can also be used for audition and performance pieces." Katie M. Deaver, feminism-andreligion.com

### *Snow White Gets Her Say*

"Why isn't anyone doing this on stage? … What a great night of theater that would be!" szferris, Librarything

"I loved the sassy voices in these stories, and the humor, even when making hard points." PJ O'Brien, Smashwords

## Deare Sister

"You are clearly a writer of considerable talent, and your special ability to give expression to so many different characters, each in a uniquely appropriate style, makes your work fascinating and attractive. ... The pieces are often funny, sometimes sensitive, always creative. But they contain an enormous load of anger, and that is where I have problems. ... I know at least one feminist who would read your manuscript with delight (unfortunately she is not a publisher), who would roar with laughter in her sharing of your anger. ..." rejection letter from Black Moss Press

## Particivision and other stories

"... your writing is very accomplished. ... *Particivision and other stories* is authentic, well-written, and certainly publishable ...." rejection letter from Turnstone Press

"... engaging and clever ...." rejection letter from Lester & Orpen Dennys, Publishers

"As the title indicates, this collection of stories is about getting into the thick of things, taking sides, taking action, and speaking out loud and clear, however unpopular your opinion may be. ... refreshingly out of the ordinary." Joan McGrath, *Canadian Book Review Annual*

## dreaming of kaleidoscopes

"... a top pick of poetry and is very much worth considering. ..." *Midwest Book Review*

## Soliloquies: the lady doth indeed protest

"... not only dynamic, imaginative verse writing, but extremely intelligent and intuitive insight. ... I know many actresses who would love to get their hands on this material!" Joanne Zipay, Judith Shakespeare Company, NYC

"'Ophelia' is something of an oddity ... I found it curiously attractive." *Dinosaur*

## UnMythed

"... A welcome relief from the usual male emphasis in this area. There is anger and truth here, not to mention courage." Eric Folsom, *Next Exit*

"… With considerable skill and much care, chris wind has extrapolated truths from mythical scenarios and reordered them in modern terms. … Wind handles these myths with and intellect. Her voice suggests that the relationship between the consciousness of the myth-makers and modern consciousness is closer than we would think." Linda Manning, *Quarry*

"Personally, I would not publish this stuff. This is not to say it isn't publishable—it's almost flawless stylistically, perfect form and content, etc., etc. It's perverse: satirical, biting, caustic, funny. Also cruel, beyond bitter, single-minded with a terminally limited point of view, and this individual may have read Edith Hamilton's Mythology but she/he certainly doesn't perceive the essential meanings of these myths. Or maybe does and deliberately twists the meaning to suit the poem. Likewise, in the etymological sense. Editorial revisions suggested? None, it's perfect. Market potential/readership targets: Everyone—this is actually marketable—you could sell fill Harbourfront reading this probably. General comments: You could actually make money on this stuff." anonymous reader report for a press that rejected the ms

## Paintings and Sculptures

"You know that feeling—when you read the first page and you know you're going to like the book? That happened when I read the first poem. … I loved 'Mona' and I could picture the scene; it might have happened that way, we'll never know …." Mesca Elin, barnesandnoble.com

## Satellites Out of Orbit

"*Satellites Out of Orbit* is an excellent and much recommended pick for unique fiction collections." Michael Dunford, *Midwest Book Review*

"… I also love the idea of telling the story from the woman's perspective, especially when the woman is only mentioned in passing in the official story, or not mentioned at all. …" Shana, Tales of Minor Interest

"Our editorial board loved it. Our readers said it was the most feminist thing they've read in a long time." rejection letter from publisher

## As I the Shards Examine / Not Such Stuff

"*Not Such Stuff* challenges us to rethink some of our responses to Shakespeare's plays and opens up new ways of experiencing them. …" Jeff, secondat.blogspot.com

"This world premiere collection of monologs derive from eight female Shakespearian characters speaking from their hearts, describing aspects of their lives with a modern feminist sensibility. Deconstructing the traditional interpretations of some of the most fiercely fascinating female characters of all time, the playwright is able to "have at it" and the characters finally have their say. And oh, what tales they have to weave. ..." Debbie Jackson, dctheatrescene.com

## Let Me Entertain You

"I found 'Let Me Entertain You' very powerful and visually theatrical." Ines Buchli

"I will never forget 'Let Me Entertain You.' It was brilliant." Kate Hurman

## ProVocative

"Timely, thought-provoking, dark, and funny!" Kevin Holm-Hudson, WEFT

"... a great job making a point while being entertaining and interesting. ... Overall this is a fine work, and worth listening to." Kevin Slick, *gajoob*

## The Art of Juxtaposition

"A cross between poetry, performance art, and gripping, theatrical sound collages. ... One of the most powerful pieces on the tape is 'Let Me Entertain You.' I sat stunned while listening to this composition." Myke Dyer, *Nerve*

"We found [this to be] unique, brilliant, and definitely not 'Canadian'. ... We were more than impressed with the material. *The Art of Juxtaposition* is filling one of the emptier spaces in the music world with creative and intelligent music-art." rejection letter from a record company

"Controversial feminist content. You will not be unmoved." Bret Hart, *Option*

"I've just had a disturbing experience: I listened to *The Art of Juxtaposition*. Now wait a minute; Canadian musicians are not supposed to be politically aware or delve into questions regarding sexual relationships, religion, and/or sex, racism, rape. They are supposed to write nice songs that people can tap their feet to and mindlessly inebriate themselves to. You expect me to play this on my show?" Travis B., CITR

"Wind mixes biting commentary, poignant insight and dark humor while unflinchingly tackling themes such as rape, marriage (as slavery), christianity, censorship, homosexuality, the state of native Americans, and other themes, leaving no doubt about her own strong convictions upon each of these subjects. Her technique is often one in which two or more sides to each theme are juxtaposed against one another (hence, the tape's title). This is much like her *Christmas Album* with a voice just as direct and pointed. Highly recommended." Bryan Baker *gajoob*

"Thanks for *The Art of Juxtaposition* ... it really is quite a gem! Last Xmas season, after we aired 'Ave Maria' a listener stopped driving his car and phoned us from a pay phone to inquire and express delight." John Aho, CJAM

"Liked *The Art of Juxtaposition* a lot, especially the feminist critiques of the bible. I had calls from listeners both times I played 'Ave Maria.'" Bill Hsu, WEFT

"Every time I play *The Art of Juxtaposition* (several times by this point), someone calls to ask about it/you." Mars Bell, WCSB

"The work is stimulating, well-constructed, and politically apt with regard to sexual politics. (I was particularly impressed by 'I am Eve.')" Andreas Brecht Ua'Siaghail, CKCU

"We have found *The Art of Juxtaposition* to be quite imaginative and effective. When I first played it, I did not have time to listen to it before I had to be on air. When I aired it, I was transfixed by the power of it. When I had to go on mike afterward, I found I could hardly speak! To say the least, I found your work quite a refreshing change from all the fluff of commercial musicians who whine about lost love etc. Your work is intuitive, sensitive, and significant!" Erika Schengili, CFRC

"Interesting stuff here! Actually this has very little music, but it has sound bits and spoken work. Self-declared 'collage pieces of social commentary'. ...very thought-provoking and inspiring." *No Sanctuary*

more at
chriswind.net
and
chriswind.com

# Also by Peg Tittle

### fiction

*Jess*
*Gender Fraud: a fiction*
*Impact*
*It Wasn't Enough*
*Exile*
*What Happened to Tom*

### screenplays

*Exile*
*What Happened to Tom*
*Foreseeable*
*Aiding the Enemy*
*Bang Bang*

### stageplays

*Impact*
*What Happened to Tom*
*Foreseeable*
*Aiding the Enemy*
*Bang Bang*

### audioplays

*Impact*

### nonfiction

*Just Think About It!*
*Sexist Shit that Pisses Me Off*
*No End to the Shit that Pisses Me Off*
*Still More Shit that Pisses Me Off*
*More Shit that Pisses Me Off*
*Shit that Pisses Me Off*

*Critical Thinking: An Appeal to Reason*
*What If? Collected Thought Experiments in Philosophy*
*Should Parents be Licensed? (editor)*
*Ethical Issues in Business: Inquiries, Cases, and Readings*
*Philosophy: Questions and Theories (contributing author)*

# Writing as Jass Richards

## fiction

(the Rev and Dylan series)
*The ReGender App*
*License to Do That*
*The Blasphemy Tour*
*The Road Trip Dialogues*

(the Brett series)
*Dogs Just Wanna Have Fun*
*This Will Not Look Good on My Resume*

*A Philosopher, a Psychologist, and an Extraterrestrial
Walk into a Chocolate Bar*

*CottageEscape.com: Satan Takes Over* (forthcoming)
*TurboJetslams: Proof #29 of the Non-Existence of God*

## stageplays

*Substitute Teacher from Hell*

## screenplays

*Two Women, Road Trip, Extraterrestrial*

## performance pieces

*Balls*

## nonfiction

*Jane Smith's Translation Dictionary*
*Too Stupid to Visit*

# Writing as chris wind

**prose**

*This is what happens*
*Thus Saith Eve*
*Snow White Gets Her Say*
*Deare Sister*
*Particivision and other stories*

**poetry**

*dreaming of kaleidoscopes*
*Soliloquies: the lady doth indeed protest*
*UnMythed*
*Paintings and Sculptures*

**mixed genre**

*Satellites Out of Orbit*
*Excerpts*

**stageplays**

*As I the Shards Examine / Not Such Stuff*
*The Ladies' Auxiliary*
*Snow White Gets Her Say*
*The Dialogue*
*Amelia's Nocturne*

**performance pieces**

*I am Eve*
*Let Me Entertain You*

**audio work**

*ProVocative*
*The Art of Juxtaposition*

# FIGHTING WORDS

notes for a future
we won't have

PEG TITTLE

Magenta

Fighting Words
notes for a future we won't have
© 2022 Peg Tittle

pegtittle.com

978-1-990083-00-6 (paperback)
978-1-990083-01-3 (epub)
978-1-990083-02-0 (pdf)

Published by Magenta



Cover design by Peg Tittle
Image by Gerd Altmann from Pixabay
Formatting and interior book design by Elizabeth Beeton

**Library and Archives Canada Cataloguing in Publication**

Title: Fighting words : notes for a future we won't have / Peg Tittle.
Names: Tittle, Peg, 1957- author.
Description: Short stories.
Identifiers: Canadiana (print) 2022022966X | Canadiana (ebook) 20220229724 |
– ISBN 9781990083006 (softcover) | ISBN 9781990083013 (EPUB) |
– ISBN 9781990083020 (PDF)
Classification: LCC PS8639.I76 F54 2022 | DDC C813/.6—dc23

# Acknowledgements and Notes

"It's a Boy" was previously published on 365tomorrows.com (under the pseudonym used at submission, Peter Tittle; the story had been rejected sixteen times prior, in each case submission having been made under the name Peg Tittle)

◆

Thanks to Catharine MacKinnon for articulating this: "The *mens rea* requirement in the law of rape ... bases its determination of rape on the perspective of the accused rapist, as opposed to that of the victim" (*Women's Lives, Men's Laws*, p34). It motivated "What Sane Man".

Thanks to June Stephenson for "It's a Boy". It was totally her idea. (Read her *Men Are Not Cost-Effective*.)

Thanks to John Callahan: if it wasn't for him, I probably wouldn't've imagined the quadriplegic scene in "A PostTrans PostPandemic World". The guy was wickedly funny.

◆

Although I don't always provide a link or footnote, every reference (to facts, to blogs, to books) is real except for the reference to *Post-Mortem Report* (in "The Women's Party").

For those reading paperback, the blog item mentioned early on in "Justified" is at trustyourperceptions.wordpress.com/2013/09/01/dudesaredoomed1. Or do a search for "trustyourperceptions 'Dudes are Doomed' part one". (My mention in "Men Need Sex" of TrustYourPerceptions actually refers to the same post. Apparently, it made quite an impression on me.)

With regard to "Men Need Sex", the increase in femicide attributed to not getting sex has been documented by Laura Bates in *Men Who Hate women* (p42-44).

The quote attributed to Abigail Bray in "How We Survived" is from *Misogyny Reloaded* (p102).

Again, for those reading paperback, the archive mentioned in "The Knitting Group Solves the Problem" is *TrustYourPerceptions*, and the post quoted is at trustyourperceptions.wordpress.com/2016/05/15/semen-mens-chemical-war-against-women-part-i-male-chemical-munitions-what-semen-does-to-females. The Giglieri reference can be found at pbs.org/kued/nosafeplace/articles/rapefeat.html. Or do a search for "Rape, the Most Intimate of Crimes" by Mary Dickson. Mention of Goldberg refers to his book, *Why Men Rule: a theory of male dominance*.

The chilling photograph mentioned in "A PostTrans PostPandemic World" is at feministcurrent.com/2018/01/04/thanks-trans-activism-2017-saw-return-old-school-sexist-dismissals-women-womens-rights. Or go to Feminist Current and search for the "Thanks to Trans Activism" post (January 4, 2018). And the $250,000 fine really did happen; see www1.nyc.gov/site/cchr/law/legal-guidances-gender-identity-expression.page#3 (or do a search for "New York $250,000 fine pronoun").

# Damages

This was a mistake, she was thinking, as she approached the house. She should never have agreed to come 'home' for New Year's. She'd refused her mother's invitation twice before in the thirty-five years since she left; she should have refused this time. But, as her mother had pointed out, they were getting on. Pushing eighty, both of them.

They'd ambushed her. When she'd come out of the forest with Tassi, at the end of one of their ten-mile walks, she saw the car, pulled over to the side of the dirt road. Assuming the occupants were lost and in need of directions—so many people thought the road went all the way around the lake—she approached.

But they didn't ask for directions. They just looked at her. Oddly. Didn't say anything.

"Do I know you?" she finally asked.

As soon as the woman spoke— She'd recognize that voice anywhere. Even after what, twenty years? It was critical, it was disapproving, it was—

How had they found her? They must've stopped at the post office and inquired.

So much for the privacy of an R.R.# address.

Her kneejerk reaction had been to be polite. She invited them down to her cabin for tea. That was her first mistake.

Too late, she realized that their presence contaminated her refuge, her sanctuary.

She didn't have a living room per se, nor a kitchen or dining room. Nothing was anonymous, nothing was for guests, so they'd had to sit on *her* couch, the couch that fit her and Tassi like an old track shoe, and they'd looked out at *her* view, the view of the lake and forest that had made her buy the cabin even before she'd seen the inside. She did most of her best work sitting on that couch looking out at that view. (The rest she did while walking in the forest.)

It had been her dream-come-true, the cabin. She'd wanted a place on a lake in a forest ever since she was a kid, spending summers at the family cottage, paddling in the green canoe or just sitting on the dock, reading, thinking, composing ...

And if her parents had held on to that family cottage for her, instead of selling it before she even had her teaching degree—

Didn't they realize how much she loved it? No. When she walked them through her cabin—it had seemed the thing to do, but was another mistake—she pointed to the photograph she'd thumbtacked to one of her bookshelves, of the winding road that had led to that beautiful paradise— They hadn't recognized it.

"It wasn't winterized," her father had said when she'd found out they'd sold the cottage and had expressed her disappointment. Her anger.

Right. As if *that* was the reason they hadn't even *considered* selling it to her.

Of course in retrospect, she wouldn't've have wanted to buy it anyway. Living there would have been a constant reminder of family. Still. The point.

That visit, the ambush, had provided the last straw. The tipping point. The trigger. The *idea*.

Because they had been, still, so oblivious, so willfully deluded. Forget apology, they hadn't even reached acknowledgement. People shouldn't be allowed to be that clueless for that long. To be that blind to the consequences of their actions. Or lack thereof. Call it negligence. At the very least, reckless endangerment.

Of course they had suffered. Their youngest daughter had walked out of their lives at twenty-one. Surely that cut to the bone. To have your own child reject you so ... completely. To wonder every day 'Was she okay?' Well, to wonder for the first twenty years. At any time in the last fifteen, they could have just googled her. And discovered she was alive and well.

But, apparently, they'd never wondered, certainly never asked, 'What did we do wrong?'

At sixteen, she'd entered one of her compositions in a city-wide competition and placed second. She made the mistake of telling them. Her mother had asked how much money she'd won. Like some gold-digger measuring value only by dollars. Her father had asked where the sponsoring organization was. Like some Neanderthal needing location data to establish territorial boundaries. Neither one of them asked to hear the piece. It shouldn't have surprised her. It wasn't the first time they failed to ... care.

She'd decided then and there never to share her joy with them again. To present to them the glistening iridescent bubble of her achievement only to have it popped. Like a pimple. A cyst. An abscess.

And yet, when they'd ended the short tour of her cabin in her music studio, she found herself, forty years later, at fifty-five for godsake, proudly handing them a copy of her latest CD. She'd been such an idiot! Why did she still need their approval, their praise? Damn it!

"What's this supposed to be?" her father had sneered at the cover, a sort of holographic musical score it had taken her two days to create using various visual art and photo editing programs. He didn't even bother turning the CD over to read the list of pieces. Several nocturnes. A duet for sax and loons. Another for sax and wolves.

It hurt.

And disappointed. She'd thought he couldn't hurt her anymore. She'd thought she was past that.

And he had no idea. That he—

He handed it to her mother, who merely glanced at it then gave it back.

"No, I meant—" She changed her mind mid-sentence. They didn't deserve the gift.

She should've asked them to leave. Kicked them out right then and there.

As they had—

Well, no, they hadn't exactly kick her out. But when she'd wanted to move out in her fourth year, her mother had said 'If you leave now, you don't come back.'

She'd been stunned. She'd always been such a good girl, quiet, obedient, doing her homework without being asked, practising the piano without being asked, never needing a curfew because she never went out because she had no friends ... It wasn't until university— Well no, their relationship had started crumbling before that. At fifteen, actually, when she started thinking for herself. That was when she started asking questions, raising objections ... But even so, she had continued to do what they'd asked of her ... For another six years. Then, enough was—

She could understand that her mother was hurt by her decision to move out. She didn't have a job in Edmonton to go to, like her brother. She wasn't getting married, like her sister. Both were legitimate reasons to leave the nest. She— She just wanted to leave. To live on her own. Was that so bad? So unforgiveable? Apparently. For an unmarried daughter. God, you'd think it had been the '20s. Not the '70s.

Once the tour was over, she'd led them to her couch. It was the only option. Seemed, at the time, the only option. She herself settled onto the floor with Tassi. (Another mistake. Teenagers did that, not adults.) They told her about her brother's successful business. Her sister's husband's recent promotion. Their kids. Their kids' kids.

She didn't even pretend to be interested.

Didn't matter.

Not once did they ask her about *her* achievements.

And not once did they ask why she'd left. Why she had, essentially, divorced them. She'd explained it all in the letter she'd written, but it seemed they hadn't read it. Hadn't understood it.

No, most likely, hadn't taken it seriously.

But now? How could they *not* take it seriously? She hadn't contacted them, not once, in thirty-five years. She'd shown no desire whatsoever to be part of the family. Wasn't that why they'd tracked her down one more time before they died? To ask *why?*

Apparently not.

She had realized, all those years ago, that her parents weren't going to change. And she herself certainly wasn't going to change. Wasn't going to turn back into the good little girl she once was. So their continued relationship would have been either a façade or a constant stream of criticism and rejection.

She'd always told herself that she respected them too much to pretend; that's why she left.

But in not speaking the truth, all these years, hadn't she been lying? Perhaps.

Still, what would have been the point?

And yet, with her silence, she'd been, to use current jargon, an enabler. She was partly to blame for their cluelessness. About so many things …

When they'd finally stood up to leave, her mother asked for a hug. If you have to ask— But, she … acquiesced. That is to say, she let herself be hugged. She did not hug back. And yet her mother's eyes filled with tears of joy.

And then she'd asked her to come home for New Year's. Yes, 'home'. Where did they think they'd been for the last hour?

Of course, she was going to say 'No' again. Maybe scream it. But then she changed her mind.

Because.

✦

She slowed as she approached the house, then drove past it. This was a *big* mistake.

No. She owed them an explanation. Should they be interested.

And even if they weren't.

Perhaps especially if they weren't.

She circled the block, then came back.

The house seemed smaller than she remembered. Less imposing. Less a given.

She parked on the street. Around the corner, actually, on Lucan Street. The corner had seemed further away, back when she'd walked past Lucan to Moore to the candy store. And she doesn't remember ever just walking along Lucan, to see whatever there was to see. It just wasn't done.

There was a sidewalk now on their side of the street. As she walked toward the driveway, she remembered her brother's white-with-black-stripes Triumph Spitfire parked at the end, tucked as close as possible to the retainer wall. Later it would be a mustard yellow MGB. And then the Norton with the metallic blue gas tank. When she wanted to buy a little Yamaha, with a cherry red tank, her father had said there was no room to park it. He'd already put a row of patio stones on the strip of dirt alongside the driveway, the grass hopelessly worn away from driving their burgundy Rambler around her brother's cars to get in and out. Eventually—she can't remember why he changed his mind—he said she could park it between the garage and the retaining wall, behind the garbage cans. She had to move the garbage cans out and then back in every time she wanted to use her bike. And more than once, given the awkward and tight fit, she pinned herself against the garage or the wall, bruising herself to get out.

As she walked up the driveway, it suddenly dawned on her: how did her brother have the money to buy all those vehicles when he was still in university? She herself had barely covered her tuition and books with her part-time job. Took her three years to save up for the Yamaha. Yes, his ice-maker job weekends at the curling club probably paid more than teaching piano, but still.

The answer punched her in the gut: her parents must've lent him the money.

It would've been at about the same time they'd said that if she wanted to continue with her piano lessons, she'd have to pay for them.

Why did that surprise her?

She couldn't go around to the back door and just walk in. Not anymore. And knocking would seem even more weird. So she headed to the front door. Yes, that felt right. She was a visitor. A stranger.

Her mother opened the door before she knocked. Watching for her, no doubt. It was her big day. Prodigal daughter returns and all that. Surely it spoke ill of her all these years to have a daughter who would not speak to her. But now she was redeemed! She *was* a good mother!

Sure enough, her mother beamed as she hugged her, not sensing, or just ignoring, her stiffness.

"Let me take your coat," she said, then gave it to her father, who grudgingly disappeared up the stairs with it, probably to add it to the pile on their bed. Or maybe he'd put it in one of what now must be guest bedrooms.

The bedroom she shared with her sister, Cheryl, had been decorated in frilly pink and white. Two dressers, two closets, two twin-sized beds. A little night table between the beds. And in that night table was a little book. *Mother's Little Helper*. Each chapter was to be read only when you reached a certain age. The chapter for thirteen-year-olds was titled 'You're a Woman Now!' and it explained menstruation. At sixteen, heavy with guilt, she finally disobeyed and read the chapter for eighteen-year-olds, thinking that it would finally explain sex. But no. It just said that one day she'd find a man to love and marry and, God willing, she'd be blessed with children. That was the extent of her education about sex.

Did her mother have any idea how inadequate that was? How irresponsible that was? Not just the failure to explain how, exactly, sexual reproduction occurs, but the failure to explain, let alone endorse, how sexual pleasure occurs.

And she prided herself being a good parent. Unbelievable.

Her brother's room was in black and green. Similarly, a dresser, a closet, a bed. And a desk, in the corner. Her father had built it just for him. The C student. Oh how she'd envied that desk. Every Saturday when she had to dust his room, she'd see it. And have to crawl under it, dust rag in hand, to reach the baseboards along the wall.

Her parents' bedroom took up the other half of the upstairs, the vanity table straight ahead when you walked in, their closets in an alcove on the left, the large shared dresser on the right, the queen-sized bed, a night table on each side, and at the end of the room, a cedar chest in one corner, her mother's sewing table in the other.

"You can leave your shoes on," her mother said, as she stood just inside the front door, but was obviously relieved when she slipped them off and tucked them under the bench by the small telephone table.

She had only two vivid memories of sitting at that telephone table. The first was when she was seventeen, just finishing grade thirteen. Peter had called to ask if she'd wanted to go to a movie with him. Her first date! She was so excited she left a message proclaiming her good news on the breakfast nook table. All her mother had to say was "I wouldn't want to kiss that face."

A few months later, he was off to Vancouver to attend UBC. She'd been accepted at the local university, WLU. They'd agreed to write to each other, and they did—long letters, forty pages by the end of her fourth year, at which point she got on a train and took the three-day trip to see him. To see if what they had was love. They'd made the arrangements by phone: she'd told him her arrival time; he said he'd come pick her up at the corner of such-and-such. That was the second vivid memory.

Wait— Why didn't he park somewhere so that after four years of writing, their first in-person meeting could be … special? With time to say hi, to talk, perhaps to touch. Instead, he'd stopped at the corner, a busy intersection, and she'd had to hustle her backpack into the back seat and herself into the front, and then keep quiet while he negotiated the traffic … It wouldn't be the first time she, their relationship, was … subordinated.

Almost forty years it's taken for that question to occur to me, she thought. Appalled.

So low were her expectations. Because when had *anyone* treated her as *anything* special?

"Come, we're in the living room," her mother said, brimming with happy excitement.

Oh no. A huge sign, WELCOME HOME, hung on the wall, covering the landscape painting that, she was sure, her mother couldn't describe without looking.

The room still had the plush gold wall-to-wall carpeting, the heavy floor-length cream-with-gold-thread drapes, the blue-green couch along the far wall, the matching large square chair in the corner, an upholstered footstool in front of it, an end table beside it, and, across from all that, along the other wall, two matching floral upholstered chairs, and the huge—well, not so huge, now—stereo cabinet in between. A long coffee table filled the interior space.

Her parents had their after-work drink in that living room. It was off-limits to the kids, not just then, but always. Except on Saturdays, of course, when she and her sister had to do the cleaning. She'd dust, her sister would follow to vacuum.

She smiled, remembering her discovery of "The Elizabethan Serenade" on her parents' James Last *In Concert* album. She'd danced around the room as she dusted, making little balletic movements, not in a little-girl-being-pretty-ballerina way, but in a—she was simply expressing the intricate, ornate, Mozartian flourishes, making the music visual, embodied. Five years later, she'd put on her brother's Pink Floyd album. It might seem a long way in just five years, but no, she'd continue to enjoy classical music (less the delicacy of Mozart, more the precision of Bach and the passion of Beethoven) as well as rock opera, and she'd go on to compose in both genres.

The end wall of the living room was a wall of shelving. She'd hated that wall. Took her half an hour to dust it. She'd have to take every knick knack out of its cubby hole, dust it, dust the five surfaces of the cubby hole, then return the knick knack. Except for the two large spaces at the bottom, each containing one of her brother's model ships. The one on the left was called the Bluenose. She couldn't remember the name of the one on the right. It was burgundy. Those she couldn't risk taking out of their cubby holes; she had to be oh-so-careful, dusting them while they were in place. It would have been so much easier with a feather duster, but all she had was the dust rag: she had to wipe the rag over every piece, gently, careful not to break off any one of them. It was agonizing work. If her brother had had to dust the damn things every Saturday, he probably wouldn't have made them. He didn't seem proud of them; he didn't even seem to like them. It was just something he did, like collecting stamps. It was a fashion, and he followed. And she was the one to pay the price for his thoughtless conformity. For as long as she lived there.

*His* chore—his one, single, chore was the cut the grass or shovel the driveway. (In addition to the Saturday whole-house dusting, she had to iron the tea towels and pillowcases on Mondays and do the 'dusting around' on Tuesdays and Thursdays; setting the table and doing the dishes was an everyday thing she did with her sister.)

And he didn't even do all of that. She and her sister took turns going behind him, clipping the grass around the trees and along the flower beds or sweeping the snow from between the railings on the porch. Why? Why didn't *he* have to do that as well? Were the clippers too much like scissors and therefore a female thing? And yes, the broom they used was the kitchen broom, because the garage broom was a push broom and wouldn't fit between the railings, but my god why couldn't a man use a kitchen broom? Or was it that clipping the grass and sweeping between the railings a small thing, and men did the big things? Because if men did or used big things, they themselves were big? And big was better because … ? Or was it that the lawn mower made noise and the clippers did not, and when men used tools that made noise, they felt loud as well, like a lion roaring? She suspected that men started to trim the grass around trees and flower beds only when, only because, those obnoxious two-stroke engine weed trimmers were invented. It was the Neanderthal thing again.

But it meant that women did the 'fussy' stuff. The stuff that required time, patience, and attention to detail. (The annoying stuff. The hard stuff.) And if it was true that women were simply better at that stuff, then what the hell were men doing dominating biology, chemistry, medicine, math, physics, architecture, engineering, accounting … music?

Among the knick knacks, there were various trophies. Bowling trophies and curling trophies, won by her brother, sister, mother, or father, all team trophies, all local league trophies. And then there was her lone public speaking trophy, won at the provincial competition. It was put in one of the cubby holes along the far edge of the wall.

They were also allowed in the living room on Christmas Day. And a couple weeks before, in order to decorate the Christmas tree. That is, she and her sister were allowed in the living room a couple weeks before Christmas Day. To decorate the Christmas tree. She hated having to do it. Hanging the ornaments wasn't so bad, but they couldn't just throw the tinsel on, they had to place each strand, one at a time, over a branch, carefully, making sure it didn't get stuck on any of the needles. Yes, the final effect was pretty, more aesthetically pleasing than if they *had* just thrown it on, but overall, she wouldn't consider a Christmas tree a work of beauty. And by the time she was eighteen, she was a confirmed atheist, so there was that … And again, why didn't her brother have to help? Again, a time-consuming, fussy task …

One that, like meal preparation and housecleaning, wouldn't even be granted permanence. Unlike construction. Of, say, a model ship.

On Christmas Day, her brother played chess with her dad. She could never understand that. They never played chess except on Christmas Day. So why did they play chess then? For some reason, it was what middle-class fathers and sons did on Christmas Day. It was a mindless ritual.

And then they watched the game. There was always a hockey game on tv on Christmas Day. Again, neither her father nor her brother were hockey fans. It was, again, just what men did. On Christmas Day. Another mindless ritual.

Meanwhile, 'the girls' were in the kitchen preparing Christmas dinner.

Mindless doesn't mean harmless.

It meant she never learned how to be strategic.

It meant she learned that winning wasn't important for women.

It meant she learned that women worked while men relaxed.

Now though, her father was reading the paper. Sitting in that large square chair in the corner, his chair, feet up on the footstool. Ignoring her presence. As always.

Couldn't he read the paper later? Of course he could. There was nothing in it that he needed to know right now. But reading it made him seem important. God knows why. And no coincidence, its size made it a wall. A barrier. The newspaper was man's best friend.

Her mother had disappeared. No doubt, to the kitchen.

She claimed the floral chair furthest from her father.

Her sister, Cheryl, and her husband, Bruce, sat on the couch. Bruce nodded at her. A perfunctory nod. Her sister did the same. Okay …

Other than the extra pounds, they looked pretty much as they had when she saw them last. She'd never really liked Bruce. Like so many men, he thought being male was enough. As for Cheryl, they'd never been close, but since she hadn't had any friends, her sister was the person she did stuff with. That stopped when her sister got married. Even so, she'd hoped they'd develop some sort of Roseanne-and-Jackie relationship. So it didn't feel strange, in her fourth year, once she'd moved out, to take her laundry to her sister's house one day. But Cheryl said she couldn't use her washer and dryer. She'd just gotten it. It was brand new. Seriously? What did she think she was going to do, break it?

And the time she helped herself to some leftovers in their fridge—she was down to just a dozen piano students and all of her income went to rent and tuition and books and piano lessons—Bruce accused her of stealing. She'd protested. It had been just a dried out corner of a lasagna her sister had made, probably the week before. "Make your own lasagna!" he'd shouted.

"This is Kevin," Cheryl said, nodding to the heavy-set younger man beside her on the couch, accusation in her voice. Wait, accusation?

Kevin said nothing.

"And that's Nathan," she nodded to the other younger man, not at all heavy-set, sitting on a card table chair beside the tree.

"Hello," he said, looking at her with interest. "This is Tanya, my wife, and Devon, our son," he introduced the woman sitting on another card table chair beside him and the teenager comfortable on the floor in the doorway. Tanya nodded politely, and Devon just stared at her. God knows what he'd been told about her. Perhaps he hadn't been told anything at all.

"You're not married?" she asked Kevin. Not that she cared. She was just curious.

"Separated. The wife is spending New Year's with her family."

"'The wife'. She doesn't have a name? She exists simply in relationship to you? No wonder you're separated."

There was, of course, an awkward silence. No doubt both he and Bruce were scrambling for an alternative to 'Fuck you'.

"Nice to meet you too, finally," Kevin managed to say, making it sound like an insult.

"What do you mean, *finally*? You could have met me before. Anytime. Google? Email?"

"Yeah, well, it was pretty clear you had no interest in meeting us."

"Not true." She looked at Cheryl and Bruce. "You didn't tell them?"

"Tell us what?" That was Nathan.

"I didn't want to be a mother, but I was looking forward to being an aunt. I told your parents they could be in charge of bowling and baseball, I could take care of books and ballet. And your father told me in no uncertain terms that I would do no such thing. He said he didn't want me anywhere near his kids. And your mother," she turned to her sister, "didn't object." She turned back to Kevin, "So if you have a problem with me not being a part of your life, take it up with them."

"Is that true?" Nathan looked at his father.

Bruce shrugged. "I don't remember that."

"How convenient," she said. Then added, "You never wondered why, after that day, I never came back? It didn't bother you that I showed no interest in your kids?"

"Nope." He looked away. Left the conversation.

Another silence.

"Kevin works at a garage," Cheryl said then, showing that she was clearly her mother's daughter. "He's good with cars. And Nathan has a degree in … Philosophy. Right?"

Nathan gave a brief, agonized nod, and Bruce snorted.

"Why the snort?" she asked.

"Well, what's it good for?" Any idiot would know why the snort.

"Everything. For starters, I'm sure Nathan could tell you a thing or two about how to figure out right and wrong. No doubt he could clarify your thinking on a number of issues." Should the man ever think about anything.

"Yeah, and when's the last time you saw a job for a philosopher?"

"There are some. That there aren't more is the fault of our society, not philosophy. If people understood its value, policy analysts at every level in every field would have to have a philosophy degree. In other countries—the UK, for instance—there's actually a PPE degree. Philosophy, Politics, and Economics."

She turned to Nathan. "Have you been able to use your degree? For income?"

"To some extent," he replied. "I have a freelance job editing articles for a philosophy journal. Best I could do without a Ph.D."

"But that's good! You get to read stuff you're interested in all day!"

He conceded that with a nod.

"'Course, it probably doesn't pay very well. Since philosophy is so useless."

He smiled.

In fact, Kevin probably made more money than he did. Because cars.

"Tanya's an engineer," Nathan volunteered then.

"That's unusual," she replied, smiling at Tanya.

"Yeah, I was in high school when the Montreal Massacre happened, so …"

"Oh. Then I don't know whether your career choice was very brave or very stupid."

Tanya laughed. "It was both, I assure you."

She smiled even more. She liked Nathan and Tanya. Too bad she'd missed—

"So you were raised by your dad?" she turned to Devon. "I mean, he was the stay-at-home parent? What was that like?"

"I don't know," Devon shrugged. "He was my dad. He was *supposed* to look after me."

Indeed. And when she saw Nathan put his arm around those shrugging shoulders—

"Doug and Anne-Marie are here!" Her mother chimed from the kitchen, scurrying to the door to greet them.

She stayed in her chair in the living room. No need, no desire, to get up to greet them. Besides, no room.

"Kimmy, you're prettier every time I see you!"

"I've asked you before. Don't call me Kimmy. I'm not a child anymore." Indeed, the voice clearly belonged to a teenager. She was the first to enter the living room. She had a retro-goth look, complete with a pair of Doc Martens she must've gotten from a second-hand shop.

"So you're my grandaunt. My other grandaunt." She reached out to shake hands. "I didn't even know you existed until this morning."

And she didn't know Kim existed until now.

"That's because I'm the devil."

Anne-Marie was a devout Baptist. No drinking, no dancing. Certainly no consorting with atheists.

"Hm." She thought about that for a moment, then walked through the living room. "Hey, Dev, what's up?" He grinned, got up, and followed her into the den.

The den. She suspected it was also the same as it once was. Although one of the walls was full of books, it was the tv room. In fact, she'd never seen her father ever read a book. And the only books she saw her mother read were by Taylor Caldwell. Where all those books had come from—a set of Funk and Wagnalls encyclopedia, two dictionaries, H. G. Wells' *The Outline of History*, the first three volumes of a Great Philosophers series— and why they had them was a mystery to her.

On the third from the bottom shelf, on the left side of the tv, there was a complete set of *The Hardy Boys*, for her brother, though she never saw him read any of them. Below that, a set of *Nancy Drew* books for her sister which also went largely unread, and below that, a set of *The Bobbsey Twins* for her. Which she definitely read. Odd that it never occurred to her to read the

*Nancy Drew* and *Hardy Boys* books, both of which she probably would have preferred. No, not odd. She wasn't told she *could* read them. She also remembered *Rebecca of Sunnybrook Farm* and *Karen*, the story about a girl with cerebral palsy. She really liked *Karen*. Identified so much with— Ah. To be a woman in a male supremacy is, of course, to be crippled.

So, not a reading room. A tv room. Every evening, her father would be stretched out on the couch against the far wall, usually reading the newspaper (again?) and her mother would be in the lazy-boy across from him, making the grocery list, mending socks, writing Christmas cards ... She and her sister, and sometimes her brother—though he was often somewhere else, in his room or out with his friends—would be sitting on the padded bench seat directly across from the tv. It wasn't exactly a family event. Nor was it enjoyable. Whenever they watched *Mannix* or *Hawaii-Five-0*, she kept asking what was going on, and her father would get increasingly irritated with her, because he didn't know. Why would he? In retrospect, she understood that. But she was raised to believe that men knew everything. And so didn't understand why her questions made him so angry.

In fact, now that she thought about it, *everything* she did seemed to irritate him. Her brother responded the same way. And it seemed like the harder she tried, to please them, to impress them, the more annoyed they became. Ah. Because the harder she tried, the more competent she became, the more she achieved. *That's* what annoyed them. It's bad enough when the son upstages the father. But if the *daughter* surpasses him— And of course one's kid sister isn't supposed to be better than you at anything.

The show she remembered most was *All in the Family*. Whenever Archie dismissed Edith, Carroll O'Connor's face screwed up with such— It was more than irritation, more than annoyance. Contempt? It drove her nuts. But her father loved it. And apparently her mother didn't notice. Or didn't mind. Worse, her father laughed along with Archie at Meathead and Gloria. Oblivious to the fact that *she* was Meathead, the intellectual and budding environmentalist, *as well as* Gloria, the budding feminist. Which meant that he was laughing at her. Making fun of her.

She also remembered one hot summer's evening, she'd put on her 'baby dolls'—just now the name registered, with all its awful implications—and her mother, catching the uncomfortable glance of her father, scolded her and told her to go cover up. Right. It's the woman's responsibility. The woman's fault. Heaven forbid men take responsibility for their reactions.

On the bottom shelf on the right side of the tv were their high school graduation pictures. Her mother had reminded her of that when they'd ambushed her. "I still have your high school graduation picture," she'd said. "I've always loved that picture."

It looked nothing like her. Not now. Not even then. It looked exactly like the person her mother wanted her to be. Prim and proper, an A student who took piano lessons and didn't have an original, let alone radical, thought in her brain.

Doug entered the living room. Over the years, she had come to realize that her brother was, in every way, ordinary. She could say little more about him.

Her mother gestured for him to sit in the floral chair nearest the doorway. Her chair. Seriously?

Anne-Marie stood beside him, awkwardly.

"Doug's son is Kimmy's father," her mother explained, standing in the doorway, clearly about to return to the kitchen. "And they're not able to be here today."

She didn't ask why. She didn't really care.

Then, "Doug has a place on the lake now," her mother said brightly. "He's doing a lot of work to fix it up." She did leave then. Anne-Marie followed.

"How are the bugs at your place?" she asked. In the silence that followed. "They're so bad where I am, I built a little gazebo, all screened in."

He didn't respond. Didn't acknowledge that she too had a place on the lake. That she too had done a lot of work to fix it up.

No surprise. Women's work is invisible. And must remain so.

And when it *was* acknowledged, it must be thought to be easier. Like most men, her brother had managed to make everything he did seem harder than it was, certainly harder than anything she did. Cutting the grass was harder than dusting. Working at a curling club was harder than teaching piano. Business was harder than Music. Did he think that if what he did was harder, that proved that he was more competent? Or was it that if what he did was harder, he had an excuse when he failed?

"I also added insulation to the ceiling," she continued, "of the cabin, not the gazebo. It originally had just those fibreglass-backed ceiling tiles. Absolutely useless. I put insulation in the crawlspace too, so the floor's a lot warmer now. You ever work with that pink stuff? Horrible job."

He ignored her. He always had. Odd how two people could live in the same house, for almost twenty years, and say not one word to each other.

"I also took out the wall between the two small bedrooms, to turn the space into a music studio. Did you take out any walls?"

"He doesn't have any insulation. Or dividing walls," Kim volunteered from the den. "It's just a trailer."

She burst out laughing. Serves him right. Always pretending to have more, to be more.

She knew then that his 'place on the lake' was just an excuse to get away from Anne-Marie for a while.

"Doug has his own advertising company now," her mother had returned. And tried again. To do what? Facilitate conversation? No. Make him the best. He was their *son*. He was *male*. Or maybe she was just trying to prove that she *wasn't* a bad parent. That *one* of her kids had succeeded. Two, though she wasn't really counting Cheryl. No surprise.

"Yeah. You told me. Being the scum of business is hardly worth bragging about." Because she *was* bragging.

"How can you say that?" she smiled.

"Easy. I just open my mouth and form the words." She waited. Nothing. "Did you mean '*Why* do I say that?'" Her mother's dependence on platitudes, which prevented her from saying what she really meant, no doubt from even *thinking* about what she really meant, irritated the hell out of her. Always had.

The smile flitted away, but returned in an instant. It was like she couldn't help it. A moment later, she left the room again.

Kim and Devon quietly returned to the room. Well, as far as the doorway. They slid down to settle on the floor. This was going to be good.

"If I were to list business activities by honour and value," she said, answering 'Why' anyway, "advertising would be dead last. Convincing people to buy what they don't really want or need— Wouldn't it be better, more respectful, to just have a directory that listed every product in every category, provided a comprehensive description, good points and bad, so people could make an informed decision, without manipulation?"

No response.

"Did you know that the pharmaceutical industry spends more money on advertising than on research and development?"

"No, I didn't know that," Doug said, a little sarcastically and clearly annoyed with the way the things were going.

"How can you not know that?" She wasn't going to let him get away with it. "Don't you read?"

"Yes, I read!" he retorted.

"Yeah? What's the last book you read? Because the paper doesn't count. It's just an advertising vehicle. As you would, should, admit."

No response.

Not even from her father, still reading said paper. Of course, she had never been worth his attention.

"And *you* dismiss *me*," she said. "Unfuckingbelievable."

No response.

"Furthermore," she continued her explanation, "I'd like to know what gives you the right to force yourself on me every time I go outside, to scream at me when I'm just walking down the street, 'BUY THIS! BUY THIS NOW!'? Worse, what gives you the right to call me at home, to send messages into my inbox … I can't fucking concentrate when I'm on the internet anymore because of people like you interrupting me all the time, insisting I pay attention to you, insisting I buy whatever-the-hell it is you're selling. How do you figure some guy's desire for money trumps my desire to be free from such constant intrusion? Your roadside billboards are literally *designed* to *distract me* from *driving*, to make me take my eyes off the road—how moral is that?"

No response.

"I'd like to hear the answer to those questions as well," Nathan said, with a quick glance at her.

"I think you're over-exaggerating," Doug said. "Most people don't even notice ads."

She waited. For just a moment.

"THEN WHY THE FUCK DO YOU DO IT?"

Because it paid well. Stupidly well.

"We googled you," Kim said, once it seemed that the conversation, such as it was, was over. "Found your website. It says you've released *fifteen* albums?!"

She turned to her and nodded. "I started with solo piano, then new age stuff, before it was called new age—my favorite pieces are three duets for sax—one with rain, one with wolves, and one with loons."

"How'd you get the wolves and loons to ... play?" Devon giggled.

"Pre-recorded tracks," she smiled, "I composed around their phrases."

"Cool."

"Yeah. Narada was interested—"

"Narada?" Nathan recognized the label.

"Yeah. They sent a letter, saying they'd heard my sampler tape and wanted to hear more of my Ruby Rose album, but it wasn't done yet. I'd just bought my cabin and was spending my days scrambling for income and my evenings with hammer and saw. I didn't even have my studio set up yet ... Anyway, I told them I was delighted with their interest and could send them more in six months—"

"But by then, they'd signed someone else."

She nodded. "I so didn't know how things worked. Anyway, then, or also, I wrote some Pink Floyd wannabe stuff."

"Seriously?" Kim was impressed. "Wow."

"Well, it isn't nearly as good as Pink Floyd," she grinned.

"It also says you were featured in *Canadian Composer,*" Kim continued. "That sounds ... big."

"It was, sort of. Back in the 80s, if you'd made a list of the top twenty indie composers in Canada, I'd be on it. So yeah, they did a small article about me. One of my albums, social commentary audio collage stuff, had made the top ten of the year at CKLN."

"I know CKLN!" Nathan said. "I used to listen to it all the time! It was the best non-mainstream station in Toronto. *In Canada!* Lots of radical stuff ..."

"Yeah," she agreed. "It was a good station."

"The picture taken for the music magazine," Kim had the site open on her smartphone, and turned it to face her. "What *is* that? On your shoulder."

"A cockroach, I think. Found it in the photographer's studio. It was dead," she hastened to add. "I was looking for a way to make the picture, to make me … unique," she finished lamely. "I thought I was. I was wrong." She, her experience—and not just with music, by any means—was *not* unique. Which was another reason for being there.

"It also says you've had *international* airplay?!"

"Well, in just a few countries."

"Did you know about this? Any of this?" She turned to Doug, then to Cheryl, and finally to her greatgrandfather. "None of you bothered to google her from time to time? Not even out of curiosity? That is so fucked up."

"Dinner's ready!" her mother's voice warbled from the kitchen.

She made a quick detour to the bathroom, passing the door to the basement on her way. She'd divided her life between the cellar and the attic. Too often she'd wanted to do her homework when her mother wanted to use the dining room table for something else, so they'd decided to set up a table and chair in the attic for her to use. She'd loved it.

She'd worked hard. Got straight As. And yet, they'd never enrolled her in any sort of gifted program. As a result, she became teacher's helper. And decided to become a school teacher—it was familiar, and she had experience. Bad choice. She was interested in the subject matter, not the students.

Also, as a result, she was always the smartest person in the room. If she'd been a boy, that might have led to arrogance. Since she was a girl, it led to embarrassment. And *because* she was always the smartest person in the room, she learned that she could never learn from someone else. So when she finally found herself among intellectual kin, she didn't think 'Hey, I can learn from these people, I can become even smarter!' All those lost opportunities …

As for the basement, that's where her piano was. The laundry room and her father's workshop took up the back half, a rec room and a ping pong table took up the front half. When they decided that 'the girls' should have piano lessons, they'd bought a used upright and set it against the wall beside the ping pong table. Every day after school, she'd go down to practice (and if she'd forgotten to close the door at the top of the stairs, someone would invariably slam it shut as soon as she began to play).

She remembered one time when her brother had his friends over, she'd heard one of his friends banging away on the keys, a bottle of beer no doubt sloshing about … She almost cried. It was just an old Heintzman, but it was her portal to the sublime. Through it, she entered an entire world of such exquisite beauty …

She also remembered the time she'd asked her mother if she could play her first composition for her. Her mother had been right there, on her way up the stairs, but no, she didn't have time, the potatoes were on. Right. Making supper was more important than listening to your daughter's first composition. And okay, so maybe it was bad timing, but did her mother say, 'I would *love* to, but not right now, sweetie. How about after supper, when I can give it my full attention?' No. She did not.

Her mother had never called her sweetie. Or anything like it.

Her parents sold the piano while she was in Vancouver. Without even telling her. When she confronted them with the … betrayal, her father was unmoved. "We bought it. It was ours to sell." She couldn't argue with that. But they had no idea what they'd done. She was devastated. Yes, once she had her own place, she'd get another one, a better one, and yes in the meantime, she wasn't there to use it and had no place to store it, but still.

She looked through the small bathroom window to the back yard. The clothesline looked so close now. She remembered on more than one occasion when it started to rain, her mother shouting to her and her sister to quick, help, get the laundry in. As if locusts were on the way.

On her way to the dining room, she passed through the kitchen. And saw herself standing at the sink, doing the dishes with Cheryl. Her sister would wash, she would dry, and she could never keep up, and Cheryl kept getting angry because there was no room in the drainer to put the next washed dish, and one time she peed her pants right there in the kitchen rather than insist on taking a break to go to the bathroom.

It took her half a lifetime before she could insist. On getting her own needs met.

A large cabinet separated the dining room from the kitchen, with a see-through cut-out in the middle making a counter top. The cabinet contained the good china. (The everyday stuff was in the kitchen cupboard.) She'd never understood the concept. If you really liked the good china, why wouldn't you use it every day? Why hide things of beauty? Again, thoughtless convention. Middle-class families had 'everyday' dishes and 'the good china'. (She herself had only what she needed, each second-hand item chosen with care: an oversized tea cup, a gold-splashed plate, an iridescent bowl.)

The small radio was still there, on the counter top, probably still tuned to the city's top ten station, CHYM. Her childhood and youth had been saturated with pop music. Saccharine romance. Donny Osmond. The Beach Boys. Imagine her surprise, her wonder, at discovering the FM band. Led Zeppelin. Emerson, Lake, and Palmer. And symphonies. Chamber music. Sonatas. Didn't happen until her late teens. Not even her piano teacher told her she could hear Bach and Beethoven on the radio.

The dining room looked the same. The rug was a muted turquoise, and she knew that under the plastic table cloth (now in off-white instead of bright turquoise), she'd see the wood-grained formica that she'd loved … (She hadn't yet seen a table made of real wood …)

Her father had put in the extender (he would always be the one to do that; why her mother couldn't, or wouldn't, she had no idea—it was another one of those arbitrary according-to-one's-sex things), so there was room for three people on either side. Cheryl, Bruce, and Kevin took the chairs on one side. Doug and Anne-Marie sat on the other.

"Kimmy," her mother said, "would you mind sitting with your cousin today?" Devon, Nathan, and Tanya were already at the breakfast nook in the kitchen.

"Kim!" the young woman insisted. Again. "I'm not a child anymore!" She happily went into the kitchen and slid onto the bench seat beside Devon.

Her father took his place at the far end of the table, flanked by Bruce and Doug—odd how that worked out—and she assumed her mother would sit, as always, at the other end, closest to the kitchen. She had no choice but to take the remaining chair. At her mother's elbow.

"Shall we say grace?" Her mother smiled, and everyone bowed their heads and folded their hands in prayer.

"No."

The bowed heads slowly raised, and everyone looked at her, absolutely astonished.

"I'm not going to pretend anymore that it's okay for you to pray to an imaginary, sadistic entity. It's *not* okay. Your religious beliefs are fucked up."

Her mother winced.

"And forcing those beliefs on children, who have no capacity to evaluate them, is—was—criminal."

"What are you talking about?" her mother smiled. Had recovered, obviously. "We raised you Roman Catholic!"

"That's what I'm talking about!"

"If you don't agree, that's your prerogative," her father spoke up, clearly pleased with his use of the word, "but we also raised you to be polite." He stood up to slice off some turkey from the platter in the middle of the table. Doug, Bruce, and Kevin followed his lead.

She stared at him. "You've completely ignored me since I arrived. Said not one word, given no acknowledgement whatsoever of my presence. But, okay, you want to talk about polite? You think it's polite to lie? To pretend to endorse something I clearly don't endorse? Something I believe is actually dangerous, genuinely harmful? If Devon pulled out a knife and started slashing, would you be polite and just ignore it?"

"Religious belief isn't—" Anne-Marie tried to help out. "God is good, we believe in helping others."

"The Baptist god, like the Catholic god, is all-loving, all-knowing, and all-powerful?"

"Yes—"

"Well, if he's all-loving, why would he let animals die a horrible death in a forest fire? He knows the forest fire is going to happen. And he's able to stop it or move them to safety. He doesn't. Explain."

"But," her mother was several steps behind, "you're Roman Catholic!" She belatedly started passing various dishes around the table.

"No!" she practically shouted, since it was not by any means the first time she'd said it. "I'm not!"

"Of course you are," she said. "Don't be silly."

"Don't tell me what I believe." She clenched her teeth. "And don't tell me I'm silly when I disagree with you and have very good reasons for my disagreement."

"But you were *born* Roman Catholic."

"No, I wasn't. One can't be *born believing* something. Newborns don't have the requisite cognitive structures, especially for metaphysical, epistemological, and ethical beliefs. We had this discussion. Thirty years ago. Weren't you paying attention? Probably not. You never did." She glared at her mother and then at her father. "Why was that? Why didn't you *ever* take me seriously?"

It was like nothing she said or did had any meaning.

"But, *we* were raised Catholics, so—"

"No doubt you were. And did you ever once *think* about what you were told? Did you ever ask yourself whether the things that you were told were sins were really that bad? Did you ever ask yourself whether you had any *evidence* for the existence of a god, a heaven, a hell—other than a book written by a bunch of nearly prehistoric men, full of contradictions and idiocies?"

"You don't know what you're talking about," her brother said.

Right. Because.

"'I am merciful, saith the Lord, and I will not keep anger forever.' Jeremiah 3:12. 'Ye have kindled a fire in mine anger, which shall burn forever.' Jeremiah 17:4. Contradiction.

"'Do not wear clothing woven of two kinds of material.' Leviticus 19:19. Idiocy."

"'They shall seek me early,'" Nathan spoke, quietly, "but they shall not find me.' Proverbs something. 'They who seek me early *shall* find me.' Proverbs something else. Contradiction."

She sent him a smile of gratitude.

Encouraged, he continued. "Don't save money. Don't plan for the future. Matthew, essentially. Idiocy."

"Have you even *read* the *Bible*?" she asked, looking around the table.

Of course they hadn't. They probably hadn't even read the bits in the missals they used every Sunday.

"Regardless, isn't that an unfathomable amount of trust to put in a bunch of people you don't even know?" she resumed. "If

I told you that I had a hundred job offers last week, would you believe me? No. And yet that's *way* more plausible than believing in some all-knowing, all-good, all-powerful god. Who advocates horrible and ever-lasting pain for people who—"

"It's just words," her father grumbled. "It doesn't mean anything."

She stared at him. Stunned. Then carefully put down the fork she'd had in her hand. Then the knife. "It doesn't *mean* anything? Telling me that I was going to burn in Hell forever, that I was going to be burned *alive*, not just until I died, but on and on, without an end, if I didn't obey you— That didn't *mean* anything?"

"We never said that!" her mother protested.

"Violations of the Ten Commandments are mortal sins, punishable by an eternity in Hell. What's the Fourth Commandment?"

"'Honour' doesn't necessarily mean 'obey'," her brother spoke up.

"Agreed. But that's how the nuns at St. Louis interpreted it. And you subjected me to their teaching—their *conditioning*—for *six years.*"

No response.

"When I got a job at the youth drop-in center, it was Friday nights and Sunday afternoons. So I was breaking the Third Commandment. Keep holy the Sabbath. '*Six* days you shall labour and do all your work ...'."

In the silence that followed, Bruce reached for the bowl of mashed potatoes in front of him, put a second spoonful on his plate, then passed the bowl to Kevin.

"Let's try one that's not open to interpretation: Roman Catholic dogma says the Pope is infallible. And the Pope says it's a sin to use contraception. So, married or not, I could be celibate or I could risk becoming pregnant. That's the life you told me I must have. When you raised me to be a Roman Catholic."

Doug reached out to take the bowl from Kevin.

"You even believe that I was *born* sinful! That simply by being *born,* I'd done something wrong. Which, when you think about it, is a good argument for abortion. But why would you think that? That people are *born* having sinned."

"We don't," her mother said. Still confused.

"Sure you do. The concept of, the belief in, original sin is central to Roman Catholicism, and you keep insisting you're Roman Catholic."

"But—"

"Okay, surely you're familiar with the Roman Catholic prayers. You were just about to say one. Let's consider the 'Our Father'. 'Our Father, who art in Heaven—' So you believe in Heaven. Where is it? Up in the sky? How far up in the sky? I mean, is it past the atmosphere? The stratosphere? Beyond the solar system? Past other solar systems? And what evidence do you have that it's there?

"'Thy kingdom come.' Okay, when? When is God's kingdom coming?

"'Thy will be done.' Which parts of it? The part when he says that if your right hand offends you, cut it off? The part where he says that if a woman isn't a virgin when she marries, she should be stoned to death?"

"Enough!" her father boomed.

"No! *Not* enough!" she boomed right back. "Not *nearly* enough!" She turned back to her mother. "My guess is you really mean '*Some* of your will be done.' You just pick and choose what to believe."

"Of course that's what we do," her father mumbled.

"How convenient." She stared at him.

He didn't understand the problem.

"On what basis do you pick and choose? Do you just believe whatever you want?"

No response.

"Then don't fucking call yourself a Roman Catholic or a Christian!" she shouted.

Her mother winced again.

After a moment, she added, "But it's just words, right? You don't really believe it. Well, way to raise a kid. Say shit you don't mean."

Hello to the consequences.

"We never said we were *good* Catholics," her father said, having finally come up with a response.

She laughed. "That may be, but if you call yourself Catholic, you still have to *believe* certain things. Roman Catholicism is a religion. Not a social club. It's a set of very specific beliefs.

"Furthermore," she muttered, "if you're going to call yourselves something, and insist that your kids be that something, you should damn well figure out what it fucking means."

"Language, please!" her mother finally had to say.

"Yes, I'm using language!" she glared at her. "And if you paid more attention to what I say than to how I say it, we might not be here, today, like this."

It occurred to her that people who paid excessive attention to form did so because they were unable to pay attention to the content.

She considered another approach while she took a dinner roll from the basket Anne-Marie passed her.

"Okay, tell me, if when you say you're Roman Catholic, you don't mean that you believe the Roman Catholic tenets, like the infallibility of the Pope, and you don't mean that you believe what the Bible says, and you don't mean that you believe the prayers you mumble every week, what *do* you mean? When you insist you're Roman Catholic, what exactly do you mean? Just that you were born to parents who were Roman Catholic? And they're Roman Catholic just because *they* were born to parents who were Roman Catholic … ?"

"I suppose we just mean we're good people." Her mother smiled. Nervously.

"Then why don't you just say you're good? To say you're Roman Catholic means a whole lot more than that. As I've explained. You can be good without being Roman Catholic. Surely you believe that. Then again, maybe you don't. When I told you I was no longer Catholic, you acted like I'd said I believe in rape, murder, and torture. Surprise. *Roman Catholics—you—* believe in rape, murder, and torture."

"We do not," she smiled again, as if she was just pulling her leg.

"Pope John Paul II said that the sexual act between husbands and wives can take place without the wife's volition. That's rape.

"As for murder—"

"The Crusades," Nathan volunteered from the kitchen.

"And torture? The Inquisition."

"You've always taken things too seriously." Her father.

She thinks about that as she takes a bite of her dinner roll. "I shouldn't have taken it seriously? Telling me you were Roman Catholics, telling me *I* was supposed to be a Roman Catholic— that was all just … for fun? Telling me I'd burn in hell, be endlessly tortured, if I went on the Pill— You were just playing with me?"

He shrugged his shoulders.

"What's that supposed to mean?"

No response.

She looked at her sister. "Are *you* still a Roman Catholic?"

Cheryl looked at Bruce, then at each of their parents. Like the proverbial deer caught in headlights. "I don't know."

"You don't know? How can you not know? Did you have Kevin and Nathan baptised?"

"Yes."

"Why?"

"I don't know, Mom said we should."

She turned to her mother.

"Why? Why did you tell them they should baptise their kids?"

"You know why! Because we're—"

"Right." She sighed. "But that means that you believe that baptism takes away original sin. How does sprinkling some water on an infant's forehead take away sin? Sounds like a bunch of mumbo jumbo hocus pocus, if you ask me."

"No one asked you!" her father shouted.

"Exactly."

She waited a moment. In vain.

So she turned to her brother. "I know *you're* not a Roman Catholic anymore."

He'd become a Baptist in order to marry Anne-Marie. Odd how that was acceptable. To her parents.

"Who knew you could change your beliefs so quickly? They must not be based on clear and critical thought. I'll bet you just *said* you believed whatever Baptists believe in order to marry Anne-Marie. Or you just *said* you believed all the other shit, before then, in order to … who-knows-what."

Did it mean *anything* to any of them to say 'I believe …'?

"Because seriously, what are the odds that one suddenly changes one's beliefs in such a specific direction? Did no one see through that but me?" She looked pointedly at her parents, then at Anne-Marie. Who was staring at her plate.

"You're all fucking hypocrites." She took another bite of her dinner roll. And saw, out of the corner of her eye, Kim's smile.

"So let me ask you this," she looked at her parents. "If you didn't really believe it, why did you pretend you did? And why the fuck did you teach *us*, tell *us*, to believe it?"

"Because," her mother was searching, "we wanted you learn right and wrong!"

"And you thought the Roman Catholic religion was the only way to do that? Was the *best* way to do that? How many other ways did you investigate before coming to that conclusion?"

More silence.

"Your hypocrisy, your utter thoughtlessness, hurt me," she said quietly, looking from her mother to her father.

They stared at her.

"Do you have any idea of the stress I felt trying to be good all the time? *Bless me Father for I have sinned, I got angry with my sister five times last week …* It took me *years* to realize that sometimes anger is *justified*. Why should it be cause for punishment?

"Do you have any idea of the anguish I experienced, knowing that I was going to burn in hell forever? First, I wanted to live forever, to postpone that awful punishment. Then I wanted to die, just to get it over with. But of course that wouldn't get it over with, because it was going to be forever. Do you have any idea what it's like to live with that knowledge? The knowledge that at any moment, if I was hit by a car, say, or if I got sick and died, that torment would begin?

"Do you have any idea of the mental contortions I went through as a teenager trying to accept so many logical impossibilities?

"I nearly had a nervous breakdown trying to be Roman Catholic."

Her mother smiled. Surely she was exaggerating.

Her father shrugged. Not his problem.

She gave up. Wasn't sure they understood that she'd exposed their hypocrisy. Failing that, their superficiality. Let alone their awareness of the injuries they'd inflicted on her, the damage they'd done to her, by raising her to be a Roman Catholic.

"I'll get dessert," her mother said, her cheery chirp perhaps a little subdued. She went into the kitchen, followed by Cheryl and Anne-Marie.

Two apple pies were set onto the table, along with a small stack of dessert plates, dessert forks, cups and saucers, cream and sugar.

The pie was served, and eaten, in absolute silence.

When everyone had finished, her mother spoke.

"Why did you come?" she asked. Quietly.

"Well, I would never have shown up uninvited." She stared at her mother, then her father, but neither one acknowledged the transgression of their ambush. "You asked me to come. Remember?"

"Because we're *family!*"

"So? What's so fucking sacred about genetic relationship?"

She thinks of social service agencies bending over backwards to keep a family together even after, for example, the father rapes his daughter.

"Everyone needs family!"

"For what, exactly?"

She waited. For her to consider the question.

"I haven't needed any of you for thirty years. I've managed to feed myself, clothe myself, entertain myself. I've obtained a graduate degree. I've obtained employment. I've even established a career. All without your help. I've managed to buy a car and keep it running. I've even managed to buy a house, keep it in good repair, and make improvements. Without your assistance. I've suffered several deep losses and, yet, have survived. Without your support. I've had several emergencies and have always managed to get assistance from people who were not family.

"Good thing," she continued, "because the one time I *did* call family for assistance, none of you came. I learned early on that strangers were more likely to help me than any of you."

"What are you talking about?" Her mother smiled as if she were exaggerating. Perhaps even making something up.

"That time I drove my bike to the cottage for the weekend, and it broke down on my way there, *you,*" she turned to her brother, the obvious choice for assistance, "couldn't take time off from your precious job at the curling club to come help. Help I wouldn't've needed if you'd shown me how to maintain my bike and make small repairs. As I'd asked you to do. But no. You never had the time. Women aren't supposed to have any mechanical knowledge, I guess. I suppose women's ignorance allows men to play the hero, but you didn't.

"You didn't come either," she looked at her father.

"And I guess you two," she turned to her mother and her sister, "forgot you knew how to drive."

"So what did you do?" Kim asked from the kitchen.

"Watched the guys play pool at the local bar until it closed, then went out to sleep on a park bench." She stared at her mother. "Didn't have enough money for a room in a hotel. This was before credit cards," she glanced through the cabinet cut-out to Kim.

"Fortunately, the waitress saw me, on her way home, asked about my situation, then said I was welcome to sleep on her couch. She was so poor she was living in a crappy trailer park. But she was more generous to a stranger than any of you were to family."

Silence.

"And the worst of it was," she said, "I accepted, I excused, your behaviour. It was so far, I was already more than half-way to the cottage. Years later, I realized I was only forty-five minutes from home. A distance I've since driven twice a day to get to and from work."

"But you've done nothing but criticize us." Her mother was clearly hurt.

And you haven't heard the half of it, she thought.

She nodded. "Which is a partial answer to the question you've never bothered to ask. Why did I leave?"

As she'd explained in the letter she'd sent when she decided to break off, to break away, she was not ungrateful. In fact, she'd said thank you for twenty years of food and shelter, thank you for fifteen years of clothes, books, piano lessons, and dance lessons, thank you for providing safety, thank you for giving up smoking, thank you for not getting drunk very often, and most of all, thank you for giving me life. But, she'd explained, a love of gratitude can go only so far. I refuse to live the life you insist I live, she'd said. We have different interests, different values, different opinions. You're not going to change; I'm not going to change. Any further interaction is bound to be unpleasant or untrue. What's the point?

So, she'd left. She didn't want to hurt them, keep hurting them, with her criticism. Of course, leaving would hurt them too, she knew that, but she'd thought lesser of two. Not evils. Injuries.

One of her friends at the time had asked why she couldn't leave, but at least keep in touch, visit from time to time, make small talk while she was there? Because, she'd replied, that would be pretending. Pretending the insignificant things were important, and the important things non-existent. People who prattle on about the weather ignore the implications of climate change. People who prattle on about sports ignore the implications of society's obsession with competition and male supremacy, because they're sure as hell not going to be talking about women's sports. People who prattle on about their kids and grandkids ignore the implications of pronatalism, the fucked-up view that having kids is a measure of adulthood. God knows she'd been treated like some sort of perpetual teenager all her life because she didn't have kids.

Of course, the biggest problem, she went on to explain to her friend, isn't that people *do* pretend; it's that they're *expected* to. That's the awful lesson of adolescence: to be an adult is to live with your head up your ass. People who *don't* pretend, people who say what they mean and mean what they say, are actually reprimanded. How many times had she been scolded for being rude when she was simply being honest? How many times had she been penalized in some way for being offensive when she was simply expressing her opinion.

"It's fine you disagree with us," her father lied, "but why don't you just keep it to yourself?"

"What, you're allowed to criticize me, but I'm not allowed to criticize you? How do you figure that?"

"When have we ever criticized you?"

She stared at him. Dumbfounded.

Then responded with a list. Off the top of her head.

Then continued. "I knew it would be hard enough to become what I wanted to become without your support. But with your constant mockery—"

And that was the rest of the answer. To the question they never bothered to ask.

"And you know what? It was easy. Leaving was one of the easiest decisions I've ever made. And not once have I regretted it. As soon as I left, I felt … light."

The way she felt at the end of a five-mile run when she took off her ankle weights.

"But—" her mother was still struggling to understand … everything, "Why didn't you *say* anything?"

"Why didn't you *notice*—anything?"

Silence.

"Besides, what would've been the point?"

The question hung in the air.

"You know," she said after a few moments, "in thirty years, not once have you wanted to discuss why I left. Why I've stayed away."

"Well," she shrugged, "we thought …"

"You thought I'd eventually come to my senses."

She nodded.

Right. As if it were a phase. As if she were a child.

"Even when I was thirty. Forty. Fifty."

That's some phase.

"I never stopped hoping."

"And you never developed the courage. To face the truth about me, yourselves, our relationship. And I let you get away with that for thirty years. No more."

They were cowards.

"I didn't love you. I *don't* love you. I don't even *like* you."

"But," her mother objected, "I don't understand—"

"Oh for once in your life," she all but shouted, "could you be honest? Failing that, precise? You *do* understand. You just don't want it to be true."

She was being harsh, she knew it. But.

"And I think if you were *really* honest with yourself, you'd find you don't love me either."

"That's ridiculous! Of course I love you!," her mother said. "You're my daughter!"

She considered that.

"I think what you mean is that you're emotionally attached to me. That's not love," she added. Seeing that it needed to be said.

"Or perhaps what you mean is you think you *should* love me. Because I'm your daughter."

"I love you," her mother insisted. "I always have."

"Well then your definition of love must not include like, because you sure as hell didn't like me. People who like each other enjoy spending time together. When did we ever spend time together? And enjoy it? When did we ever go for a walk together, go for a bike ride, sit down for a cup of tea and just talk, discuss a book we'd both read, a tv show we'd both watched?"

"I often asked you to come shopping with me—"

"Exactly. I hate shopping. I always have. See?"

"But—"

"And you know what? I don't remember either of you ever smiling at me. I mean *really* smiling. You were both always angry, frustrated, *annoyed* with me. There was no warmth. No affection."

"Well, we—"

"You said we didn't support you," her father interrupted. "Who do you think put a roof over your head—"

"You did," she conceded. "For twenty years. And I thank you for that. But it was the same roof over your head."

He didn't get the point. She moved on.

"I wasn't talking about material support. When I moved out, you told me I couldn't come back. Not even to practise." She'd even promised to come only when they weren't there. "I was one year away from my Associate!"

"What's that?" her father screwed up his face.

"Again, see? Right there." She explained, then, with sarcasm. "It's just the culmination of fourteen years' hard work. After the grade ten certificate, you can get an Associate diploma. What did you think I was practicing four hours a day for?"

Still no response.

"I understood that if I moved out, I wouldn't be allowed to keep teaching out of your house, and I was okay with that."

She started giving lessons in her students' homes, biking from house to house in the spring, summer, and fall, running in the winter.

"But if I couldn't keep up with my practice, I wouldn't've been able to obtain the Associate. And if I'd had to rent a practice room—"

"Well, you should've thought of that before you moved out," her father said.

"Seriously?" She stared at him. "You really would've wanted me to stay at home just because it's cheaper?"

He shrugged. Obviously a decision he would have made.

Fortunately, every single one of her students' parents had said 'Yes, certainly, you can use our piano for a bit of practice after the lesson, we'd love to hear you play!'

We'd love to hear you play. Hearing that had—

"So let me get this straight," Kim called out from the kitchen. "They kicked you out because you wanted to leave."

"Yeah, what do you call that?" she turned to look at her.

"Win-win."

She grinned at Kim, then turned back to her mother.

"To answer your question, I came to tell you that I'm suing you."

Initially, she'd thought she'd come to give them a last chance. To acknowledge that they weren't the parents they thought they were, that they'd treated her like shit. If they'd acknowledged that, maybe even apologized for it, maybe she wouldn't go ahead. But she'd changed her mind. Such behaviour shouldn't be excused. For any reason.

And maybe a lawsuit— She wasn't doing it for the money. She didn't want their money. In fact, she'd already decided that if, against the odds, they'd included her in their will, she'd just give her share to the grand- and great-grand-kids.

She was doing it to make them see, to make them understand—

"What?" her mother smiled. "You can't be serious!"

"And again. There. All my life you haven't taken me seriously. My opinions, my values, my ideas. Dismissed. Ignored."

"But—I don't understand."

"And there." But at least this time she was being honest. "You have no comprehension of the harm you've done, the injury you've caused. What do you think happens when someone is always ignored? Never taken seriously? She grows up to think she doesn't matter. To think she has no value."

No response.

"And you," she turned to her father, "you've done nothing but mock me. My opinions, my aspirations."

He shrugged.

"See? Right there. Right now. You're dismissing me." Funny how his shrugs could mean so many things.

Another shrug.

"And again."

"Well, obviously I disagree."

"Right, but why?"

"What does it matter?"

"And there you go again!"

Silence.

"It matters, god damn it!" she exploded. "What I say, what women say, matters!"

She glanced at Cheryl. To no avail. No surprise.

"Your attitude," her glance took in both of them, "amounts to perhaps not abuse, but certainly neglect."

"Oh, come on!" her brother protested. He'd had enough.

"Oh, come on, what? You wouldn't know neglect if you tripped over it. For almost twenty years we lived in the same house, and you barely acknowledged me. In all those years, I heard only one compliment from you. You said 'not bad.' Such high praise.

"And whenever we passed each other in the halls at school, you looked right through me." It made her feel like shit. Or invisible. She never figured out which was worse. "Apparently I was so disgusting, or so worthless, I couldn't even be acknowledged."

"It wasn't—"

"Then what was it?"

He couldn't say.

"It *was* that. Being a man means ignoring women. Bros before hos."

She paused.

"Do you remember that time— We were having dinner, at this very table, and I was talking about running—can't remember why— and I said, sharing a new and important understanding, that you run *on* your legs *with* your arms. You laughed. With such scorn.

"Didn't matter than I was quoting a famous coach. Didn't matter that *I* was the runner, not you. *I* was the serious athlete. *I* was the one on the cross-country team, the track team, the basketball team, the gymnastics team. What the fuck team were *you* on? Oh, right. None. But you're male. Ergo, you know more about sports than me, than *any* woman. How do you figure that?"

"Well, you *don't* run with your arms," Bruce laughed. He and Doug reached across the table for a high-five and, in the process, knocked over the gravy pitcher. Anne-Marie jumped up to get some paper towels. After a moment, Cheryl joined her.

Wow. Had anyone else seen what had just happened? One man had joined another man in making fun of a woman, they'd cemented their brotherhood with a physical gesture of victory, as if male-female relationships were a competition, and in the process, they'd made a mess, and then expected someone else, a woman, to clean up after them.

"I don't have to listen to this," her father said, getting up from the table.

"No," she agreed, "but I think you should."

She saw the look her mother gave him.

"All right," he sat down, with a heavy sigh. "Let's hear it. What is it you think you're going to sue us for?"

My god, he couldn't help it. Well, all the more reason.

"I don't *think* I'm going to sue you for anything. I *am* going to sue you."

"For what?" Her brother's tone suggested, as it always had, that she was crazy.

"One, emotional and cognitive abuse due to religious indoctrination. I think I've covered that.

"Two, discrimination on the basis of sex and marital status. If such discrimination is a violation of human rights in the workplace, it's surely a violation in the home. In both cases, the person's opportunities are diminished."

"You can't—"

"The sovereignty of the home has been challenged, successfully, specifically with respect to marital rape and child abuse."

"We never abused you!" Her mother protested.

"Weren't you listening before?"

Of course not. Not really.

"Being raised Roman Catholic, being *indoctrinated*—" She sighed. Then started over. "Roman Catholicism is a misogynistic cult full of sick and contradictory beliefs with no basis whatsoever, that encourages blind obedience, punishes critical thought, demeans women— And you forced that mindfuck on a child!"

Her father shrugged his shoulders.

"No!" she almost screamed. "You don't get to do that anymore."

"What?" he shrugged his shoulders again, grinning.

And at that, that grin, she almost got up and walked out. But.

She didn't see that Nathan and Tanya almost did the same. Nor had she seen them silence Kim a few times. As for Devon, he'd been too surprised to say anything.

"You don't get to avoid my questions by implying that the answer is obvious. You've done that all my life. *Articulate* the answer you think is so obvious, and let me consider it, let me hear your reasons—"

Every single interaction she'd had with her parents had been superficial. Just day-to-day management. Not once had they even come *close* to having a conversation of substance.

She remembered the time her mother came home after work to find her sitting at the dining room table having a conversation with two strangers. They'd come to the door giving away copies of a magazine titled *The Plain Truth*. When she took one, opened it, and actually started to read a bit, they asked if they could come in. She'd said yes. They didn't laugh at her questions about God, right and wrong, life and death. For two hours they talked. It was the best conversation she'd ever had.

The closest she'd come to an exchange of any importance with either one of her parents was when her mother had called her a slut. She was in her fourth year at the time, she'd already moved out, and she'd gone to Toronto for the weekend with her brother's friend. Why her mother had a sudden interest in what she did, she had no idea. But she cautioned her, asked her to think carefully about her questions, told her she would not lie. And yet her mother had persisted. Did you stay in a hotel? Did you share a room? Did it have two beds? And then— Her mother had practically spat the word. Then left the room. 'Mom, please— Let's talk about it.' But no. 'I can't even look at you!' was the end of it.

It hurt. Of course it hurt. Up to that point, she'd respected her mother. Wanted to please her. Wanted her to be proud of her.

Yes, she *had* been *a slut*. That is to say, she'd had sex with men she wasn't married to. Men she had no intention of marrying. She wanted to know why that was cause for such disapproval. She didn't lie to the men she was with, she never pretended she was offering anything more than a one-night stand. She suspected that her mother's response was an unexamined reflex, an inherited attitude, perhaps based on the belief that women who gave it away decreased the price of those who sold it, for marriage. Which made sense if you needed a husband for financial support while you were raising kids; if there had been paid maternity leave, then state-provided daycare ... In any case, if you had no intention of raising kids, that whole argument fell apart. So—

Just then, it hit her. Her mother wouldn't've been *able* to explain, let alone justify, her pronouncement. It *was* just an unexamined reflex. And maybe that's why her father just shrugged his shoulders so often. It was a cover-up.

Their lack of substantive discussion, their relentless superficiality— It wasn't because they refused, it wasn't because they thought she wasn't worth discussion of any consequence. It was because the surface was all there was. There wasn't anything *to* discuss. They had no thoughts on the matter. No reasons for their opinions, their values, their actions, or lack thereof.

They didn't arrange for her piano lessons because they loved music. It's just that that's what good middle-class parents did. Piano lessons for their daughters so they could entertain guests. Clarinet or trumpet lessons for their sons so they could play in the band.

Same for having the cottage. They didn't feel any love for the lake, the forest— It was just a middle-class convention. They packed the car and kids on Friday after work and arrived Friday night; her mother spent Saturday morning cleaning the cottage, went into town that afternoon to do some shopping, then made dinner, while her father spent the day cutting the grass and then fixing things, and in the evening, they played cards. Oblivious to the sunset. They could've done all that at home.

And the wall of books in the den … They probably just belonged to some book-of-the-month club. Because that's what middle-class people did.

All of which would suggest that they may not have engaged with her brother in any substantive way either. But they sure as hell took his opinions and aspirations more seriously.

"You also said you're suing for sex discrimination," her brother said. Challenged. "How do you figure that?"

"Seriously?" She stared at him. "They've always treated you differently. Better.

"I wasn't given money for spring break at Daytona Beach. For starters.

"You got a genuine Ingo sweater for Christmas. Cheryl and I got knock-off Warrens.

"You got Adidas. We got knock-off Cougars. Did you even *try out* for the track team? For *any* team?" she added.

"So," she looked at her mother, then her father, "did you just figure he was … entitled? To better? Because he was male?"

Silence.

She turned back to her brother. "Everything you did was automatically better."

Then she turned back to her father. "You even thought his degree was somehow more of an achievement than mine."

"Well," he replied, shrugging his shoulders.

"Well *what?*"

"He was in Business."

"And, what, Business is harder than Music? Is that why he quit the clarinet after a year?

"Besides which, he got a C average. I got straight As. Did he get any scholarships? No. Did I? Yes. And yet you persist in thinking he was the better student."

No response.

"I remember one time you cut the grass, and I was surprised because that was *his* chore. His *only* chore, I might add. You said you did it because he had to study for his exams. How did it not occur to you that I had exams too?"

No response.

"Not once, *not once*, did you— I remember that you attended a few piano recitals and that you came to one of my gymnastics competitions. That's it. And honestly? I got the impression you felt compelled to do so."

Her mother looked a little sheepish.

"I certainly didn't get the impression you came because you had a genuine desire to see me, let alone cheer for me.

"But when Doug put together a model ship one weekend, you oohed and aahed and put it on permanent display."

Her father shrugged again. Ships versus piano and gymnastics. It was a no-brainer.

"He got a chemistry set for Christmas. We got Easy-bakes. What message did you *think* you were sending?"

"It's just what one did then!" her mother protested.

"Yeah. I get that. What *you* don't get is that that doesn't make it right. You think conformity trumps morality?"

Again, no response. Perhaps they didn't understand. But she couldn't say it any more simply than that. And they weren't *that* stupid. They just weren't thinking about what she said. They never had.

"If I'd been black-skinned, adopted, and you treated your other two kids, white-skinned, with more attention, more encouragement, more praised, more money, you don't think I'd have a case for a civil suit because of discrimination on the basis of race? Skin colour?

"This family, that the two of you made, is a perfect reflection of sexism in our society. Congratulations."

Her mother smiled.

Seriously? Maybe she *was* that— In which case—

"Parents have to prepare their kids for the world that exists," her father spoke up, "not some ideal world."

"So that makes it okay to tell your daughter to subordinate herself to men?"

"We never did that."

She turned to her mother. "You told me, on several occasions—and they were clearly reprimands—not to let my intelligence show."

"Because men don't like—"

"Exactly."

She waited a moment, then summarized.

"You taught me, and I learned, that because I was a woman, I wasn't as important as a man. Any man. All men. I was less. Less important, less capable, less worthy.

"My opinions— didn't really matter.

"My aspirations— didn't really matter.

"My achievements— didn't really matter.

"I was supposed to get married and have kids. I was supposed to subordinate myself to a man and to my reproductive capacity. End of story.

"Which brings us to discrimination on the basis of marital status.

"I wasn't given a fridge," she turned back to her sister, "or an expensive stereo," she turned to her brother.

"It was a wedding gift!" her sister protested.

"Precisely. But think about it. What does a fridge or a stereo have to do with being married? Do single people not need fridges? Not want stereos?"

No response.

"They're setting-up-a-household gifts. But they're given only to people who *marry*."

Silence.

"Furthermore, my guess is one or both of you were given an interest-free loan for a down payment on a house."

She saw that she was right.

"So, what," she looked at her mother, "I don't need a house? I'm supposed to live on the street? Or rent an apartment for my entire life?" She looked at her father. "You'd be the first to point out what a waste of money that would be. A lifetime of rent payments and nothing to show for it."

"That's it!" her father burst out as he shoved his empty dessert plate away from him. Why did men do that? It looked like a denial of responsibility for things once they'd gotten what they'd wanted. It was if to say that cleaning up after themselves, that the consequences of their taking, their actions, was not their concern. "I've had just about enough of this!"

"Of what? Truth? Honesty? Criticism?"

The irony.

"It's a stupid idea," her brother said. "Everyone I know would be subject to such a lawsuit."

She nodded. And thought of all the people who, as kids, had had it worse, *far* worse, than her. Maybe they too could get some … satisfaction, closure, if not justice.

"If you go ahead with this," Anne-Marie agreed, "people are going to think twice about becoming parents."

She nodded again. "You say that as if it's a bad thing. I hope that happens. I hope people *do* think twice about whether they become parents, not to mention whether they have an inalienable right to reproduce."

"So you think the government should regulate who can and cannot reproduce?" Nathan asked. In an impressively neutral tone.

"I think people who want to be parents should meet some minimal standards, yes. Don't you think it odd that we allow people to manage, to be responsible for, a child's physical, cognitive, emotional, and social development, from birth, for a good fifteen years—with no particular knowledge about that development whatsoever?"

"I do."

"People have to study for two years and obtain a diploma," she continued, "before they can get a job looking after kids in a daycare centre. Why should the bar be set higher for raising *other* people's kids than for raising your own? Are other people's kids more important than your own?"

"It is an indefensible position, isn't it," Nathan agreed.

"Without any training, my guess is that most people raise their kids pretty much the way they've been raised. My guess is—"

"And what, that's not good enough?" her father challenged.

She was, again, dumbfounded.

"You're just not getting it, are you? No. Your parenting wasn't good enough. It wasn't even *close* to being good enough."

"No one's going to tell me how to raise my kids!"

"Why not? You don't *own* us."

"I sure as hell had to pay for you! I worked every day of my life to support you!"

"Not exactly true. I remind you that I had to pay for everything but food and shelter once I turned sixteen and got a job.

"And as for that shelter, you would've bought a house anyway, right? Did you have to build an extra wing for me? No. Was the mortgage higher because you had kids? No. Did you have to pay more for house insurance? No.

"So other than my food, clothing, school supplies, and health and hygiene products, what great expenses did you have to bear? Until I got a job of my own?"

No response.

"Yes, you worked all your life, but you would've had to do that anyway. What did you have to do that you wouldn't've done if you hadn't've had kids?"

"Lots of things."

"Name ten."

"I stopped smoking because of you."

"And he stopped drinking so much," her mother added.

"Both of which you should've done anyway, but thanks. Is that it? That's what entitles you to raise me however you want?"

"I put food on the table," her father repeated, "and a roof over your head—"

"And," her mother was so upset she interrupted, "your father never ... you know, like we hear so much of these days, we never hit you—"

"*That's* the bar? Food, shelter, and *we didn't hit you?*"

Silence. She was tempted to invoke the Roman Catholic distinction between sins of commission and sins of omission.

"Seems to me you've done okay," her father grumbled after a few moments. "We must've done something right."

"Oh no, you don't," she said tightly. "You don't get to take credit for what I am, for what I've done. I became what I am in spite of you. Not because of you.

"And think of how much better I might have done with your support, your help, hell, with even a little encouragement. I might've become the next Laurie Anderson."

She didn't see Tanya nod ever so slightly.

"Do you really think a diploma can replace love?" her mother asked, leaning forward slightly.

"No. It adds to it." She paused. "It proves it."

"So you really don't think having kids is a human right?" Nathan asked, curiously.

"I really don't. I think it should be an acquired right, an *earned* right. A privilege."

He nodded.

"And I certainly don't think it's an inalienable right. And on *that* point, our system is already in agreement. Sometimes kids are taken away from their parents and put into foster care."

"You just wait," her mother said, leaning back. "Once you have kids of your own ..."

She stared at her in disbelief. "I'm not going to have kids."

"You don't know that!" she smiled.

It irritated the hell out of her. That smile. And in this case—

"Just how old do you think I am?"

No response.

"Fifty-five. Past menopause. So I *do* know that," she added.

"Quite apart from I was on the pill before I started having sex. And I had a tubal ligation at thirty. You talk as if one has no control over reproduction. You do know how babies are made, yes? You don't find them in the cabbage patch, and the stork doesn't deliver them to your door, you—"

"Enough!" Her father said once again.

She ignored him. It felt good.

"I get that because you were Catholic, or rather, because you *thought* you were Catholic, and/or because it was the 1950s, you didn't have access to contraception or abortion, but even so, having kids or not is *well* within your control. If you don't want to have kids, don't have sexual intercourse." She looked at her mother, then stared at her father. "It's that simple."

"We did the best we could," her mother protested.

"And that's supposed to excuse you? Absolve you? So if I walked onto a plane, insisted on being the pilot, and then crashed it, causing serious injury to several people—that's okay? If I did the best I could?"

"It's not the same," Doug scoffed.

"How so?"

"No one forced you to pilot the plane."

She waited. In vain, apparently.

"Am I missing something?" She turned to her parents. "Did someone force you to become parents? Did someone force you to have sexual intercourse?"

Of course, they couldn't identify the cultural forces at work. Let alone resist them. One gets married and has kids. The implication is that anyone can do it. Since the belief is that everyone should do it.

"You're an embarrassment. Both of you."

Because it seemed they had truly never thought about it. Any of it.

"And whether your utter thoughtlessness is due to stupidity or laziness, I don't know. And I don't really care."

She looked at one and then the other.

"But there's a price to be paid for such thoughtlessness, for such mindless conformity. *Should* be a price to be paid. Because it has had consequences for others. Painful consequences. Injurious consequences."

She looked again at one and then the other.

"I think you should leave," her father said, standing up. Not looking at her. "You're not welcome here."

"Then why the fuck did you ask me to come?" She stood up as well.

"We thought—" her mother didn't finish her sentence.

"What? What did you think? What did you hope would happen here, today? Apparently not reconciliation, since you didn't even begin to address the elephants in the room. Did you think I'd pretend they aren't here? That I'd forget why I'd left?"

No response.

"You're right," she turned to her father. To her father's back. "I'm not welcome here. Never have been. And when I realized that, well, that's why I left. Why I've stayed away."

She went upstairs for her coat. And heard her father ask Doug if he wanted to play a game of chess. And then heard the clatter of dishes as her mother started clearing the table.

Nathan was waiting for her at the bottom of the stairs, Tanya and Devon at his side.

"I'm sorry my parents treated you the way they did," Nathan said to her. "I would have liked to have known you while I was growing up."

"Thank you."

"Me too," Devon said.

"Me three," Kim added as she came to join them.

"Are you driving back?" Tanya asked. "I mean now? You're welcome to stay overnight at our house. We have a guest room. Perhaps we could spend some time together tomorrow? I mean, if you'd like that."

She considered the invitation. "I would like that, yes, thanks." She smiled at them.

"Can I come too?" Kim asked. "For overnight and—tomorrow?"

"We'll have to ask your grandfather," Nathan replied.

"He's not the boss of me!"

"He kinda is," Devon said, grinning.

They sorted out the logistics. She put on her shoes and fastened her coat.

She paused at the front door before she left. Her mother had not come to see her off. No doubt she was in the kitchen, perhaps fighting tears. She glanced into the living room. Her father was pointedly engrossed in the chess game. He looked old. So had her mother. This was cruel. The public humiliation of a lawsuit would break them. Yeah, well, years of private humiliation had broken her.

And countless others who had parents just like them.

# Home for Unwed Fathers

About a month after, they came to get him.

"Hello, is there a Rob Ellis here?"

He heard the polite voice at the door.

"Yeah," his mother replied. "Rob!" she called up the stairs.

Rob came down the stairs and warily approached the two people standing at the door.

"Rob Ellis?"

He nodded.

"Would you please come with us? We have an order to escort you to the Home for Unwed Fathers." The taller woman turned the tablet to face them both, so they could read the order if they so wished. They did not.

Instead, his mother turned to him, rage on her face. "You—"

He said nothing. Just stood there. Unsure—

"Go!" his mother shouted at him. "Get the hell out of my house!" She reached out then, grabbed him, and practically shoved him out the door. "You fucker!" She spat. She actually spat at Rob's feet.

Rob stumbled across the threshold.

"You're allowed to bring one suitcase if you like," the other woman said to him.

"No! Let him go as he is!" His mother slammed the door.


Once at the Home, they put an ankle monitor on him.

"What's this for?" he protested. "I'm not on house arrest, am I? I haven't done anything wrong!"

The woman stared at him. Eventually, he looked away.

"It's for your own good," she said then. "If you try to go back home, there will most likely be worse consequences."

Well, she was right about that. But maybe he could go stay with Tyler. No, his parents wouldn't exactly welcome him either.


Next, they branded him. A small 'U' on one cheek, an 'F' on the other. Unwed Father. Or, as his mother would surely say, Unwed Fucker.


For nine months, he had to live in the Home. It was an older house, renovated for its current purpose. On the ground floor were the administrative offices, a kitchen, and a dining room. The upstairs was divided into four small bedrooms, each with two bunk beds; a large communal bathroom was in the middle. The basement had a small utility room, and, now, two large areas that served as school rooms during the day, recreation rooms in the evening.

The house was full: sixteen guys, their ages ranging from thirteen to just shy of eighteen. Several other Homes were scheduled to open that month, as soon as the accelerated renovations were done. The demand was quite high.

There were rules about what to do when. Everything they did had to be supervised. They couldn't even go outside into the fenced yard alone. It was like they were kids. He was seventeen, for fuck's sake.

He spent the mornings and the afternoons in class, with no spares: he had to keep up with his regular courses in order to pass the year and graduate, and there were a ton of extra courses, every one of them mandatory: child development—physical, intellectual, emotional, social; nutrition; first aid; parenting skills for a newborn, an infant, a toddler, a child, a teenager. They had some good laughs about that last one.

Once a week, they were all encouraged to go on the day trip. They'd pile into two mini-vans, each with 'Unwed Home for Fathers' emblazoned on the side, and spend the afternoon at the mall or, more likely, attending the Saturday game of some local sports league. Every one of the guys wore an over-sized hoodie and a baseball cap, but still, it was obvious. Who they were. What they had done.

He talked with some of the guys, mostly Mitch, his bunkmate.

"It's not fair!" he'd protested early on. "I don't even know if she's pregnant." Though, he supposed, she must be, if he was here. She must have identified him as the father. That's how they knew to come and pick him up.

"Yeah, we all fucked someone," one of the other guys said. "Big deal, everyone does it."

It seemed that all of the guys had pretty much the same home situation and so were actually content to be there in the Home. And as for when they got out? Don't know, don't care.

Rob would have said the same thing, had someone asked, but hearing it from so many others, it started to sound … inauthentic. He didn't know what was going to happen when he got out of there, but truth be told, he did care.

About eight months in, one of the women came down to the classroom and asked him to come upstairs to one of the offices. It was the same woman who'd put the ankle monitor on him.

"Have a seat, Rob."

He sat.

"So … Kaley has survived childbirth."

He was caught by surprise. He hadn't expected that to be what he'd been called to the office for. Honestly, he hadn't even thought much about Kaley, her being pregnant, going through childbirth. And the word 'survived'—had there been a chance she *wouldn't* survive?

"You don't know it's mine! I wasn't the only one bangin' her."

Again, the woman stared at him. Again, eventually, he looked away.

"We do know. A paternity test was done. Back when." And since every male's DNA was on file …

So now what, he wondered.

"Now we wait for her to confirm her decision. Whether to keep the baby or give it up."

Well, if she decided to give it up, what the fuck had he spent almost nine months in stupid parenting classes for? Actually, even if she decided to keep the baby, what the fuck had he spent almost nine months in stupid parenting classes for? It was her body. Her baby. *She* should be the one in parenting classes.

The next day, he was asked again to come to the office.

Again, "Have a seat, Rob."

Again, he sat.

"Kaley has decided to give up her baby."

Yes! He was off the hook!

But then he was, again, caught by surprise: another woman entered the office, holding a newborn.

"As you know," the first woman continued, "when a woman gives up her newborn, it automatically goes to the father."

The other woman held out the baby to him. "Her name is Cindy."

"But—" He did not reach to take the baby. "No— It's not my fault!"

The first woman spoke, while the second one took a seat, carefully holding the baby. "Are you saying that Kaley, a fifteen-year-old girl, somehow overpowered you, restrained you, brought you to erection, and then to ejaculation into her vagina?"

"No, I—" Did they have to be so blunt?

"Even if that were the case," she continued, "perhaps because she put something in your drink, you willingly put yourself in that position, no?"

"No! I mean— I used a condom!" He actually couldn't remember if he had or not. Probably not. They weren't cheap.

"Yes, well, sometimes condoms break. There's a chance with *any* contraception that it won't work. That's the risk you take when you engage in sexual intercourse."

"But— I don't want it." He didn't even look at the baby.

"Well, you should have thought of that before. Before you ejaculated into Kaley's vagina."

"I didn't— We were just fooling around, having fun!"

Yet again, the woman stared at him. "You didn't know how babies are made?"

"No— Yes— I'm not stupid!"

She kept staring at him.

No one spoke.

"Okay," he leaned back in his chair and crossed his arms. "If she can give it away, so can I." He glared at them.

"No," the first woman said, "one of you has to take responsibility for it. Ideally, both of you take responsibility, but that's not an option here, apparently. Kaley got first choice, since it's been her body the baby has been using, but since she said no, well, it's … yours."

"Why didn't she ask me first? I'd've said no. Then she could've had an abortion! I would've *told* her to have an abortion!"

"Rob," the second one spoke up, gently, "you know that's impossible. Abortion's been illegal for years now."

"Well, I won't take care of it," he insisted. "I'll just … leave it somewhere."

"That's your choice, of course, but as you should know by now, the baby will likely die without your care. And then you'll be charged with infanticide. For which the penalty is assisted suicide."


Since Rob hadn't planned for any of this, they arranged transfer to a 'Tier 2' Home, one that had the appropriate facilities and resources for babies.

"I figure I'll get a job," Rob said to Mitch, thinking out loud as he packed his stuff. Because no way was he going to live in another Home and— Actually, he didn't know what that future would look like. "I'll get an apartment, hire a babysitter for during the day, then—"

"You won't get a job," Mitch scoffed. "No one will hire you with those," he nodded to his cheeks.

"Why not? If I work hard—"

"If you do it again, they'll be the ones have to pay for this," he gestured at their situation. The house. The program.

Rob looked puzzled.

"It's the law."

Oh. Rob sat down heavily.

"Even if you *could* get a job," Mitch continued, "you probably wouldn't make more than what you'd have to pay the babysitter.

So you'd still be out rent, food, diapers …"

Rob exploded back onto his feet and started pacing the small room. "So how the fuck am I supposed to do all the stuff I gotta do?! For the baby?"

"Ah," Mitch sighed, "an age-old problem. With an age-old solution." There was a crooked grin on his face.

"What, I get married? I suppose that would work …"

Mitch scoffed again. "Good luck with that."

"Why? I'm good lookin'," Rob glanced at the mirror, as if for reassurance on that point.

"You're damaged goods is what you are," Mitch replied. "Who's gonna want someone who's got a kid to look after?

"And even if you didn't," Mitch continued, "even if Kaley had kept the kid, who's gonna take a chance that you won't be a Fucker again?

"Who's gonna want someone who's pocketing only part of their wages?"

"What?" Rob stopped pacing.

"If Kaley had kept the kid, they would've taken your wages to support her and the kid, *your* kid, for six years, then just the kid, *your* kid, for another twelve. Don't you know anything?"

Rob sat down again. Slowly. Thinking this through.

Mitch waited, the crooked grin back on his face.

Rob saw no way out. "Okay, genius, so what—"

"Didn't you pay attention to your Women's History course?"

Ah. But Rob just snorted. Then protested, "I ain't a woman!"

# Fighting Words

She was so tired of it. They all were. Every day, as they walked from one classroom to the next, or to the cafeteria, or to the gym, "Hey, ho!" "Gonna do me?" "C'mere, I got somethin' for you!"

Then from school to the bus stop. "Y'all jus' bitches, you know that, right?" "*She's* a slut!" "No, *she's* a slut!" Laughter. Always laughter.

And as they wandered through the mall. "Hey, look, a bunch of cunts!" "Yo, slag, c'mere!" This last, with a British accent.

Of course, they'd all tried to respond in kind. Problem was, there was no 'in kind'. 'Asshole', 'dick', and 'prick' just meant idiot. 'Stud' was a compliment. There was no word—

Then one Saturday afternoon, when she and her friends were standing in line to see a movie, one of the older boys they knew called out to a guy, "Oh, look at the little puss-in-boots!" The guy was a young man, actually, not someone from their school. And he completely lost it.

Someone called 9-1-1. Everyone got it on their cell phones. Mall security managed to stop the fight and hold onto the two of them until the police arrived. Shortly after, the paramedics wheeled them both away, and they read all about it in the following weeks.

There had been a number of nasty punches, resulting in one very broken nose and one seriously bruised kidney.

The boy charged the young man with assault.

The young man responded with the 'fighting words' defence.

And won.

They looked up from their smartphones. He won? The same eureka-moment flickered on each of their faces. They started googling, as they settled into more comfortable positions in Teague's room.

Women had tried suing men for defamation. After all, surely relentless sexual insult 'causes injury and damage to the woman's character'.

"It fucking *dismisses* her character," Teague muttered when they start read the definition.

"Maybe the courts didn't see it as making *false* statements," Sophe suggested as she continued to read the rest of the definition.

Teague and Em stared at her. Fuck. She could be right.

"It also says," Sophe read aloud, "'The statement must have been made with reckless disregard for the truth, meaning the person questioned the truthfulness but said it anyway.'"

"Right," Teague said with disgust. "How often do men question the truthfulness of *anything* they say?"

Em nodded.

"They've been bullshitting so long," she added, "they believe their own bullshit."

"But," Em pointed out, reading, "damages include 'pain and suffering', which covers 'personal emotional reactions such as shame, humiliation, and anxiety'." She looked at them.

Yeah.

"And," she continued, "'being ostracized from a social group'."

"*That* certainly applies," Teague said, angrily. "Every time a woman is called a cow or a cunt, she's ostracized from humanity."

"So," Em said thoughtfully, "wouldn't sexual insult be cause for a class action suit?"

"You'd think so," Sophe murmured, tapping away, "but the charge seems to stick only when lost income is at issue. Figures." She looked up at them. "Money. Business. The world."

In any case, they discovered that defamation was considered damaging only when the statement was public; one-to-one didn't count.

"Maybe it's just as well," Sophe said, leaning back, "because do we really want to limit freedom of speech? I mean, remember that article we read in class? 'Freedom to Offend'? The way to deal with something you don't agree with is to make a counterargument."

"But when they call us sluts, they're not making an argument," Em pointed out. "So there's no—

"True, but—"

"And remember Stoltenberg's comment," Teague added. "*Exceptions* to freedom of speech exist because some speech causes harm that cannot be redressed or undone by more speech. That's why defamation is illegal."

They turned back to their phones.

Women had also sought remedy on the basis of 'intentional infliction of emotional distress'.

"Also called 'outrage'," Sophe announced happily, looking at her screen. "'This cause of action may be available for cases that involve just words or in cases that involve both words and acts'," she continued with optimism, then deflated: "'In order to be actionable, the defendant's conduct must be extreme, meaning that it exceeds all bounds of decent behavior.'"

She sighed and leaned back.

"And that's the problem," she said. "This sort of thing has become *normalized*."

"Yeah. Wonder how that happened," Teague said bitterly.

Because they knew the answer. The internet had made porn easily available, and therefore (therefore?) widely viewed. And it had become, almost all of it, so completely degrading: women were invariably presented as subservient, doing, willingly or not, whatever disgusting thing the men wanted them to do. And apparently boys, and even men, were unable to distinguish reality from fantasy: they came to believe that women actually existed to please men, sexually; they came to believe that they were *entitled* to women's bodies. And so boys, and even men, routinely reached out and touched women's bodies. Grabbed women's bodies. Not only their behinds, but also their breasts. Thus routinely proclaiming that girls, and women, were sexually available to them. Hey ho.

"Hang on," Em had a thought. "Schools already have rules about bullying …" She started tapping at her phone again.

Sophe nodded and joined the effort. "Here we go. 'Bullying can be defined as repetitive, aggressive conduct growing out of an advantage in power and a desire to control. Said conduct can include the repeated infliction of verbal abuse such as the use of derogatory remarks, insults, and epithets.'"

"Perfect," Teague said.

"'While the techniques of bullies vary,'" Sophe continued, "'their object almost always is to gain control over the victim by engendering shame, anguish, fear, and/or humiliation.'"

"Our entire sexist society bullies," Teague said. "It's *designed* to *enable* bullying. *By men. Of women.*"

Em nodded.

Sophe continued. "'Most victims of bullying experience guilt, shame, fear, embarrassment, and diminished self-worth. These effects can lead to anxiety disorders, depression, and insomnia. The targets have an increased risk of suicide and other forms of self-harm.'"

They looked at each other. Anorexia. Cutting. Two girls killed themselves last term.

Not to mention the self-fulfillment prophecy. Call a girl a whore often enough …

They found dozens of articles in law journals about bullying. But not one presented a gendered analysis of the phenomenon. Not one specifically addressed males bullying females.

And bullying in itself was not a crime.

Go figure.

"Why can't we just charge them with hate speech?" Em asked, then turned back to her phone.

"'A hate crime'" Em read, "'is a criminal offence committed against a person or property that is based solely upon the victim's race, religion, nationality, ethnic origin, sexual orientation, or disability.'"

There was a moment of silence. Then Sophe pointed at the elephant in the room. "Sex isn't on the list."

"How can that be?" Em was aghast. She looked it up again. And again.

Five definitions later, she echoed Sophe. "Sex isn't on the list."

"Which explains why Reddit banned GenderCritical as hate speech," Teague grimaced, "but continues to allow AntiFeminists and StruggleFucking. Previously called RapingWomen," she added with a grimace.

"Wait," Em was catching up, "how was GenderCritical hate speech? Gender isn't on the list either."

They looked at each other. Blankly.

"So," Teague concluded a long moment later, coming full circle, back to their starting point, "'fighting words' it is."

Em nodded. "If 'puss-in-boots' is considered an instance of 'fighting words', surely 'cunt', 'slut', 'ho'—"

"Not necessarily," Sophe interrupted.

"What? Why?" Em asked.

"They'll consider the context. For a man to be called a woman is more insulting than for a woman to be called a cunt."

Sophe was right. And they both knew it.

"A lot of men genuinely believe that," Teague added anyway.

"So a judge might decide that calling a woman a cunt is … okay," Em said, with disbelief, "because it's just …"

"Fact." Teague's voice was hard. "Women are sexual. They are to be fucked. They are to be incubators. End of story."

Geezus. How the *hell* did they get here?

"Even 'girls' is used as an insult," Sophie said. "And 'ladies'. When they say it … The *way* they say it. You know what I mean."

They did. Bottom line, it was insulting just to be called female. What do you do when what you *are* is an insult?

"Regardless," Em said, "it's a *defence*, right? 'Fighting words'? So we have to be hit first?" She wasn't keen on that part.

Sophe started tapping again. "'Fighting words alone are not considered assault,'" she read, "'but may be folded into an assault *charge*,'" she emphasized the word, "'if accompanied by threatening acts, for example, raised fists—'"

"A grabbed crotch?" Teague suggested.

"What about a smirk?" Em asked. "A facial expression is an act, right?"

Sophe sighed again. "That would probably be hard to prove." And she wasn't sure what 'folded into' meant, exactly.

"Wait a minute," Teague said, "I thought I saw … Here it is. 'Fighting words are words intentionally directed toward another person which are so venomous and full of malice as to incite him/her to immediately retaliate physically. … The offensive language is such that the person temporarily loses control of their actions.'"

"And that's exactly why women are at a disadvantage," Sophe said with frustration, leaning back again. "We're more mature than they are. We have greater self-control."

Em nodded.

"Which is truly ironic," she added, "given the laws against contraception and abortion, which *deny* us self-control …"

"Well, we'll just have to change," Teague announced. "The critical factor isn't the retaliation per se, it's that the resulting fight is a breach of peace." She'd continued reading. "We just have to make a fuss. We have to breach the peace."

"And," Sophe was thinking it through, "we just have to do it often enough to convince the courts that it *may* happen."

"Exactly." Teague consulted her phone again. "'Provocative words may be justification for an assault, provided the person uttering the words *understood or should have understood that physical retaliation would be attempted.* The words must be 'fighting' words.'"

"And," Sophe was getting on board, "since the court uses the reasonable person standard ..."

"What difference does that make?" Em asked. "I mean, it's not always reasonable to retaliate—"

"Because the 'reasonable person' in courts of law has always been assumed to be the 'reasonable *man*'."

"Ah." A reasonable *man* would retaliate.

"That's interesting," Teague said. "Maybe we've been *un*reasonable *not* to retaliate. By ignoring it all these years, we've been doormats. We've *let* them insult us."

"And so stayed alive," Em protested. "Atwood."

Yeah. Men are afraid women will laugh at them. Women are afraid men will kill them.

"Hang on," Sophe said, backing up. "Isn't it the case that if escape is possible, assault *isn't* justified?" She started tapping away again. Teague and Em, as well.

"Here it is," Em said. "'According to the Castle Doctrine, victims threatened with physical aggression are required to retreat if they can safely do so, before responding with force. If the victim were to respond with physical force when she could safely retreat, she would be charged with a crime concomitant with the amount of force used and the harm done to the aggressor.'"

"Oh, sure, *in that case* they identify the person as 'she'!" Teague said with disgust.

"But it's everywhere now," Em said, thinking about retreat. "Where are we supposed to go?"

Teague agreed. "Some days I feel like I'm spending all my time trying to avoid these assholes."

"Wait," Sophe said, still reading. "It's changed. The Castle Doctrine has given way to the Stand Your Ground Doctrine. 'In the last ten years, most states have extended the Castle doctrine to both public and private places. In these jurisdictions, everywhere a person stands is his or her castle. That is, most states have jettisoned the duty to retreat.'" She looked up at them, a smile creeping onto her face, then continued.

"'The major justification for Stand Your Ground laws is summarized most succinctly by the Supreme Court of New Jersey in State v. Abbott', which says 'The law should not denounce conduct as criminal when it accords with the behavior of reasonable men'" —she grinned at Teague— "'The manly thing is to hold one's ground, and hence society should not demand what smacks of cowardice. It is obvious that the interests to be protected by stand your ground laws are dignity and pride.'"

Sophe looked up to see both Em and Teague smiling, then finished the paragraph. "'So, if pride is a protectable interest … why should the law not protect other emotional and psychological interests …?'"

"Yes!" Teague almost shouted. "Why shouldn't we be able to defend our dignity and pride and everything else required for our emotional and psychological well-being? Especially since defending one's physical well-being is allowed!"

"Wait—" Sophe sounded discouraged again. "'Although the law is currently *without* protections for those who use physical force in defense of their emotional and psychological well-being,'" she glanced up, then resumed, "'*jurisprudence*'—that's the lawyers and judges—'has always vindicated the idea of physical force when certain non-physical interests of the victim are at stake.'"

"Aha!" Teague raised her fist.


They organized it on social media. On one of the 'by invitation only' sites.

"I don't know," ChatCat posted. "I've never hit anyone in my life."

"I'll do it," NotYrPrincess posted. She was a boxer.

"Me too," HockeyStick posted.

"Keep in mind that we don't have to really fight," Teague posted. "We just have to retaliate in a way that causes a fuss. The point, if we understand it correctly, is that the insult disturbs the peace or whatever."

"And if you don't feel comfortable with the physical part of it," Sophe added, "that's okay. You can be one of the people at the edge getting it all on your phone. We need people to post the incidents online."

"We also need someone to call 9-1-1," Em chipped in. "You can be that person." *She* was going to be that person.

"And we need people who can write about it," Sophe said. "So everyone who blogs, tweets, spins ..."

"We have to be prepared," Ruby49 cautioned. "The backlash will be vicious."

"Agreed. Hell hath no fury like a man one-upped by a woman." Sportster described an incident wherein she was playing basketball in a mixed league. She'd set up such a perfect pick, the guy ran right into her. Hadn't seen it coming at all. He was understandably embarrassed. But *so* embarrassed, so *humiliated*, by *a woman*, that he actually came at her and proceeded to plow her right off the court. No foul was called. Duh. She withdrew from the league.

"And that's how they do it," ButListen remarked. "They don't even have to pass any laws, to keep us offside ...."

"Yeah," Sportster replied, "but it wasn't fun anymore. As it was, the guys hardly ever passed the ball to me."

"A metaphor if there ever was one," said ButListen. And everyone heard the sigh.

The first reported incident was textbook perfect. If there'd been a textbook about this sort of thing.

"Hey ho!"

She glanced at her friend to make sure she was recording it.

"What did you call me?"

"A ho!" he laughed.

She started to walk toward him. Three other young women walked with her.

"Take it back!" one of them said.

"No!" he laughed again.

So she shoved him. So hard, he fell down.

Then, as predicted, all hell broke loose. His rage!

Someone called 9-1-1. The young man's broken nose was tended to. The young woman's black eye was tended to. They were both wheeled away for various x-rays.

And they were both charged with disorderly conduct and assault.

The young woman's lawyer argued that 'fighting words' had been uttered. Six different videos proved it.

Within an hour, said videos had been posted. Everywhere.

Accompanied by commentary that placed the blame, the responsibility, clearly on the young man. None of this 'A woman was raped' shit. No, it was 'A man, with malicious intent, provoked an assault, with complete disregard for women's moral right to be free of sexualized insult …'

Even so, the young woman lost the case.

But the idea spread like wildfire.

Early on, someone suggested organizing 'Take Back the Day' marches, reminiscent of the 'Take Back the Night' marches of the '70s. Someone else suggested that 'Take Back the Public Space' was more accurate. But it was 'Take It Back!' that caught on.

"But we don't want them to say it in the first place," Sophe had lamented.

No matter. 'Take It Back!' got its own hashtag.

Social media exploded with videos and reports … 'Men triggered five fights today …' Then ten. Then twenty.

It was hard, though. Women had to overcome a lifetime of 'Don't hit,' 'Don't hurt'…

"And that's how they've kept us subordinate all these centuries," ButListen posted.

And so the women who'd already broken through helped the others.

"Aim for their knees," JustDoIt7 posted. "Once a man's down, their upper body strength isn't as much an advantage!"

"Men have a weak spot," FightFire posted, "front and center, that we have *not* taken advantage of. It's time. Surely, it's time."

Schools had to hire extra security personnel. They'd already had to hire guards to oversee metal detectors at the entrances because so many young men came to school with weapons. Now they had to have personnel walk the halls all day.

Malls had to do the same. They too had already put guards at the entrances to watch for 'trouble-makers'. Now they had to have circulating guards.

Every day, the police lay more and more charges. Breach of the peace, disorderly conduct, causing a disturbance … and, always, assault.

Apparently, men couldn't help themselves. They kept up the insults, and once they were shoved, they could *not* just walk away. Let alone take it back. As requested. Said request seemed, universally, to elicit a 'Fuck you!' Which didn't help matters.

When was society going to get fed up with their young men? ('Young' as in 'under forty'. That seemed to be the age at which misogyny— Well, no, it didn't disappear, it never disappeared, it just … went underground. Still.) When would they be shamed for their immaturity?

"I get it," a prominent black man posted. "I've been called a nigger my whole life."

"Thank god for the SNCC, right?" a prominent black woman responded.

"You know it, sister!" He attached a smiley face.

"You do realize," the prominent black woman then posted, "that Stokely Carmichael said the only position for women in the SNCC was prone? Stokely Carmichael, the *civil rights* leader? What does that tell you?"

Apparently the prominent black man had logged out. No doubt, he had something important to attend to.

"I get it," a prominent gay man posted. "I've been called a faggot more times than I can count."

"All in one day?" a woman asked.

"And when it happens," another woman asked, "do they reach out and grab your penis when they say it?"

Apparently he too had logged out.

And, as predicted, the men upped their game. First, by outnumbering the women. No insult was made unless there were ten of them present. They were used to acting as a gang.

Women responded in kind. No retaliation was made unless there were twenty present.

"No fair!" The beaten men cried.

"No fair?" One blogger responded. "But gang rape—*gang rape*—*that's* fair?"

Then the men made sure they were armed. Baseball bats were too obvious, knives and guns could be discovered, and would most definitely lead to more serious charges, so they started putting palm-sized stones in their pockets.

Women responded in kind. And discovered it was relatively easy to swing a purse full of marbles.

Even so, fearing cracked skulls, those who already had pepper spray started using it.

Men started wearing face shields. And using acid.

And then, in a long-awaited landmark case, a judge was convinced that the young man before him *should have expected* retaliation. He should have *known* that a scuffle (yes, 'a scuffle') would ensue when he called the young woman in question 'a fucking cunt'.

The young woman in question won her case.

Sexual insults were considered fighting words. No question now.


And then, much to women's surprise, and delight, several of the lawyers who had been involved in pushing the 'fighting words' defence, pushed for sex to be added to hate speech legislation. Pushed to make the insults themselves an offence.

They succeeded.

Sexual insults were considered hate speech. No expectation of retaliation required.


And then, surprisingly, wonderfully, years later, when men no longer routinely called women sluts and hos, when they no longer heard other men routinely call women sluts and hos, they just … stopped thinking of them in that way.


But not after many, too many, young women had died from their injuries. They were appropriately remembered as martyrs to the cause. One headline that made mainstream news said it all: "Young woman dies defending our humanity".

# Comedown

*illions of us watched, eyes glued to the nearest television. At school, at play, at work. Everywhere. We held our breath.*

*"It's looking good … Drifting forward just a little bit … That's good …"*

*They had less than 30 seconds of fuel left.*

*"Houston, Tranquility Base here. The Eagle has landed."*

*The Eagle has landed! We did it! We landed on the Moon! People cheered!*

*Then we saw Neil Armstrong going down the stairs. And then those words, for all the world to hear, and remember, forever.*

*"That's one small step for man, one giant leap for mankind."*

*And then Buzz Aldrin bounded in slow motion across the surface. The surface of the Moon!*

*They took samples of the dust, collected some rocks, drilled for core samples. And planted the flag. The American flag. There on the Moon.*

It was such a … comedown. All those years, SETI listening so closely, so persistently, people everywhere excited every time they mistook a comet or a meteor for a UFO, and then this.

A surprise visit.

No one saw it coming.

Suddenly there was a small ship in the sky, heading our way. Well, not *our* way. It looked like it was going to land in the States. Washington, probably.

So everyone scrambled to meet it. The President, of course, with lots of security. Men with guns. And some sort of first contact team. A linguist? An anthropologist? A biologist? Robert J. Sawyer? Of course not. More men with guns.

And press. Lots of press. And aides pushing last minute speech revisions at the President.

And people. My god, Americans like to crowd. If Woodstock had had 500,000 people, Washington had ten times that. Five million people. Waiting. For what?

Well, that was the question, wasn't it.

*Every time people watched the now-famous footage, they stopped talking when the flag was planted. It was a sacred moment. They'd stand and put their hands over their hearts. And if someone didn't, well …*

*"Hey, aren't you proud to be an American?"*

*"I guess." An awkward silence. "I'm glad to be an American, sure, but—"*

*"Well, stand up then. Show some respect. That's our flag."*

The ship landed neatly. Uneventfully. After a while, the door opened. A ramp unfolded. It was just like all the sci-fi novels said it would be.

A figure appeared. Humanoid. It looked out at all the people, then focused on the ones nearest to him. All of whom were just staring. Stunned, I suspect.

"This is yours, yeah?" It did something to the tablet thing it was holding and the American flag wavered in the air, projected as a hologram. "I'm in the right place?"

The President took a step forward then, and launched into his speech, in the stentorian voice that got him elected.

"We greet you, we *welcome* you, to this *great* nation, the *United States* of *America*. A nation of which we're *proud*—"

"No—"

"A nation *strong* and—"

"Well, that's all very good, but—"

"And *free*—"

"No, you've got it wrong, I'm—"


*National pride, my ass. That's what the American public was supposed to think when they saw the flag being planted. Either that or 'Victory!' They were competing with the Russians, and they won.*

*But every government in the world knew otherwise. The flag was a claim to ownership, pure and simple. This was the U.S., remember? Capitalism? The right to life, liberty, and the pursuit of profit? It was like in* Far and Away, *that movie with Nicole Kidman, when the pioneers raced across the land trying to be the first to get to the section they wanted so they could put a stake in it, so they could claim it as theirs. It was like during the gold rush, when miners would stake a claim wherever there was something promising, just in case.*


"Collections."

"And a nation—" The President stopped speaking.

"You're in arrears?" It consulted its tablet. "For ... sixty orbits. Hm. Comes to—oh my—967.3 trillion." It looked at all the blank faces.

"U. S. dollars," it added helpfully.

They still didn't get it.

It tried again. "Property taxes?"

In the long and awkward silence that followed, one of the aides suggested that they retire to the Oval Office. Or the nearest Tim Hortons. Well, actually, they don't have Tim Hortons in the States, but you know what I mean. Someplace where the world couldn't watch whatever was about to happen. Because, as the aide correctly surmised, it wasn't going to be pretty. Let alone glorious.

"Sorry, but no thanks," the Collections Agent said to the invitation, "I'm on a schedule. So … how would you like to pay?"

"Um, ah, we don't have that kind of money," the President stammered. Unpresidentially.

"Oh, well, then, we'll just garnish your …" it tapped away on its tablet, "loan repayments."

"Excellent," the Secretary of the Treasury stepped forward with surprising poise. "I'm sure you'll find that that will cover the amount in full."

The agent tapped on its tablet … then tapped some more…

"Actually," it seemed to be scanning a long list, "none of your creditors appear able to pay in full. Not the way you've calculated their interest." It looked up then. "I'll just garnish the principals and consider the loans paid in full," it said cheerfully.

The Secretary of the Treasury fainted.

"There are 500 American billionaires," someone called out. With pride. Or not. "If each of those donated a billion dollars …"

"You'd still be short," it called back. "By 966.8 trillion," it added. Helpfully.

Again, silence.

"What about your natural resources?" it asked.

"What do you mean?" the President said. Stupidly.

The agent had resumed tapping. "No, I can see you … you're getting your water from Canada?" It looked up from its tablet. "But—" He turned back to it and tapped a bit more. "You used what you had to fill swimming pools in California instead of irrigating crops—*food* crops—in the Midwest? Why would you do that?" It looked up again, genuinely puzzled.

Awkward silence.

"And you haven't figured out yet how to desalinate?" It was amazed. And still tapping away.

"Actually, sir, m'am—" the Science Advisor to the President stepped forward, eager to correct the bad impression that was clearly being made, "we have. Figured out how to desalinate."

"And you're not doing it because …?"

The Science Advisor stepped back. Quickly.

It consulted its tablet yet again, then looked up in disbelief. "And you've already used up all your oil? In just—" it did the math, "ten seconds?"

"What?"

The Science Advisor stepped forward again, this time to speak quietly into the President's ear. "Relative to the presence of humans, if encapsulated into one day."

"What?"

"And you haven't figured out sun panels? Not even windmills and watermills? How the *hell* did you get to the moon?"

The Science Advisor muttered to himself. Then left. Just walked away.

"Look," the Agent sighed, "I'll give you some time, um … twenty-four hours, to come up with a plan for repayment." It retreated to its ship for a much needed drink.


Late that afternoon, a group of Nobel Laureates presented a carefully prepared plan. They were willing to engage in a one-way exchange program, to share their knowledge, as payment.

It was a heroic thing to do. Very patriotic. The President promised huge rewards upon their return. But they didn't do it because it was heroic or patriotic. They were trying to redeem humanity in the eyes of the alien.

When the Agent told them they'd be perfect for their teaching their six-year-olds, they beat a hasty retreat. After a moment of humiliating paralysis.


That evening, as a last resort, the President offered their weaponry. Really, what else did they have? Inventory after inventory was solemnly passed to the Agent. The pile in its (two) arms grew. And grew.

"Have you guys been spending *all* of your allowance on guns?" it quipped.

Yet another awkward silence. To which it raised his eyebrows.

It seemed, at least to the only woman on the President's staff, that the meaning of raised eyebrows was multiversal.

Finally, with considerable ceremony and much-to-do, the President offered the last inventory: one hundred state-of-the-art next-generation brilliant bombs.

"I think you'll find that covers it," he said. Weakly.

It flipped through the specs.

"'Fraid not," it said. "The museums won't pay *that* much for these."

"Museums?" the President said, then clutched at his heart.

"Hey!" the Agent had an idea. "We could turn you into a tourist destination. Sort of a theme park for our kids."

"Yes, we can do that!" the Vice-President had stepped up. Over the President's body. "We have lots of theme parks! We can add more! How many more would you like?"

"No, I meant—*you'd* be the entertainment. Just as you are."


Pity, the only woman on the President's staff thought to herself, at around midnight, the debt couldn't be paid with the American male ego.

Actually, that's kind of what happened. There was no way—no *fuckin'* way—men, especially *American* men, would be somebody's amusement. So the economists and accountants put their heads together, and reconceptualized this, and pretended that, and, by morning, said they could pay the arrears after all. Overnight, the U.S. became *not* the most powerful nation on the planet. And since they'd been the ones refusing to reduce emissions (4% of the planet's population and they were responsible for 25% of its carbon dioxide emissions), refusing to accept fact, scientific findings about global warming ... And then dominos did what dominos do, and China, well on its way to owning pretty much half of the U.S., also became not the most powerful nation on the planet. And since they'd been even worse with their emissions ...

# What Sane Man

She pushed the chair against the wall. It was a sturdy armed chair; that's why she preferred this motel. Then she helped him, still a bit groggy from the drink she'd doctored at the bar, from the doorway to the chair. Using zip ties—impossible to loosen, let alone break—she lashed his wrists to the arms, then his ankles to the legs.

When the sedative wore off, she put on the boxing gloves and started to hit him. First, a few jabs to his shoulders, to get his attention.

"What the—"

Then one to his stomach.

He struggled for lucidity. Then he struggled against the restraints.

She concentrated on his face. She broke his nose, one of his cheekbones, his jaw. He'd heal, but it would leave a mark. Not exactly a disfigurement, but people would be able to tell. He'd been beaten.

"Smile," she said.

"Fuck you," he drawled, then spit out a tooth.

She broke a few ribs. Then pummelled his shins. *That* hurt.

"Smile," she said again.

At the beginning, he'd shouted. Then he'd screamed. Then he cried. Finally, he just moaned.

When she was done, she took off the gloves, bagged them, snipped the ties, then left.

She didn't ask for his number.

She didn't even know his name.


At first, the men who'd been beaten didn't report it. They were embarrassed. Ashamed.

Then a few started doing so. But the police laughed at their claims. Dismissed them as cover-ups for intoxicated who-knows-what. S&M gone wrong or gang-related retaliation, they didn't really care.

In a few cases, when the victim was actually believed, no charges were pressed. Because how could it be proved? Had the victim recorded it on his phone? Had a credible witness been present? (Besides, what had they been doing in a bar in the first place?)

And because even when the incident *had* been recorded—and posted online at one of the many websites dedicated to such things—Boys, Boys, Boys, Beaten; Another Dad Bites the Dust; Black Men and Blue; Knocked Out Dudes—the women got off.


"And did you believe he was consenting?" the woman's lawyer asked. In a crowded court room.

"Well, yeah. A friend told me he was into this sort of thing."

"And you believed her?"

"Sure."

"It didn't seem implausible?"

"Nah. You see it all the time. Men fighting, punching each other … They like it."

"But that's crazy!" the victim cried out with indignation. He'd intended to assert his objection by rising forcefully to his feet, but all he managed was a painful crouch. "Who would consent— To this?" He pointed to his face, still swollen and bruised.

The judged looked pointedly at the prosecutor, who nodded then gently pulled at the man. "Sit down and be quiet," he hissed.

"But I said 'Stop!'," he protested. "I'm sure I did!" He met his assailant's eyes.

She shrugged. "'Stop' means 'Continue'. Your face said 'Continue'. Your screams said 'Continue'. Your moans— You *enjoyed* it! You know you did!"

"What sane man would have consented to what you did?" He stared at her in disbelief. "Let alone enjoy it?"

"For centuries," the woman's lawyer continued with her case, initiating a slide show on the projector screen, "men have enlisted in order to fight—"

"But *this* man isn't a soldier," the prosecutor interrupted.

"They have voluntarily entered the ring to be hit again and again—"

"But—"

"And every day we see movies and video games—a great number of movies and video games, all easily accessible— depicting men willingly engaging in physical fights."

"That's TV!" the prosecutor objected. "They're actors! Acting! Real men don't—"

"And although they often minimize their injuries, it's clear they're very proud of them. Win or lose, the men, and their injuries, are imbued with the heroic."

"There is nothing heroic about this!" The prosecutor presented one of his own images, the victim's chest, an ugly mess of purple and yellow.

"Regardless," she continued, "as my learned counsel well knows, it's the *mens rea*, the state of mind, of the *accused* that determines whether or not a crime has been committed here. She believes he consented. Perhaps with good reason, perhaps not. Either way, ergo, no crime was committed."

And so the woman went free. As did the next woman. And the next. And the next. Not convicted of a crime, nor even of a tort: when damages were mentioned, lawyers pointed out that at least the defendant hadn't left victim with a squalling infant to look after.

Worldwide, women went about beating up men. After all, that's what men were for. Fighting. Being beaten up. Women took out their frustration, their anger, on men. Television and video games started showing women beating up men, started showing men *enjoying* being beaten up by women. It became common. It became normalized. One in four *actual* men were beaten. By women. Few reported it. What would be the point?

# Sweet Sixteen

It's John's sixteenth birthday tomorrow. He's coming of age. His cousin, Jane, who lives just down the street, won't come of age until her eighteenth birthday, and everyone said at the beginning how unfair that was, but truth be told, and John knows it, guys can do a lot of damage between sixteen and eighteen.

"It's your sixteenth birthday tomorrow," his mother had said that morning, in a carefully neutral voice. "What are you going to do?"

"I don't know!" he'd screamed at her, as if she'd asked the question a hundred times before. Then he stomped out of the house, slamming the door on his way out. Standing in the middle of the yard, he'd called a few of his buddies, but they were all away. Summer camp, vacation, whatever. So he'd climbed into his old treehouse and sat there, alone, fuming. It was all he could do not to kick the walls out.

What happened was, in 2035 organized religion finally went too far. That might seem like an odd thing to say, given the institutionalized misogyny of Judaism that had Jewish men thanking their god every morning for not making them female, the Vatican's decision to prohibit contraception and permit pedophilia, the routine defrauding done by various Protestant evangelists, the Taliban's practice of beheading people, the Puritans' tendency to cut off people's ears and bore a hole in their tongues with a hot iron, the Inquisition's habit of dislocating limbs and burning people alive, the witch 'trials', the human sacrifices of the Mayan, Inca, and Aztec theocracies …

Ironically enough, it was the Americans' ramped-up military engagement with Islamic countries that made the long-time similarities between Christianity and Islam suddenly all too apparent. People started to see the my-god-versus-your-god subtext and were hard-pressed to prove their own god was the one true god. It wasn't something they were used to doing, providing support, actual evidence, for their beliefs.

(It didn't help that 'salvation challenges' became all the rage: people would challenge each other to jump off a cliff, each appealing to their god to save them and thus justify their faith. It was hard not to notice that the winners were always atheists. They were the ones with hang-gliders.)

So what, you may ask, was the thing that was considered going too far? Because really, how much further can you go beyond torture and mass murder?

It was this: the American president was not only refusing to sign anti-nuclear accords and pro-environment accords, he was actively pursuing nuclear and environmental destruction to ensure that the Biblical prophecy of the apocalypse would be fulfilled. He would thus prove once and for all that the *Christian* god was the one true god. That there would be no one left alive to appreciate such proof seemed to have escaped his notice.

Immediately upon discovering this insanity, the Scandinavian countries organized a global boycott of everything American, and, upon further thought, of everything from every country that claimed, one way or another, to be a nation under god.

The world became atheist overnight.

And then philosophy finally, *finally*, took its true place in society. The 'Philosophy for Children' programs run by various fringe 'wingnuts' were suddenly mandatory. The brave initiative in Canada in 1995 to introduce philosophy into the high school curriculum, an initiative that flashed then faded, blazed back into popularity: both senior courses became mandatory not only in Canada, but also in the United States, and courses were developed for grades nine and ten as well. At universities, Departments of Philosophy and Religion finally separated: Philosophy became a department on its own, and Religion was added to Folklore Studies or completely subsumed into invisibility by Ancient History.

And people, *ordinary* people, began to *think*.

Almost overnight, instead of hearing people talk on and on about sports, you could hear them, here and there, talk about things like how sure you had to be about something before you could say you knew it. Epistemology in the pubs!

And without religion to issue decrees, suddenly questions of right and wrong were, well, questions. Recourse to legal moralism was common among the lazier minds, but the presumed equivalence between law and morality did not go unchallenged.

People also talked a lot about rights and responsibilities. It was almost as if they had been wanting to do that for a very long time, but had lacked a vocabulary. The sudden proliferation of philosophy courses, as well as philosophy blogs, philosophy newspaper columns, philosophy talk shows, and even philosophical counselors (after all, many mental health issues are simply the result of not thinking things through clearly) gave them that vocabulary.

One of the first things to go was the right to reproduce.

"The Smiths and their Biochem Cubes" had become a staple in the grade eleven Philosophy course:

Suppose the Smiths make biochem cubes—biological-chemical cubes about one metre by one metre with an input for the resources required for sustenance at one end and an output for the unusable processed resources at the other. Why do the Smiths make biochem cubes? Good question. Truth be told, the cubes are unlikely to make the world a better place. And the Smiths don't sell them.

Should we make allowances for the Smiths with regard to money (salaries, taxes, subsidies, etc.)? After all, they have, let's say, five biochem cubes to support. If the cubes are to stay alive, the Smiths need to provide sustenance. They need a bigger house. More electricity. More food.

Should we encourage their 'hobby'? Perhaps even consider it respectable, a rite of passage to maturity?

Or should we censure it? Because once their biochem cubes become ambulatory, the rest of us have to go around them in one way or another. And when we're all dead, the Smiths' ecological footprints will have been at least 50% larger than that of those of us who don't make biochem cubes. Even larger, if the cubes they made go out and make other cubes …

Suddenly everyone was aware of Oliver Wendell Holmes' famous comment, 'Your right to swing your fist ends where my nose begins.' That is to say, suddenly everyone understood that the crux of the matter for rights was that, and how, others were affected. No right was absolute because no person was an island. Everything, everyone, was connected. Maybe not directly, maybe not immediately—if the change in the Earth's climate had taught us anything, it had taught us that—but connected, nevertheless.

So a *right* to reproduce? No. It was a privilege. One had to earn it. And even so, it could be taken away.

Shortly after, the abortion question was finally seen as a simple matter of competing rights: the right of the fetus to develop versus the right of the woman to carry on with her life as she wishes.

And once it was decided that the fetus' right *didn't* trump the woman's right, that the fetus didn't *automatically* have a *right* to develop, a right to *life*—why would it? just because some man ejaculated into some woman and started the process?—it was a very small step for people to realize that they themselves didn't automatically have a right to life. After all, *everyone* was just the result of some man ejaculating into some woman. Everyone was just someone's biochem cube.

A lot of people resisted. They struggled to argue for a right to life, an *inalienable* right to life. But there was simply no basis for it. Absent a god to grant it.


John wasn't aware of any of this, of course. He just knew that once he came of age, he had to prove somehow that he had a right to live. He had to be useful or valuable in some way. You got a free ride until then, that was the deal. But once you turned eighteen, or, if you were male, sixteen, you had to *earn* the right to life, you had to *prove* your life was worth—well, worth the resources you used and/or worth the negative consequences you inevitably caused for others.

It was easier for girls, John thought. Jane had been useful since she was old enough to wash and dry the dishes, standing on a stool at the sink. She had a whole list of chores to do: dishes every day, dinner twice a week, dusting and vacuuming on Saturdays, babysitting on Sundays …

She'd even learned to play the piano. By the time she was fourteen, she was practicing an hour a day, and the last time he was at her house, she played something by Mozart for him. She was useful *and* valuable. And she wasn't even sixteen yet.

When John saw how good Jane was at the piano—she'd even played some retro Supertramp for him once—he decided he'd become a musician too. So he got a guitar. But he had no idea how to play it. A friend of a friend finally showed him a few chords, but even after fiddling with it every now and then for two whole weeks, it was hit-and-miss, so he gave up. Clearly, he had no talent. Jane was lucky, he thought, she could do shit like that.

He didn't know why it was different for girls. Maybe all that stuff just came naturally. Guys were different. For example, a couple weeks ago, he and his buddies broke all the windows at their school. Every last one of them. They'd had a race to see who could break the most. And just last week they had a great time turning over everyone's garbage. He always felt a little bad the day after they did these things, seeing the mess they'd made, but a guy's entitled to have a little fun, right?

It had taken Jane a good two hours to pick up all the stuff that had overnight blown onto their lawn. Wads of tissue, scraps of soiled, unrecyclable packaging— So, he thought, philosophically, he'd given her the opportunity to be useful. Didn't that make *him* useful?

Long ago, his parents had told him that he had to cut the grass, but he'd said 'Fuck that!' and took off. They didn't insist. Truthfully, they were a little afraid of him.

All of the young men who in earlier times might have proved themselves useful as soldiers didn't have that avenue open to them now. There were no wars now. Killing someone— remember, everyone of age had earned the right to live now, they'd proven themselves to be useful or valuable—killing someone, taking away someone's right to life, was the quickest way to get your own right to life revoked.

And once people started thinking, they realized that football, hockey, soccer, basketball—these things did nothing to improve humanity. So that avenue for young men was also no longer open. The entertainment defence for that level of sport, for that concentration of resources for sport, was tried, but it failed. As it did for pornography. There was simply too much violence involved—and in the latter case, too much degradation—to grant entertainment value to anyone but vicarious sadists.

Even so, at the beginning it was easy for guys like John. On their sixteenth birthday, guys like John would just start roaming the highways picking up the garbage that littered the ditches. But a generation later, well, the kind of people who had earned the right to live weren't the kind of people who tossed their garbage out their car windows.

The more ambitious guys got jobs. But jobs weren't that easy to find now. Certainly John couldn't find one overnight. Even more certainly, he wasn't doing well enough in school to argue that he was going to become a scholar, a scientist, or even an entrepreneur.

And the truth of the matter was that John wasn't unusual. A great many men by the age of sixteen hadn't done anything, not one thing, to improve life for humanity, to justify their existence.

The same was true, of course, of a lot of young women. Especially the ones who'd expected to get a free ride just by being somebody's wife and/or somebody's mother. In fact, Brittany, one of John's classmates, would have trouble a couple years from now. In a previous time, she may have been useful as a prostitute, but once pornography became illegal, prostitution quickly followed. The similarities were clear, once people thought about it, but also, the demand for it had significantly decreased.

Even so, even now, in certain cesspool corners of the world, to which John and Brittany could escape if they'd known about them, Brittany could have, would have, found herself useful. But she would've been raped to death within six months.

And then John would have discovered just how useful *he* could be.

Now, he just kicked at the walls of the treehouse. Now he wished his parents *had* insisted. Again, and again, and again if necessary. That he cut the grass. Or whatever. It was their responsibility to make sure he was useful, wasn't it? They created him. It was their fault he was in this situation!

He looked back toward the house. Then came down out of the trees. And went on one last rampage.

Tomorrow he'd be sixteen.

And he wouldn't be missed.

# Ballsy

"I'd like to thank all of you for coming," the smartly-dressed woman smiled warmly at the several people seated around the board room table, each with a prospectus in front of them. Only one was a man.

"As all of you know, my name is Mariette Chandler. Kristina Bolaenko, legal counsel, is at my right, and Chen Li, financial advisor, is at my left. We're hoping that after today's presentation, you'll agree to invest in this exciting business venture. Based on similar ventures, the returns promise to be high, very high indeed. And yet, our venture is, dare I say, innovative.

"We have arranged a visit to one of our clubs, for those of you who want to see first-hand what we're talking about, but before—"

She paused as her assistant arrived with a rolling cart of refreshments.

"Please, everyone—" She gestured with her hand for those in attendance to partake, then waited as the young woman made a quick tour around the table, then took a seat at the back of the room.

"Thank you, Alyssa."

Alyssa nodded, then took out her tablet, ready for whatever notes she'd need to make.

"At 'Ballsy'," Mariette started her power point presentation—an image appeared on the screen behind her, an attractive building with the name emblazoned across the front—"members will be able purchase the opportunity, typically for half an hour or an hour, to kick a man in the groin, or do whatever else they want, whatever else gives them pleasure, and," she smiled at the room, "I must say that some of our clients have been rather imaginative—"

"You can't do that," the man spoke up, brimming with self-righteousness. "It's assault!"

Ah. Mariette had suspected as much. The man was a reporter. No matter. He'd discover that his editor would refuse to print any explicit descriptions. So she just nodded to her colleague. "Kristina, would you …"

"Certainly," Kristina said, then turned to the man. "We appreciate your concern," she smiled at him, "but I assure you that all of our employees will have signed a contract containing the appropriate clauses."

"But—"

Mariette cut him off by clicking to the next image. "These clips are from our flagship club here in Montreal. Within a year, we hope to have a 'Ballsy' in every major city. Within five years … who knows?" She smiled.

The screen showed a man with his arms raised and tied to a crossbar over his head, his legs spread and shackled to the floor, his genitals exposed, and already bruised and misshapen. A narrow foot shot out from off-screen.

The man present gagged and rushed to the wastebasket by the door.

"I supposed it's an acquired taste," Mariette said and smiled at the room.

The man in the video grinned, then panted, "Kick me again."

The next clip showed a man on all fours, a corkscrew hanging from his bloodied rectum.

Halfway back to his chair by then, the man quickly turned around.

During the next clip, he made it all the way back to his chair, staggering slightly and wiping his mouth with a tissue. He glanced at the screen, then stared at Mariette. "That one looks drugged," he accused.

"Oh, we don't allow drugs on the premises. *That* would be illegal," she laughed lightly. "And what our employees do on their off-time is surely none of our business."

A few more clips played.

"You won't be able to find enough men—"

"Our data suggests otherwise. As you know, unemployment among young men is increasing every year. We provide jobs. At well above minimum wage. Most of our men make more money in a day with us than they would in a week at a call center."

"But," one of the women spoke up, "I'm not sure I'd want my son to ..."

"Oh, no, your son will surely have other options. We're not here to recruit!" She laughed again.

When the opening image returned to the screen, Mariette began the next part of her presentation. "As we develop the brick-and-mortar," she smiled with excitement, "we will also develop the virtual. 'Ballsy' will be online. Chen?"

"Thank you, Mariette," Chen took the hand-off gracefully. "Adding the virtual will be virtually without cost," she smiled at her wordplay, "as we will simply record the live sessions and post them online."

"With the participants' contractual agreement, of course," Kristina added, smiling at the man.

"At the same time," Chen continued, "it will be immensely profitable. We already have advertisers clamouring to be a part of this."

"And we have discussed off-products," Mariette inserted smoothly, as the image on the screen changed, "posters, calendars, magazines— Imagine seeing 'Ballsy' images on buses and bus shelters, in your corner store's magazine rack, perhaps even in your kids' teachers' lounge …"

The man was horrified. "But— You can't *do* that!"

"But we *can*. Do that," Kristina said. "Precedent has been set. Our business, and all of its services and products, would be protected by freedom of speech."

"How is *that*," he nodded to the image currently on the screen, "*speech?*"

Kristina shrugged, then continued. "Traditionally, arguments to prohibit have been rejected, replaced with arguments for equal access. Well, here we are!" She swept her open hands around the room, then behind her to the screen, where the video clips taken at the club had resumed.

"But some of them are just boys!"

"All over-age, I assure you," Kristina said smoothly.

Mariette didn't say that the younger, the better. The more pliable. She didn't say that none of them lasted very long. Many, sadly, just lost their *je ne sais quoi* and had to be let go.

What she did say was, "At the moment, this may seem … offensive to some, but in a few years …"

"Indeed," Kristina said. "We anticipate that copycat franchises will develop, but," she assured the room, "we will fiercely protect our brand and strive to make 'Ballsy' everyone's first choice."

"Truthfully," Mariette said, "we welcome competition. Such growth would actually be to our advantage, as it would mean that such clubs have become commonplace, that the provision and use of such a service, has become normalized. Imagine a world in which there's a 'Ballsy' wherever you go!"

# Justified

It was inevitable.

By 2035, almost overnight, all of my classes were two-thirds female, one-third male. We'd finally achieved the critical mass I thought wouldn't ever happen. Correction. I thought wouldn't happen in time. I was middle-aged when the most powerful county in the world elected for President not the former Secretary of State, but a business mogul who denied climate change. People would rather die than be led by a woman.

Not that all of my female students were feminist. You'd always have the barbies, it seemed. But, now, enough of them were. Would be.

I say it happened almost overnight, but of course there were signs. Geneticists had known about the Y chromosome for decades. By 2013, it was, as one blogger called it, "a trainwreck of about 45 hangin'-on-by-their-pinkies genes."

At roughly the same time—call it synchronicity, call it intersectionality, or call it all-about-relationships and you'd really nail the irony—there was an increase in chemical pollution, specifically endocrine disruptors such as dioxin.

Blithely released into the ecosystem by companies run by men, dioxin was thought to mess with the Y chromosome (as well as a great many other things).

Couples had been needing IVF for decades. Of course, men thought it was the woman's fault, not being able to conceive. They didn't know, refused to believe, that it was because they didn't have enough sperm or because the sperm they had was swimming in the wrong direction. (Never mind that so many of them jerked off every day to online porn. They didn't know, refused to believe, that every ejaculation reduced sperm quality.) No sperm delivery, no Y chromosome delivery.

All of which is to say it was almost completely the men's fault.

Of course, they'd always been a minority, but 30% as opposed to 49% made them *visibly* a minority. And for people who depend on strength in numbers (the gang mentality), for people so subject to the herd mentality (possibly related to the former), for people so focused on the quantitative, this was, in a word, terrifying.

You'd think the remaining men might anticipate that they'd be treated like royalty. Correction. More like royalty. After all, they'd become rare. And it's too easy to equivocate being rare with being precious. Women would compete for them. (Well, the barbies would.) And so they could've. Become more like royalty. Because, well, do the (male) math: there were now two women for every man.

But, as I've indicated, they blamed women. Of course they did. It's always the woman's fault. (When the porn users discovered they couldn't get an erection any more with a real woman, they blamed those real women. And pressured them, expected them, to turn themselves into porn robots.) (Alas, all too many of them did.)

And so—even so—they started (started? continued.) killing them. (And they say, have been saying for centuries, that *men* are the rational ones.) (Their preference for sex with a make-believe female over sex with a real female, when their goal, one of their goals, is procreation— Well, it boggles the mind. The rational mind.)

It didn't help that testosterone levels had risen. Partly, this was a result of the growth hormones being fed to the animals that men ate (because real men eat meat) (as if they'd killed it themselves): the onset of puberty came earlier and earlier. Partly, it was a result of the boost provided by Viagra, Cialis, Levitra, and the other seven, now on the market: it wasn't just older men were losing their beloved erections. (And sexuality was that integral to their identity: I fuck, therefore I am.) But mostly, it was a result of the increase in the use of testosterone gels (an easy step from the oh-so-common use of steroids) among men whose natural testosterone production was in serious decline. (Because oh, the horror.)

It also didn't help that there was an increase in the use of porn. Partly this was due to demand: porn is addictive—which means that more and more is needed. More in terms of quantity, more in terms of quality. Though I hesitate to use the word 'quality' in this context. More accurate would be in terms of 'ability to stimulate'. And partly this was due to supply: the internet made it easy. So easy that every second, about 50,000 men were watching porn. (Up from 30,000 in 2016.) So easy that 90% of all men, and boys (they started at eight), watched porn every day. (Up from 80%.) Someone once said that every new technology would eventually, or perhaps initially, be used as a weapon. I doubt they included male masturbation aids in their definition of weaponry. They should have. Because 85% of all porn specifically humiliated and degraded the women portrayed. And 95% showed her being physically hurt. (Both, 5% increases.) And of course, what you expose yourself to affects what you think, what you do …

And on top of *that*, the gaming industry exploded. Well past car chases, so many of the games featured pornified women who could be raped by the male player. (*Player.*) Extra points if they killed her.

So.

Every week, every day, some man went on a killing spree. Most were members of some group—the Incel Rebels, the Brothers of Lepine, the O-Jays, the Bundy Bunch, Jack's Men—groups that had formed like cancerous tumours. Like stage four cancerous tumours. The word femicide came out of the closet.

At first, maternity wards were favourite targets. Because there were only women there? Or because the women there were birthing more women? Or because they weren't birthing men? Hard to say. Quite possibly all three.

Then they targeted schools. At first, the young women tried not to clump together, tried to position themselves in the middle of a group of men. But of course, that backfired. Used to be that only—my god, did I say *only?*—used to be that only one in three men would rape if they thought they could get away with it. Now it was two in three. And the percentage of rapes that resulted in conviction, let alone the percentage that was actually reported? It was a joke. To them.

So I was ready.

I'd carefully considered the seating plan and put the boys at my far left, closest to the door. I put the barbies in the middle two rows, and at my far right, my precious 'grand-daughters', the women who would save the world. Marie was becoming a brilliant biologist; Kim, a mathematician or maybe a physicist; I figured Brett for psychology or sociology; Chandra, music; Ming was our class poet, nay, our school poet if my opinion counted for anything; Meg, likely an engineer …

I moved my desk close to the wall, brought in a coat rack, squeezed it between my desk and the wall, then permanently hung my raincoat on it.

And I was tired.

For thirty years, the boys in my class had demanded, hogged, my attention. They showed up late, swaggering into class, daring me to send them to the office for a late slip. (For which *I'd* be reprimanded: 'But *why* don't they want to come to your class on time?') They interrupted me, they challenged me on every bloody thing. 'Are you sure that's right, *Ms.* Bennett?' Too soon the mockery they slid into the 'Ms.' wasn't enough: they called me bitch, cow, cunt. Openly.

Was it just me? The last time I peeked into Janet's room, I saw the wall behind her desk covered with dried and hardened spit balls. So I'm guessing no.

They didn't do the work. They didn't even try. And then they were outraged when they received a failing grade. I stopped failing them after one took a knife to my tires. Even so, the following year, another one took a knife to me. Apparently, he wasn't happy with the C+ I'd given him.

Worse, every time one of the girls, one of my granddaughters, spoke up, they put her down. Called *her* a bitch, cow, cunt. Threatened to shut her up. For good if that's what it took.

So when I heard the pops in the distance, I quickly moved to the coat rack and grabbed the automatic also hanging there. And when the pimple-faced boy with scraggly blond hair calmly opened the door and walked into my classroom, I started firing.

I killed him. Along with every one of the boys in my class. There was no doubt in my mind that every one of them would eventually kill several of my granddaughters. One way or another. In fact, as soon as the pimple-faced boy entered the room, three of them pulled out their own guns. And not to shoot back.

That they were killing us, had been killing us for centuries, (as well as each other), proves that our lives are more valuable than theirs. They are irrational. As I've indicated. They are selfish. As I've indicated. They are a danger to society. To a thriving society.

And so, yes, I was justified.

# It's a Boy!

*It was understandable, really. By far, most of the crime—97% in fact—was committed by men. Prisons are expensive to build and maintain. Prisoners are also expensive—they don't work while they're in prison, so we have to support them. Then there's the expense of the police forces and courts needed to get them there. And the emergency services that take care of all the gunshot wounds, the knife slashes, the broken jaws …*

She pushed. And pushed. The hospital room was white and sterile. The attending doctor said something to the assisting nurse from time to time, but things seemed to be progressing normally. But that didn't mean it wasn't excruciatingly painful.

Her husband mopped the sweat off her brow, and encouraged, and reassured.

"And push again," the doctor said.

"It better be a girl," she grunted as she pushed again when the wave of pain struck her.

"Don't worry about that now, honey" her husband said. "Just focus, you're doing good …"

*Then there was all the environmental stuff. All those beer cans, empty cigarette packs, fast food cartons—most of the litter along the highways was put there by men. And that's just the tip of the iceberg. What are they driving on those highways? Big cars and pick-up trucks. Gas-guzzlers with high emissions. And the companies that dump toxic waste, and clearcut forests, and dam river systems …? All run by men.*

"But I want a girl," she cried. With exhaustion. With worry.

"Oh come now," the nurse said. "Boys are harder, I know, had two of 'em myself. Holy terrors half the time, but you love 'em just the same."

"Another push—"

*The insurance companies opened the door when they implemented higher premiums for men between the ages of sixteen and twenty-six. They were the ones more likely to cause an accident. Can't argue with the facts and figures.*

"No, it's not that," she gasped, "It's the money."

"Shh, honey, we'll find a way, it'll be all right," he wiped her brow again.

"One more, I think—"

She gave one final push then fell back against the pillows, drenched, exhausted. She waited anxiously for the announcement.

"It's a boy!"

*They called it the Gender Responsibility Tax—a $5,000 surtax was levied on each and every male. Payable annually, from birth. By the parents, of course, until the boy reached manhood.*

# Men Need Sex

We got so tired of hearing that. Men need sex. There were so many iterations, so many variations …

In 1943, Maslow, in his hierarchy of needs, included sex among the physiological needs that must be satisfied before anything else. Unfortunately, his theory, along with an unforgettable pyramid illustration, became accepted as fact, men loving both hierarchy and sex, and dominating, along with everything else, the science of psychology. Worse, psychology was the social science elective most often taken by business students, and the influence of the business worldview is near insurmountable.

Prostitution defenders, porn apologists—they too shouted that men need sex. Never mind that they might have *created* the need.

The mantra was used, consciously or not, to justify not only men's relentless sexual overtures in general, but also specific instances of pressure and coercion. Rape. First by husbands of their wives, then by boyfriends of their girlfriends, then by any man of any woman.

It was even used to justify the expectation that we sexualize ourselves. Not just at night, but during the day, all day, every day. It became our responsibility to keep men in a constant state of arousal. If men needed sex, they needed first to be aroused. Bizarre, really. If you don't have an itch, you wouldn't feel the need to scratch. Yes, there is pleasure—well, relief—not the same, note—when you scratch an itch, but wouldn't you rather just avoid getting itchy? Who would intentionally roll around on a patch of poison ivy?

And of course when I say 'sex', I mean 'sexual intercourse'. Penis-in-vagina. Apparently masturbation won't do. An equally indefensible stance.

Which is, of course, why they were so hell-bent on calling it 'a need' rather than simply 'a want'. Calling something 'a need' increases the chance that you'll have it met. Saying you *need* something makes it so much harder for others to refuse to give it to you. Because needs are, well, things one *needs*—they're *required*. Needs take priority to wants. And, so, people with needs are important. And all too many men simply *must* feel important.

Of course the argument could be made, indeed *should* be made, that one's moral obligation to meet another's needs holds only when to do so is not at one's own expense. But we're talking about women meeting men's needs. In a male supremacy—and let's face it, that describes every country in the world—women are expected to meet men's needs. We are, after all, according to the two religions that, combined, claim membership of half the world's population, *made* for men.

More than that, we are expected to sacrifice ourselves for others. Yes, in times of war, young men are also expected to sacrifice themselves for others, but at least to do so in that case comes with payment and honour. Women are expected to do so daily, throughout their entire lives, with not so much as a thank you. Let alone a medal and veteran's benefits.

Case in point: pronatalism. Despite the risks of pregnancy and labour, not to mention motherhood—loss of actual life in the former, loss of independence and aspirations in the latter—

women are expected, pressured, coerced (through the withholding of contraception and abortion) to become pregnant, to go through labour, and, unless one takes drastic action (such as leaving your newborn on a park bench), to be a mother. If women's rights—specifically the right to be free of harm and the right to autonomy—were as important as men's rights, impregnating someone without her explicit and expressed, nay, enthusiastic, consent would be illegal. Not 'an accident'.

So it did no good to speak up—and we did, loudly, clearly, and frequently—about women's wants, women's desires, women's preferences. It did no good to say 'What about *women's* needs?'

And since the argument (about obligation being limited by expense) was *not* made, at least not by most men, need implied entitlement. Which simply increased the prevalence of coercion.

Of course many of us responded—screamed, actually—no, you do *not need* sex. You need food, water, and shelter, but you do not need sex. You won't die without it. As Signme Uplease said on Feminist Current, "No man has ever died due to a lack of sexual access to women."

Well, guess what.

In 2014, Elliot Rodger killed himself. Due to a lack of sexual access to women. He said as much in the explanation he left: "I decided to go out in Isla Vista in an attempt to lose my virginity before I turned 22. *That was the only thing that could have saved me.* I was giving the female gender one last chance to provide me with the pleasures I deserved from them. ... I will punish all females for ... depriving me of sex."

Many women argued that Marc Lepine, who in 1989 killed himself, was patient zero. None of the reports at the time link his death to a lack of sex, but one must keep in mind that most, if not all, of the reporters were male. (It's almost always men who write the stories, edit the stories, 'make' the news, manipulate our world view.) So even though Lepine killed fourteen women, they didn't link his action to misogyny; they reported it as a crazed shooting, not premeditated femicide. But any woman who reads the letter Lepine left behind can see quite clearly between the lines— "I have decided to send the feminists, who have always ruined my life, to their Maker. For seven years, life has brought me no joy ..." —that he was a so-called incel and fatally frustrated by his unmet need.

Regardless, similar incidents started occurring. Many of the men identified their actions as part of the 'Incel Rebellion' started by Rodger, and the police identified the incidents as 'copycat crimes'. But given the exponential rate at which the incidents were occurring, it was soon apparent that the (male) police had misnamed the incidents. Rather than imitation, we were seeing infection. An epidemic.

It was also soon apparent that the infection was affecting not just incels. Any man who didn't get sex when he ~~wanted~~ needed it was at risk. The epidemic became a pandemic.

At first, the prostitution business boomed. Not that it wasn't already flourishing better than every other business in the world except porn. (Though of course, the distinction between the two was becoming more and more ... obscure. Untenable. Given the cross-over in personnel, business practices—kidnapping, trafficking—and content.) Mega-brothels such as those in Germany offering an 'all-you-can-fuck' option on their menu appeared on every continent, in every country, in every city ...

But the boom didn't last. As mentioned above, by mistaken logic, need implied entitlement, and men figured they shouldn't have to pay for something they were entitled to. After all, they pointed out, we don't pay for the air that we breathe. Nor, typically, the water we need. That we *do* have to pay for food, as necessary for survival as air and water, seemed to escape them. Perhaps because most men didn't do the grocery shopping.

The porn industry also boomed. The illogical prerequisite need for arousal, remember? Of course the rational thing would've been to just stop watching porn. But men aren't very rational. 'Course, neither are women, but then we aren't the ones proclaiming superiority in that regard.

Since the men so often killed women before killing themselves, some fathers armed their daughters. Alas, this was most often motivated not by love, but by outrage. At the theft and dishonour. As in the case of rape, femicide was considered to be a crime against men, not women; in this case, against the deprived fathers, not the deceased daughters.

Happily, since women typically have better hand-eye coordination than men, the girls often shot the boys first. Surprisingly, in those cases, there was no problem arguing self-defence. Why now? Why not when girls and women killed their abusing boyfriends and husbands, and their would-be rapists? Was it because now the men were about to *kill* them? Surely not. Many an abusing boyfriend/husband ended up killing their girlfriend/wife, and many a would-be rapist would have killed his victim. Perhaps it was because by this time, there were more women serving as the arresting officers, the prosecutors, the judges and juries.

In any case, the wives looked on as their husbands armed their daughters, considered the matter, and armed themselves. Almost overnight 'domestic abuse' petered out. Unfortunately, that meant there would be no justified use of the forementioned arms. But if the forementioned wives didn't kill their husbands, the forementioned husbands would, eventually, soon, kill themselves. The wives figured it was better that way.

Even so, women asked—begged—for stronger gun control and a curfew for men (men seemed more affected at night, but that was probably due to cultural tradition, not the infection), but since the gatekeepers to legislative change were, still, for the most part men, their requests didn't even get to the point of official debate. There was no way men would suggest, let alone agree, that their right to bear arms or their freedom of movement—their *freedom!*—be limited.

So women curfewed themselves. That is to say, they curfewed themselves *more*.

In fact, they essentially *quarantined* themselves, by establishing girls-only schools (and what an unexpected wonder they were!) and women-only businesses, mostly for essentials. Such places had to have armed protection, but many young women were more than happy to become qualified and provide such protection.

And then something strange happened. The rampages got shorter. The men seemed to have less and less time, during which they killed others, before they were overwhelmed by the urge to kill themselves. Soon, the men were able to kill only themselves. Yay, mutation.

Of course, not all men. Not all men were infected. With the belief that men needed sex, were entitled to sex. Some seemed to be naturally immune. Others seemed able to resist. It became a kind of litmus test. Many women were unsurprised when their husbands, their boyfriends, became infected. They were secretly—at first—not so secretly as time went on—pleased, or at least relieved, when said husbands and boyfriends killed themselves. But many women were surprised. Dismayed, actually. Especially when it was their sons who proved to be infected.

Our best minds continued their efforts to understand the infection. *Was* it an infection? If so, was it viral? Bacterial? Something else? Was it contagious? What caused it in the first place?

Of course typical infections, whether viral or bacterial, are immune to belief. Which is why many thought it was something else, some sort of prion infection, perhaps.

But the vectors of contagion were unclear. In fact, the very real possibility of *social* contagion severely muddied the waters. We knew that many opinions, beliefs, attitudes, and desires—and the behaviors, the actions, motivated by those opinions, beliefs, attitudes, and desires—were due to a sort of peer pressure rather than to any independent, conscious consideration. Especially among young people who were plugged into social media sites

24/7. Could the infection be caused by a sort of social virus? If so, the cure would be what—social isolation?

Perhaps it wasn't an infection, per se, but an addiction. This was one of the leading theories. We knew that addition could literally rewire the brain, and we *certainly* knew—well, *women* certainly knew—men seemed to keep their heads firmly buried in the sand about this—that watching porn was addictive. We knew that watching porn changed men's attitudes—toward women, toward the acceptability of violence toward women ... We also knew that smartphone companies had entire departments researching dopamine triggers (a neurological update of the old-fashioned manipulation sought by advertising) in an attempt to get and keep our attention ... It would be no surprise if porn companies had been doing the same. In which case the addiction to porn would be physiological as well as psychological (though of course, there was no clear distinction between the two). It did seem that watching porn messed with men's chemicals, a consequence very likely exacerbated by eating meat, ingesting the steroids fed to livestock ... If this theory were correct, the cure would be simple: stop watching porn.       Not gonna happen.

Another leading theory, developed by Soong Malm, was that the Y chromosome, deformed from the get-go and long disintegrating, was making a desperate, and final (as it may turn out), bid for survival. When the Y chromosome disintegrates to a certain point, she hypothesized, a hitherto dormant virus was activated that makes sexual reproduction—and hence survival of the Y chromosome—an urgent need. The theory was supported by all the selfish gene arguments, popularized by Richard Dawkins, and by the work of the famous, but pseudonymous, TrustYourPerceptions. Since the end result, in the case of the need being unmet, is the death of the male, it's obviously a defective strategy, but then we would expect no less from a defective chromosome. Regardless, this theory similarly doesn't point to a cure.

There would be a certain satisfaction in thinking that the cure could not be found because of ongoing, persistent sabotage—for surely every male scientist had a number of assistants, surely at least one of whom was female. Such sabotage would be even more possible as time went on, because as the male population decreased, so many jobs, including high-level research positions, had to be— *could* be, finally—filled by women. It made a difference. Especially when a certain critical mass was reached. Eventually whole teams, whole departments, whole companies (mainstream, not just the forementioned small essential ones), were run by women. Most women were surprised at the change they couldn't, at first, put their wedding-ringed finger on when they walked into, for example, a bank staffed entirely—*entirely*, including every single one of the managers—by women. But some women, mostly radical feminists, were not surprised at all. Such places were … relaxed. But we simply do not know. Whether sabotage is occurring.

What we *do* know is that few women are upset by the lack of a cure.

After all, most crime has been committed by men. Most violence has been committed by men. Men, by and large, have created and sustained the porn industry which overwhelmingly portrays women being hurt and humiliated. As entertainment.

The truth of it is that men are not only destructive, they are *self*-destructive. Case in point: what they have done to our planet. Its food, its water, its very air. So, the mass suicides are just a personal expression of what they've been doing all along.

So, we're just … waiting.

# How We Survived

You're wondering how it happened. How did we survive? How did our population suddenly plummet from six billion to half that. Enabling our natural resources to recover and, eventually, support us. All of us.

In 2020, all of the indicators pointed to our imminent extinction. We had to reduce our greenhouse gases by 50% before 2030 in order to have just a hope in hell of avoiding what would otherwise become inevitable in 2050, eventual human extinction. And in 2020, we were nowhere near being on target. The U.S. continued to deny that there was a problem; Canada continued to allow the production of greenhouse gases just for fun (via snowmobile, PWC, and ATV use; in fact, the government had gone so far as to designate 121,000 kilometres of crown and private land specifically for snowmobile use).

And so there continued to be—and every year, more—devastating droughts, forest fires, heat waves, floods, superstorms, and pandemics, as well as all the rage that typically accompanied such events—riots, assaults, mass shootings …

In the middle of all this, single mothers just … gave up. They'd had enough. Enough part-time, temporary, casual work for which they earned half of what men would have earned. (No, what am I saying? Men would never be offered, would never have to *accept*, part-time, temporary, or casual work. Not if they had kids to support.) Enough of no pension, no benefits. So no affordable medical care. Enough of looking after other people's kids as well as their own, but needing to do so in order to *feed* their own. Because no affordable daycare.

They'd had enough of fighting for child support every fucking month. They'd had enough of the men, the absent fathers, still calling the shots. For example, preventing them from moving back to where they could get the help of their extended family, because said family was in a different state or a different country and they, the men, wouldn't therefore be able to see their kids as often, as easily. (Suddenly that mattered.)

They'd had enough of living in a culture that "values work that contributes to the destruction and exploitation of life over and above work which nurtures life," to quote Abigail Bray. And Marilyn Waring. And how many other women who had been ignored.

They'd had enough of being considered, treated like, damaged goods and sluts.

Why were they single, you might ask. Their husbands, the kids' fathers, had abandoned them, saying they just weren't cut out to be fathers.

Or they'd left their husbands, the kids' fathers, after years of abuse, psychological and physical, that hadn't started until the first pregnancy.

Why were they mothers, you might ask. Their husbands had refused to use a condom. They'd said they'd pull out, but didn't. Usually, they just raped them. It was their right, after all. (The consequences, apparently not their responsibility.)

So the next time their kids were with their fathers for the weekend, they just … disappeared.

You might think it would tear them apart. Well, they were already torn apart.

Yes, their daughters would likely be raped. That would've happened anyway. Eventually. The famous 'one in four' had crept to 'one in three' as men got angrier and angrier with the world at large.

Yes, their sons would be raised to be misogynistic psychopaths. That too would've happened anyway. The porn culture enabled by the internet had turned most men into misogynistic psychopaths. Which was no surprise, if they'd been watching women being humiliated and hurt, and apparently liking it, since they were eight. Which was the case now for most males.

And then it wasn't just the single mothers. Married women started divorcing their husbands and insisting that said husbands, their kids' fathers, assume full-time custody.

"I'll take them every other weekend," the women would say, magnanimously.

And oh my god, was it wonderful. They'd work from nine to five, and the rest of the day, the evening, was theirs. All theirs. To do as they pleased. The housework, the laundry, the cooking—it was surprising how little was needed for just themselves. And the quiet. It was … bliss.

In a way, it seemed that women had started getting over themselves. Truth be told, in most cases, the kids would be no worse off with their fathers. It's not like they, the mothers, had been doing a stellar job. Their kids were, across the board, oh so ordinary. At best.

In a way, it seemed that they'd finally realized they'd been suckered into believing that raising children was something that only they could do, something that they could do best, being women, being mothers …

"You know, it's strange," Ann said to Beth during their cof-fee break, as they read the latest statistics on the phenomenon.

"It's like all these women, single and married, suddenly don't love their kids anymore."

"Yeah, well, love," Beth replied, cynically. "Oxytocin by any other—"

And that's when it hit them.

They did the research (suspending, for the moment, their development of an air-borne contraceptive, with a somewhat onerous and impossible-to-regulate antidote, like holding one's breath for 60 seconds every hour for 24 hours straight, that would change the default from having to do something *not* to get pregnant to having to do something *to* get pregnant), and sure enough.

There had been a decrease in oxytocin. For many, that bond was all that had been holding mother-and-child together. Once it started to dissolve, once their oxytocin started to decrease, well, it was … easier. To just give up. Give up their kids, leave them with their fathers. It actually didn't tear them apart. Quite so much.

We should have seen it coming. After all, we'd been using pesticides, handling plastics, wearing cosmetics (that turned into a nice irony: you want us to look attractive all the time, well, okay, but … it's gonna cost ya), and coming into contact with god knows how many other industrial chemicals for almost a century.

We even knew that many of these chemicals were endocrine disruptors: they could increase, or decrease, certain hormones (special signal-sending chemicals); they could interfere with the signals hormones were supposed to send; they could even turn one hormone into another.

In fact, we had proof way back in the 1940s that DDT, for example, caused problems for bees, and in 1962, biologist Rachel Carson sounded a strong alarm about such pesticides (and was dismissed as hysterical for doing so). It took ten years for the U.S. to ban DDT. And another forty to make the link to breast cancer.

But, well, research into women's bodies was not exactly a priority. The first-ever statement about *women* and heart disease—the signs of heart attack in women are different than in men—was published in *2016*. And we had Viagra (and Cialis and Levitra and Stendra ...) long before safe contraception. And—

Simply put, women weren't as important as men. It was an opinion that was, apparently, impossible to change. After all, Viagra (and Cialis and Levitra and Stendra ...) was covered by health insurance plans ten years before any of the various contraceptives were covered.

As more and more women entered the sciences, there were attempts to change that, but men continued to dominate the funding decisions. (Ann and Beth had resorted to crowd-funding for their research.)

As for research into *mothering*, that was *especially* emasculating. Only a wuss would choose to do *that*! I still remember when I first read Levitt and Dubner's *Freakonomics*, in which they present an astounding connection between access to abortion and the crime rate: twenty years after Roe v. Wade, the U.S. crime rate dropped. Astounding indeed. That men were surprised by that. What did they think would happen when a woman is saddled with a squalling baby she does not want, on an income she does not have, *because* she has a squalling baby she does not want— She'd get a 'Mother of the Year' award?

So. Oxytocin is a chemical produced by the hypothalamus. It motivates and reinforces attachment. Therefore.

Their conclusion was validated when almost overnight, the proportion of *new* mothers (single or married) with so-called post-partum depression went from one in seven to four in seven. That's over half.

We'd only recently hypothesized that post-partum depression could be caused in part by low oxytocin. Turns out that it's not so much that low oxytocin *causes* post-partum depression as that high oxytocin *masks* post-partum depression—the reasonable (healthy) response to the forementioned state of being saddled with a squalling baby ... (Especially reasonable when you were absolutely exhausted from having just birthed it, in part because you went into that labour in a weakened state due to the multiple stresses, emotional and physical, of being pregnant for nine months in the first place.)

Those who thought post-partum depression was just a medicalization of not wanting kids were right. Maybe, just maybe, women's sole responsibility for that squalling baby explains why they experienced "a loss of energy, changes in sleep patterns, a diminished ability to think or concentrate, and recurring thoughts of suicide." I mean, duh.

So when the increase in oxytocin that typically accompanied pregnancy and labour didn't occur ...

Almost overnight, most new mothers acted like those with post-partum depression. Or like men. Quite simply, they weren't all that interested in their newborns. They saw them as the demanding shit-machines that most new fathers, truthfully, had always seen them as. ('Honey, I have to stay late at the office again, sorry.' Right. Code for 'I can't stand another minute of its crying. You're different, you're a woman, it doesn't bother you, just like you don't mind changing its diaper ....' Right.)

And, simply put, most women did not want to have to look after a demanding shit-machine twenty-four/seven. Who would? Looking ahead, they saw nothing but exhaustion, frustration, resentment, anger, rage ... Being completely responsible for a completely helpless human being for years ...

So, many women just left their newborns with their husbands.

"If you didn't want to look after it, you shouldn't've had it!" Dave said when Diane told him she was going back to work the next day.

She waited a few moments, then saw that she had to say it out loud. "Same to you."

And then in the morning, when she was on her way out ahead of him—in many households, there was actually a race for the door—he objected. He'd obviously not taken her seriously the night before. But then, when had he ever?

"But … this is crazy."

She stared at him. "Don't do that."

"Do what?"

"Dismiss as 'crazy' anything you don't agree with. As if you're the standard of sanity."

"I didn't—"

"You did."

"But … I can't stay home, quit my job. I make more money than you!"

"Yeah, pity you never joined the fight for equal pay for work of equal value."

"But—"

"And," she sighed, "it's not all about money."

Many women took their newborns to their rapists. In many cases, in many countries, that meant the same as leaving them with their husbands. But in many other cases, it meant taking the infant to a male relative, a 'friend', an acquaintance … As statistics have shown, in most cases, women are raped by someone they know.

"You can't leave it here!" Tyler said. "I don't want it!"

"Then why'd you make it?"

"I didn't make it!"

She waited just a moment. "Do you really not know how babies are made? When sperm—"

"I know that shit! Do you think I'm stupid?"

"Well, unless you taught your sperm how to swim backwards …"

It was amusing, though appalling, that so many men seemed to assume that women had some sort of innate control over fertilization. That getting pregnant was their choice, hence their fault.

"Why didn't you take care of it?" He glared at her.

"I *am* taking care of it. I'm giving it to you."

"You know what I mean."

"Then say it. Say what you mean."

"Why didn't you get an abortion?"

"Why didn't you get a vasectomy?"

"I thought you were on the pill or something."

"Why did you think that?"

He shrugged.

"Well, shouldn't you have made sure? Before you put your sperm into my vagina?"

In many countries, women organized and took their newborns, en masse, to their legislatures. They walked in, close to a hundred at a time, and set their infants, strapped into carriers, baskets, and car seats, onto the long meeting tables.

"What's this?" The Man-in-Charge would say.

"The babies you forced us to have by prohibiting abortion."

"Well, *we* don't want them."

Then you shouldn't have forced us to have them."

And then they started to walk away.

"Wait! You can't just walk away! What kind of mothers are you?"

"The unwilling kind. The coerced kind."

And then with great self-righteousness, the Man-in-Charge would call Security and have the women arrested for abandonment. Right then and there. They'd be taken away to holding cells. Sentenced for, possibly, five years. With smug satisfaction, the Man-in-Charge would turn back to—

The babies were still there. Now wailing. Every one of them.

Oops.

Initially, it was concern for the kids that received all the media attention. (Of course. Even fertilized eggs are more important than women.) Women with post-partum depression don't bond with their newborns; as a result, said newborns don't thrive. They are likely to have a wide range of cognitive, emotional, behavioral, and medical problems: lower IQ scores, attention problems, mood disorders, anxiety disorders, substance use disorders, conduct disorders, my god the list goes on. (Tell me again why mothers, if they're so very important, are 'paid' just room and board.)

Most women fully understood the importance of the first six years; they were the formative years. Literally. But why were *women* best suited for those first six years? Why was *one* woman best suited for those first six years?

And if those years were so fucking important, they said, they screamed, why did men keep undoing what women did? With advertising—sugar-sweetened drinks and cereals, fat-laden and nutrient-poor fast food ... With toy stores—stocked with gun-wielding action figures on one side and pretty pink princesses on the other ... With television, intentionally attractive, intentionally addictive—the more kids watch tv, the worse their social skills, their language skills, their school performance, their physical fitness ...

Of course, many women argued that the 'What about the children?' response was just a guilt trip, and a way to keep so many of us sequestered, segregated, in the home, overworked, too tired to care about, or to do anything about, anything else. And not an expression of genuine concern for the children, for those formative years.

And so ... the men found out what it was like. To be home alone with one, two, three kids who demanded their attention every minute, every second. They'd had no idea how exhausting it could be. Physically, psychologically ...

What did they do? Some desperately hired other women to look after their kids. But ten hours a day, five days a week, it added up.

Naturally, those who were married expected their now-working (wait, *now*-working?) wives to pay half the mortgage, half the electricity, half the insurance …

"I can't afford that. We'll have to sell the house, move, find something cheaper."

"Sell the house? But—"

"And of course I won't be paying half the nanny's salary."

"But they're your kids too."

"I can't afford it." It was true.

Suddenly men were speaking out for equal pay for work of equal value. Suddenly they were insisting their wives get pay increases and promotions. Suddenly they were appalled at the jobs their wives didn't get hired for.

"But you're qualified! More than qualified!"

Duh.

"Can't you pay at least *part* of the nanny's salary?"

"Why should I? It was your decision." Because oh, the rage. Their husbands were paying some stranger more than they'd ever paid them. To do the same work.

And, again, "If you didn't want to look after a kid, why did you make one?"

And, of course, it wasn't just about money. Unless they hired a 24/7 nanny, the men whose wives had left found they no longer had their evenings and weekends to themselves. To put it mildly.

When hiring a nanny proved impossible, the men stayed home. What choice did they have? Many were fired because they didn't show up for work. Or couldn't stay late. Or had to leave suddenly in the middle of the day for an emergency. (Fortuitously, this opened positions for all the women now seeking paid employment.)

Suddenly men were speaking out for, demanding, state-funded daycare.

They insisted that their estranged wives pay child support. But when the arrears for 24/7 nanny services to date had been calculated, minus their portion for all the joint expenses, in most cases, the men still owed the women. No child support would be forthcoming.

Regardless, most men found they simply couldn't handle the non-stop neediness of babies, infants, toddlers, their relentless whining presence … When their infants wouldn't stop crying, some men threw them against the wall. Or worse.

So when *that* proved impossible, the staying at home with them, they just started leaving them alone during the day. And often during the night. Some men just left the house at one point and didn't come back.

The kids died. Of course they died.

Some starved to death. Some died of thirst. Some had fatal accidents. They fell when they tried to get out of their cribs, or they drowned when they slipped in the tub, or they died in a house fire when, so hungry, they tried to make supper …

Call it 'failure to thrive'. In a big way.

So, yes, the incidence of infanticide increased. The incidence of child abuse and neglect increased. More prisons were required. More foster homes were required. Proposals were made to bring back orphanages.

The number of street kids increased. More social services were required.

Juvenile crime increased. More young offender facilities were required.

Governments were overwhelmed.

Of course, early on, almost immediately, actually, the men realized they hadn't wanted kids after all. Not really. They'd just wanted the badge of respectability, the measure of maturity.

And they realized they'd been duped by the association between the two: being able to get a woman pregnant had nothing to do with respectability. Or maturity.

And they realized, now, that if they *did* have kids—that is, if they did create some new human beings—they'd have to look after them for a good fifteen years. Actually *look after* them.

And *then* what happened?

Nations that had hitherto spent half their budgets on weapons found that they had the money for state-funded daycare.

Legislation was passed for equal pay for work of equal value. And enforced.

Legislation was also passed for equal opportunity for promotions. And enforced.

Contraception became not only easily available, but free of charge.

Abortion became legal. And available. On demand.

And, finally, there was an increase in vasectomies, from a global rate of 2.2% to 81.9%.

And *then*, zero population growth.

# The Knitting Group

There were no knitting needles in sight. Thanks to a multitude of people across the planet, again and again … (Even so, there was a well-developed black market in contraceptives. You could even get them on eBay. Search for 'pink yarn'. Your purchase will arrive concealed in a skein of … pink yarn.)

But of course they couldn't call themselves the Radical Feminists Group. They'd be killed. Or at least subject to rape and death threats on a daily basis, joining a multitude of women across the planet, again and again …

So, the Knitting Group it was. The name was like a Romulan cloaking device. No, it was better, because instead of being invisible, they appeared as harmless fuddy-duddy old ladies. Better still, no man, trans or cis—oh how they hated those words, conflating, as they did, sex and gender—would even *think* of joining them.

◆

"I say we arm ourselves. Instead of a frickin' make-up kit, give every girl a gun. Teach her how to use it."

They were discussing the problem of male violence. Against women. (As for male violence against men, they figured that was *their* problem to solve. And frankly, it was to women's advantage if it remained unsolved.) (Though their solution to the first problem might end up solving the second problem.) (You're welcome.)

"No, that won't work. They'll just kill us. More often. With *their* guns."

"Yeah."


"You know how a couple weeks ago we were discussing AIs and robots and how of course most men seem to want them, use them, as fuck toys?"

Several women nodded. There had also been discussion of the use of pleasant, borderline seductive, female voices, for virtual assistants. To whom men would happily give orders all day.

"Well, why don't we just give each man his own personal fuck toy? Then they'd each have something to—"

"Because they'll think they can do whatever they do to them *to us*. They'll expect *us* to be their own personal fuck toy."

"Agreed. After all, that's what's happened with porn, right? Instead of decreasing their sexual use of real women, it's increasing it. Along with horrendous expectations."

"Actually, some of our studies show that men who are addicted to porn *prefer* it to real sex. And so actual sex is *decreasing*."

"At least in the case of young men."

"Hm. Regardless, that solution would just address rape, not all of the other physical assaults against women."

"Yeah."

"My grand-niece had a suggestion," her eye twinkled. Or maybe it twitched. It was hard to tell. "She said we could just ask them to stop."

The room erupted with cackles and guffaws.

"Did you explain to her that we've been asking them to stop since forever?"

"Individually and collectively?"

"Pretty much every day?"

"I did. She wasn't interested in 'since forever'."

"Is this the same grand-niece who explained to you that bikini waxes were empowering?"

"No," she couldn't stifle her groan, "that was a different one."

They all sighed.

"Then she asked me why I hate men."

They waited.

"I told her. I said that I hate that until recently, they refused to let us go to school, vote, get a job, open a bank account, own property, drive a car. I don't think she believed me."

They all sighed again.

"I told her that they sabotage our success, and when that doesn't work, they dismiss our success. They constantly reduce women to sexual parts and functions. They hurt and kill animals, and enjoy doing so. They hurt and kill people, and enjoy doing so."

They nodded. That pretty much nailed it.

"Then I asked her why she didn't. Hate men."

"And?"

"She said not all men were like that."

More sighs. A few curses.

"Did you give her the statistics? At least point her toward some of the websites that ..." She trailed off. Most of the websites had disappeared.

"I did. I tried."

There was a moment of silence. For the loss. Of hope.

"You know, *that's* why we're not making progress. It's two steps forward, two steps back."

Someone nodded. "Daughters will always rebel against their mothers, reject whatever they have to say."

"I don't see the sons rebelling against their fathers," another someone pointed out. "They're happy to be welcomed into the boys' club of male supremacy and misogyny."

They considered that.

"Friedan, Millett, Dworkin—they're all a generation before several of us here, and *we* don't reject whatever *they* had to say."

"We don't reject them at all. We're trying to refine them."

"Well, no, we're trying to resurrect them."

"Yeah."


"How about a few well-chosen legislative changes?" one of the lawyers among them suggested. "Take away their guns, for starters. Implement a curfew. Prohibit gatherings of two or more men."

"I agree with the first one, absolutely. Children should not have guns."

"Indeed. When will we insist our boys grow up?"

"Maybe they can't. Maybe *they're* the inferior sex. Among other things, they have less impulse control."

"Yeah, why did it become common to call *women* hysterical? *They're* the ones throwing tantrums!"

"All the more reason to take away their guns."

"They'd just use other things. After all, they've weaponized even sex."

"And as for the curfew, they're violent in broad daylight."

"But the 'two or more' thing is worth consideration, isn't it? They *are* very susceptible to the herd mentality. Most of their violence is committed when they're trying to prove themselves to their buddies."

"At the very least, we should constrain their behaviour between, say, fourteen and twenty-four. Those ten years seem to be the most ... explosive."

"You've got that right."


"Though," someone said a few moments later, "those ten years aren't the only— I found an archive the other day, titled Trust Your Perceptions, and there was one post that was impressively ... succinct." She pulled out a sheet of paper and began to read. "'The Number one cause of death for females ages 15-59 worldwide is males. More specifically ... *being fucked by males*.' HIV. 'Number two is pregnancy and/or childbirth. Number three is HIV-related tuberculosis. Number four is suicide/being burned.' And," she looked up, "I suspect men play a role in both of those. 'Number five is cervical cancer from HPV. Number six is murder.' By males," she looked up again. "And that doesn't include the figures for women killed in men's wars."

She passed the paper to the person next to her; it would make its way around the room.

"Men have to go," the person next to her said, once she'd skimmed the paper then passed it along. "That's the only solution."

"Agreed," the next person said.

"How about a plague?" one of the biologists suggested. "Something that targets only those with a Y chromosome."

"Isn't that a bit extreme?"

"If wolves were the number one cause of death for human beings, we'd exterminate them in a heartbeat. No questions asked."

Several women nodded.

"Even if, roaming free, they *injured* one in four people, we'd exterminate them. Again, no questions asked."

They all recognized the 'one in four' statistic. And they all knew what questions *were* asked.

"But how— You've got some sort of deadly virus in mind, yeah? Would we put it into the water supply?"

"That wouldn't work. Rural people have their own wells."

"We could put it in the beer! Enlist the night cleaners to put it into the vats or—"

"Some of us drink beer …"

"What if we made it like, I don't know, a special kind of salt. We're the ones preparing the food, serving the food …"

"At best, we'd just reduce the number of men."

"Still …"


"Mandatory sex-selective abortion would be easier."

"Easier? Let me see you get *that* legislation passed!"

"Well, we'd have to wait a while, until the men currently alive die off …"

"But in the meantime, there'd be more men. Boys. Being born."

"And a lot of women would *never*—"

"And we don't have time to wait. Because the men currently alive, especially those with power, are destroying not only us, individually, but the planet. Which we'll need."


"What about," suggested one of the geneticists, "instead of some deadly virus, a testosterone inhibitor? The comment about fourteen to twenty-four being the most explosive years suggests that maybe the problem isn't the Y chromosome per se, but testosterone. The sudden surge—"

"Yes! We *know* testosterone increases aggression, right? 'Roid rage and all that?"

Someone nodded. "Ghiglieri is convinced that testosterone is a kick-starter for violence. She goes so far as to say it *forces* aggressive behavior."

"So we could insist men take, I don't know, some sort of blocker ..."

"Or ... there's this device called a burdizzo. It's a surgical clamp used on baby male livestock to break the spermatic cords and blood vessels leading to the testicles, so they just ... wither away. Then instead of being slammed by testosterone at puberty, the animals remain their calm and sweet-tempered selves; they don't fight and scuffle amongst themselves like most male animals do. And they still grow up to become beautiful healthy animals ..."

"Well, then. There we go." She looked at the others. "And proof positive that testosterone is the problem. The reason for their violence, their aggression."

"Actually, testosterone increases not only aggression, but also competition. And of course, the two effects could also be related: the drive to compete, to win, drives aggression."

"Yes! Men are *obsessed* with competition, win/lose, one-upmanship, saving face, reputation ..."

"And, therefore, they spend so much time bullshitting, spinning, they become incapable of truth."

"Agreed. Most of them have spent so much time bullshitting, they believe their own bullshit."

Another nodded. "Most of them don't even realize they're lying. It's their norm, their normal. The 'pick-up line' for instance. It's perfectly acceptable. To them. Google 'how to get a girl to say yes' and you'll find hundreds of sites, all essentially telling guys to lie. They plan a whole charade, a whole script of lies to get what they want. What*ever* they want."

"Or maybe they know they're lying, they just don't think it's wrong. If everyone does it—and if among men, everyone does—then fair's fair: to compete, to win, they have to do it too."

"So what are we saying, competition precludes morality? Not only are they incapable of truth, they're incapable of right, wrong, good, bad ..."

Someone nodded. "Not even on their radar."

"That explains so much!"

"So very much. In fact, it might even explain why men aren't very introspective. If they're singularly focused on winning, nothing else matters. They don't *have* to think about right and wrong, good and bad. They don't have to examine their feelings, their reasons. And if their level of introspection is so minimal, it would follow, perhaps, that their self-consciousness, even their sense of self, is also minimal. From there, well, I'm not sure where to go ..."

"Self-awareness is prerequisite for self-control ..."

"But they do have free will! I'm not ready to absolve—"

"Maybe they're just *weak*-willed. Not as strong as they like to think."

"Regardless, I do think we're onto something here. Goldberg says that fetal masculinization of the central nervous system makes males more sensitive to the dominance-related properties of testosterone. That's why they compete. They can't help it."

"So ... they'll never co-operate. Except with others in their own tribe, to compete against another tribe."

"And women will never be part of their tribe."

"They'll never think about others. Except the others in their tribe."

"They'll never consider the long term. Because winning in the short term is all that matters."

"They'll never consider quality of life. Victory is the only quality worth achieving."

"And worse, I think it's self-feeding. Testosterone increases competition, and competition—winning, at least—increases testosterone."

"Both of which increase aggression."

They considered all of this.

"I dunno … all of that because of a single chemical?"

"Didn't the changing proportion of estrogen and progesterone through the month affect your behaviour? Didn't you feel a strong urge in your early twenties to reproduce?"

"Dawkins, the selfish gene, hijacking our bodies to reproduce itself …"

"And weren't you glad to finally be able to say goodbye to all that when you hit menopause?"

"And you could suddenly see men clearly? Without the blinding effect of sexual attraction?"

"Yes, but—"

"I know it's just more anecdotal evidence, but women who start taking testosterone report changes along the lines of what we're saying."

"Oh, we don't have to depend on anecdotal evidence. We've done the research. We've identified *several* correlates of high levels of testosterone: not only impulsivity and a lack of interest in others' feelings, which we've mentioned, but also impatience, unreliability, recklessness …"

"Surely, though," she persisted, "socialization is to blame as well. Men are *encouraged* to be masculine, to be tough, to be immune to feelings—"

"Other than anger—"

"Men who *don't* compete are called wusses—"

"Or worse, women—"

"Yes, but my point is that if their aggression is due to socialization, then *that's* the solution. We should focus on the way we raise them, on all the influences at school, and in society …"

"But we already do that. No one here raised their sons to be monsters, but—"

"And most teachers, especially during the critical years, are women, so—"

"Men control society."

They sighed.

"Look. Maybe you're right. Maybe it isn't hardwired. But then they could ... be otherwise. Why aren't they?"

They waited.

Had waited.

Would wait no more.


"So, but, even if we use testosterone inhibitors, or blockers— They won't be able to change a lifetime of habit overnight. If truth and morality have taken a back seat since puberty, when testosterone started flooding through their bodies, their brains, they're not going to suddenly be able to—"

"No, but surely without the drive to compete, they'll be able to focus on truth and morality. If they wish. Over time, they might become ... good people," she trailed off.

"In any case, the sooner it's done, the better."

The considered that.

"Perhaps if the burdizzo procedure became as common as circumcision ..."

"Perhaps it could be done at the same time ..."

"But it would be fifteen years before we see the effects. We don't *have* fifteen years."

"So we need both. Before puberty, the burdizzo. After puberty, testosterone inhibitors."

"But how can we ensure they'll take the inhibitors?"

"Could the surgical route not be used after puberty as well? A vasectomy is a quick and painless procedure. Wouldn't cutting off the blood supply to testes be as quick and painless?"

"Yes. There's no incision. They numb the area, so there's no pain. An ice pack prevents swelling afterwards. And as with a vasectomy, there's no visual difference."

"So, what, we kidnap all the men and ...?"

"No, we legislate and ..."

They sighed.

"Still. I can't believe we've become so … essentialist. Isn't that exactly what feminism has rejected all these decades? That there are inherent, innate, differences between men and women?"

"Yes, because they got the differences wrong. They said women were naturally stupid, passive, subservient."

"And, to use an ugly metaphor, we threw out the baby with the bathwater. Because surely we can accept that our behavior is to some extent controlled, or at least predisposed, by what's going on in our bodies, the biochemicals … Consider the chemistry of depression: dopamine, norepinephrine, serotonin. The chemistry of affection: oxytocin. So why not the chemistry of aggression?"

"But— It's so draconian. What we're planning."

"Agreed. But listen— When I went through menopause, something got out of whack, my hormones didn't change right or something, and my sexual urges went through the roof. They say that post-menopausal women have an increased libido because finally they need not fear pregnancy and maybe that's true, but in my case, since I had a tubal cauterization at thirty, that couldn't've been the reason.

"Anyway, I started masturbating. Big time. Next thing I know I'm sending covert glance at men in the grocery store to see if any of them notice that I'm lingering over my choice of zucchini and cucumber. I even put clothespins on my nipples and my clit. When I went out for a walk, in public, for fuck's sake!

"For a week or so, it was intriguing. Then it got annoying. I couldn't concentrate. You all know I'm freelance: if I don't produce, I don't get paid. My work slid for a week or so, but I thought I'll just make up the difference next week, but the next week was worse.

"There was this non-stop compulsion pounding away in the back of my mind, no, not in the *back* of my mind, but front and center. I was visiting porn sites, reading and getting excited by stuff that I would normally consider humiliating. I was this close," she pinched her thumb and forefinger almost together, "to contacting one of those personal ads giving some stranger my address and telling him to come make me his sex slave."

Someone—

"Don't laugh. I'm deadly serious. It was that bad. That unrelenting. And that perverted, given my normal baseline.

"And I thought, if this is what it's like to be a man—because we know that testosterone is responsible for one's sex drive—how do they get anything done? And maybe the question isn't why do they rape so much, but why don't they rape more often? I wonder if maybe we haven't given them near enough credit. Maybe given their level of testosterone, and their greater strength, they exhibit an impressive amount of self-control."

There were several sharp intakes of breath.

"Hunger has no conscience," someone said. Summarized.

There was silence all 'round.

"So what did you do?"

"I decided that I'd go to my doctor and say, 'Give me something. Please.' I'd ask, I'd *beg*, for some sort of biochemical ... castration. Exactly what we're suggesting here."

They considered that.

"Put that way, we'd be doing them a favour."

She nodded.

"So why aren't *men* going to their doctors and begging them to do something?"

"Because they don't know any different. They don't consider it *abnormal*. Like I did."

Someone nodded. "Maybe if they felt it rise and fall on a regular basis throughout the month ..."

"Or not. Because once they hit male menopause and feel the waning, what do they do? Buy little blue pills and steroid patches!"

"Indeed. They *love* their testosterone!"

"Maybe they become addicted to it."

"And, too, they've been socialized not only to accept that off-the-chart level of testosterone, to consider it normal, but also to consider it *desirable*, a measure of masculinity."

"And masculinity is good, if you're a man. It makes you a *real* man."

"And because their capacity for introspection is minimal, they have uncritically accepted that socialization."

"And it's *not* abnormal. For men. You talked about the selfish gene hijacking us. Well, there it is. Hijacking them."

They sighed.


"But back to 'not all men' … Surely we should give them a chance! What if instead of making it mandatory for all men, we make it mandatory at the very first act of violence. Even the proverbial pulling legs off a fly?"

"The very first act of violence that's not self-defence."

"Yes."

"And we could give them, or the parents, a choice: the burdizzo or suicide."

"Well, once they're adults, they'd rather die than—"

"So be it. Their choice."

"I agree. Because, as mentioned, we couldn't trust such a person to take regular testosterone inhibitors."

"I disagree! Vehemently! Because— *Give them a chance?! Give them a choice?!* They've had centuries of chances! They've made centuries of choices! No more!!"

"And even if men *aren't* violent, most are still obsessed with competition, with winning, and, therefore, negligent about other far more important stuff. Truth. Morality."

They sighed.

"Yeah."

"We could just wait. It looks like men will soon stop making sperm altogether."

"And we'll develop parthenogenesis?"

"Doesn't mean they'll stop making testosterone. Does it?"

"No, that won't work. Waiting. Remember Leona Gom's *Y Chromosome*? All the men started dying from a Y-chromosome defect caused by ecological degradation, and when they realized the future belonged exclusively to women, they started destroying everything. *Everything.* Infrastructure, hospitals, libraries …"

"My god, that sounds like *Planet of the Apes*. Remember when the guy activates the atomic bomb? He says something like 'It's better to destroy everything than have the apes win'?"

"God, that's sick."

"And one more reason. For the other solution."

"In case we need one more reason."


"Pity we can't just redesign— Wait, some of the COVID vaccines used messenger-RNA— I can't believe I didn't think of this before," she muttered., then looked around the group. "It sends a message to increase the production of certain antibodies. We could design RNA to send a message to reduce the production of testosterone. Put it in a vaccine. Inject all the men. And the boys. Done." She leaned back. Smiling.

"Except for follow-up shots every six months."

"Maybe not. We could make the RNA self-replicating."

"Even so. Injecting all the boys, no problem, we appeal to the mothers. But how are we going to inject all the men?"

There was a moment of silence. It was a very short moment.

"We tell them it's a testosterone booster."

# The Mars Colonies

As it turns out, once Earth had passed the tipping point and was sure to become uninhabitable for humans (our own damn fault) ('our' as in 'not including me'), there were several attempts to colonize Mars. Several attempts because, since said attempts were run by men, there couldn't be just one co-operative effort. No. Men had to compete with each other. To be the first on Mars. To be the biggest on Mars. Whatever.

(And why were these colonization attempts run by men? Seriously? You have to ask? The male modus operandi is 'Trash it and move on.' In the meantime, someone else would clean up their mess, at which time they could return.) ('Someone else' meaning 'some *woman*'. Because 'cleaning up' is beneath men. It's emasculating.)

(Actually, a better response is provided by the brilliant Sarah Sharma: "Exit," she says, "is an exercise of patriarchal power [that] stands in direct contradistinction to care ... which responds to the uncompromisingly tethered nature of human dependency and the contingency of life.")

So. The several attempts to colonize Mars.

One group failed because the men forgot to include women. No surprise. Men have been forgetting to include women since forever. "Remember the ladies," Abigail Adams had to remind her husband in 1776. Apparently, he forgot anyway. Twenty years later, when he became President. Because women weren't granted the right to vote until 1920. Read *Invisible Women*: men forget to include women in medical research (consequently, many people die because their female symptoms aren't recognized or because the male cures don't work); they forget to include women in economic analyses (consequently, their data is misleading, their policies ineffective); they forget to include women when they design, oh, pretty much anything—cupboards, pianos, seatbelts, bullet-proof vests ...

Another group also forgot to include women. They *did* remember to take a bunch of women's eggs with them, and a bunch of artificial incubators, but no one wanted to look after the babies once they were born. Because, well, real men don't do that. Look after babies.

Most attempts to recruit women failed, because who in their right mind would want to spend seven months in an elevator with a bunch of men in order to then live with said men in small apartment for the rest of their lives?

One group finally managed to include several women. Yay. But as engineers, geneticists, microbiologists, and so forth, said women understandably didn't want to spend their lives being incubators or babysitters. When they refused, citing the importance of their terraforming endeavours, the men got angry and killed them.

Another group also included women. Of the right kind. Accidentally. What happened was the planners decided to include a strip club in their Mars colony. And comfort women. You know. For massages. Within a few generations, their colony had become so dumbed down, it just sort of petered out.

Then a group decided to deal with the 'problem' by recruiting teenagers. A ready-made next generation! Every one of them killed themselves. They were bored to death.

And then, finally, a group had the eggs, the incubators, the caretakers ... There were concerns that once the kids hit puberty, the whole 'I didn't ask to be born' (let alone 'I didn't ask to be born *here*') thing would be a problem, but it turned out their concerns were completely ... unnecessary. None of the kids reached puberty. Apparently, the men forgot to read up on human development before they left. Well, more precisely, before they created new humans. (As was their habit since forever. There'd always been a huge disconnect for men between ejaculating into a woman's vagina and pregnancy, childbirth, responsibility for what they'd done, the human they'd created ...) Here's the thing: kids' bones develop because of gravity. Which Mars had little of. So the kids were, almost literally, jello. (Which, upside, meant that the inner ear malfunctions that would've resulted due to the low levels of sunlight and that would've led to continuous nausea—irrelevant.)

So. None of the trips to Mars resulted in a colony per se. All those 'visionaries'? They didn't *colonize* Mars. They showed up, did some shit, then died. Mostly because there wasn't anyone to do the shit that actually needed to be done for their survival. Things like, oh, I don't know, grow food. Because they, the 'visionaries', sure as hell weren't going to do *that*!

Of course, anyone who's heard of seasteading would realize that for the 'visionaries', going to Mars wasn't so much about the enabling the survival of the human species as it was about avoiding governance, being able to run their companies, manage their wealth, without interference. (Did they not realize that the very governments whose laws bound them, and over which, it must be noted, they had a great deal of control, were also the governments who subsidized them?) (Of course they did. So?)

However, par for the course, and ironically, short-sightedness prevented the *'visionaries'* from realizing that in destroying Earth (because for sure those bound for Mars included oil and beef barons), they'd destroyed their market.

At some point, those who *were* interested in enabling the survival of the human species pointed out that it would be far more intelligent to set up a 'Mars base' in the middle of Nevada or some such. Terraforming a ravaged Earth would be more likely to succeed than terraforming Mars. The background radiation would be lower. The ingredients for water, air, soil ... all of it was already here, more or less ... And the money saved by not having to *go to* Mars could be added to the terraforming effort. The clean-up effort. (Let's call it what it is.)

So when the next group had all their stuff ready to go, a bunch of women stole it. 'Course, it's not really stealing if you have a right to it. And they surely did. All the unpaid labour they'd provided since forever ... In addition to paying taxes once they were allowed to work, and so have an income, and so own property ...

Did they remember the men? Of course. How could any woman ever forget about men? Said men were denied the right to vote, of course. Though that didn't really matter, because there were so few of them. So few were necessary. The women hadn't even had to— By the time men of a certain sort realized that the women's effort was worth attention, worth conquest, it was impenetrable. And since it's emasculating to live among women, only the right sort of men were ... living among them.

# A PostTrans PostPandemic World

It was a matter of coordination, which most women were very good at, but it was also a matter of critical mass, which had finally been achieved, thanks to transactivism. The movement made a huge leap into the mainstream when Bruce (Caitlin) Jenner won a Woman of the Year award in 2015, and by the mid-2020s, women—enough women—were fed up.

Fed up with transwomen insisting they were women. (Because they *felt* like women.) Fed up with men—with or without surgical modifications, with or without even chemical modifications—insisting that they be allowed access to women's washrooms, women's changerooms, women's shelters, women's sports …

For some, the tipping point it was the man—sorry, the woman—who insisted that female estheticians wax his balls. His *lady* balls. Why didn't he go to a (probably male) esthetician qualified for that procedure? Obviously he wanted *women* to handle his balls. As a result of his legal action (he claimed discrimination on the basis of gender identity), one woman had to close her business. (Another had paid him, $2500, per his request, to withdraw his complaint.)

For others, it was the dead rat nailed to the door of Vancouver Rape Relief's shelter (followed by 'KILL TERFS' and 'FUCK TERFS' written across its windows—TERFs being the radical feminist who insisted on excluding transwomen from women's spaces). No doubt, transactivists felt empowered by the city council's decision to reduce the shelter's funding on the basis that it refused to provide services for men who identified as women. (No matter that the city's funding was used for their public education programs, from which *no one* was excluded.)

And for others, it was the widely circulated photograph of a march, in which men—sorry, women—carried pink and blue baseball bats while wearing bloodied t-shirts proclaiming "I punch TERFS". (And they accused *us* of violence toward *them*.)

But for most, it was $250,000 fine imposed on those who refused to concede to pronoun preferences, who refused to refer to a man as 'she' just because he said to.

So one day, over a hundred thousand of us applied for a change in our passports, claiming that we felt like men now. As soon as we received our changed passports, we applied for another change, a change back, because now we felt like women again. Passport offices ground to a halt.

We did the same thing at driver's license offices across the country.

We could have applied for a change on our birth certificates as well, but many of us feared that that would, if not now then at some future point, render us ineligible for health services specific to those with female bodies. We wanted our mammograms, our pap smears, our female-specific contraception, our prenatal care, our birthing assistance, our postpartum care …

Next, worldwide, female athletes claimed they felt disabled.

(As well as male.) Along with their entry forms for events in the Special Olympics, they sent photographs of Robert Ludwig, allowed to play in a women's basketball league, Craig Telfer, allowed to compete in women's track, Gavin Hubbard, allowed to compete in women's weight-lifting, and Will Thomas, allowed to compete in women's swimming.

The women won every single event. Gold, silver, and bronze. Along with several lucrative endorsement contracts.

Enraged, male disabled athletes went to their beloved leagues—the NFL, the NBA, the NHL—insisting that they felt able and demanded the opportunity to try out. Every season had to be postponed. At the time of writing, one able-bodied quadriplegic is still trying to complete the first of fifty push-ups.

At every university with aboriginal scholarships, we applied for them, claiming that we felt aboriginal. We like to wear moccasins, we said, we feel at peace in the forest, we go canoeing in the summer …

"But you're not aboriginal!" Chief Calm Lake screamed at one woman.

"Yes I am," she replied. "Because I *identify* as aboriginal." After all, back in 2020, the Australian Academy of Science— *Science*, note—adopted the definition of 'woman' as "anyone who *identifies* as a woman", and the UK, the US, and Canada followed suit.

"And my name is Hawk Feather," she added, "not Diane."

At first, it was all angry backlash and dismal attempts to educate people about the ridiculousness of gender identity when it referred to actual gender (because you don't need an *identity*, let alone *a publicly proclaimed* identity, in order to have or develop preferences and interests that are stereotypically aligned with, expected of, members of the other sex) and when it referred to sex (because you can't *change* your *sex*, your *chromosomes*).

But when we realized that people couldn't discriminate on the basis of sex if they couldn't determine sex …. (I say 'we' but of course those of us who had become feminists in the '70s had long known this, which is why *we* had advocated for sex-neutral pronouns, as well as the use of first initials rather than full first names.)

And that's when the pandemic of the early 2020s became … fortuitous.

For years, women had been infiltrating men's online discussions, using male names and avatars, so it seemed that men were becoming kinder, gentler, less sexist. And perhaps, we thought, that would spread; we hoped that maybe in another two or three generations, men really would become kinder, gentler, less sexist.

But it was becoming clear that we didn't *have* another two or three generations. Men had to change *now*. They had to reject the masculist mode that had enabled, *encouraged,* so much competition and hence so much destruction (win at all costs)—*now*.

Because of the pandemic, most education had gone online. Classes were held on Skype, Zoom, InClass, whatever. Most one-to-one interaction occurred online as well, via video chat apps.

So we said we were men. Our cameras didn't work, we said, and we loaded an avatar or an image plucked off the internet. Many chose an androgynous image, but those wanting to make the point with more punch, or with humour, used images of Sylvester Stallone and Dolly Parton. For example.

We also loaded voice modification software, that not only had male and female settings, but a number of accents and 'specials' to choose from. Including Donald Duck.

Of course, that might not have achieved its goal because the cameras of male students always seemed to work, but, learning from transmen (who'd been largely silent in the transactivist movement—no surprise: as women by nurture, they weren't loud and/or antagonistic; as women by perception, still, they were silenced), women cut their hair, tossed their make-up, and stopped plucking their eyebrows. They also stopped wearing sexualized clothing. And were surprised at how similar male and female features really were.

Sex-neutral pronouns were already in use. 'Ze' had easily replaced 'he' and 'she' because it was an ambiguous pronunciation of 'he' and 'she'. (And because it was an acceptable work-around the trans thing.) A replacement for 'him' and 'her' was problematic until someone pointed out that both words, as objects, were always used with prepositions (to, from, with, etc.), so 'ze' would serve quite nicely as the object pronoun as well (to ze, from ze, with ze, etc.). The same argument was made for replacing 'his' and 'her': as possessives, they were always accompanied by a noun, so why not just use, again, 'ze'? Women speaking other languages similarly introduced sex-neutral pronouns (with more or less difficulty, depending on the language).

So John sounded like a man and looked like a man, but insisted he was a woman, and Mary sounded like a woman one day and like a man the next or claimed to be a man one day and a woman the next. The students kept correcting their professors, who finally threw up their hands in confusion, and disgust, and just started referring to all of their students by their student numbers.

But numbers were too impersonal, so women chose androgynous names. But of course that didn't work either (just as the use of first initials didn't work) because most of the men held on to their male advantage, their male identity, their male names: for the most part, male names indicated men, female names indicated transmen, and androgynous indicated women.

Consequently, again following in the footsteps of transmen, women started using male names, adopting male identity, receiving male advantage: attention, primarily, inclusion.

All of a sudden, 99% of the student body seemed to be men. Of course, that was impossible, but to many people's surprise, and frustration, they couldn't tell the difference. They'd thought they could, by competence, but suddenly there were a lot more competent people: those previously known to be men, as well as many of those now sex-unknown, many of whom, of course, were women. It didn't help—that is to say, it *did* help—that many women had started interrupting others, hogging the air time, throwing tantrums.

We're not sure—because how would we know?—but we think women's scholarships became unnecessary. And although there had already been as many female students as male students in law and medicine (no doubt partly due to the arguably awful tv show *Ally McBeal* that started in the late '90s and the somewhat better *Grey's Anatomy* that started a few years later), that became the case in pretty much every discipline.

The workplace had similarly gone virtual: job interviews were conducted online, and so were also amenable to the use of image and voice modification. Which meant, we think, that those female law and med students were hired as often as their male counterparts. The same would surely be, or become, true for engineering, business, all of the sciences, and so on. In short, more women were, or soon would be, hired for positions typically dominated by men.

And since, post-pandemic, many people did their jobs from home, teleconferencing only as needed, supervisors often had no idea what sex their subordinates were or even claimed to be. Nor what ethnic ancestry they had, nor what colour their skin was. It was all very ... good.

As a result, promotions were no longer aligned with sex, ethnicity, and colour. Pay differentials disappeared. Expertise— real and perceived—became redistributed among the population.

Women were able to support themselves even if they had kids. Their standard of living rose to that of men.

Government, and politics, had also gone online, so women experienced the same advantages in terms of attention, inclusion. Generally speaking, when people didn't know whether they were dealing with a man or a woman, they erred on the side of respect. It was nice. And about fucking time.

Men's attitudes toward women changed. Though, often, they didn't know it.

Of course, many men objected. One such man ran his election campaign with the slogan "I've always *been* a man and I'll always *be* a man!"

But, so, when millions of men, maybe, started shouting for abortion on demand, well, it wasn't long in coming. Ditto for free and widely accessible contraception.

Within a few years, over half of the key positions were held by women. (We think.) Because additional legislative change was far-reaching. And enforcement was thorough.

And there stopped being a *Woman of the Year* award.

# Unless

So what happened was one day a huge pile of weird stuff showed up. It just—showed up. In someone's back yard. Left by Jodi Taylor's time travellers? Because they ~~accidentally~~ spritzed themselves with what the Professor had concocted (*No Time like the Past,* p29)?

Next time the pile filled a whole block. The remains of a Hollywood scifi movie production? Because, you know, Hollywood is so head-up-their-ass with their own ~~make-believe~~ bullshit, they've totally lost touch with reality and don't even *think* about the consequences of their actions?

And then it was the entire acreage between one town and the next that was full. Of weird stuff. A crop-circle conspiracy by the oil ~~barons~~ psychopaths and the meat ~~producers~~ psychopaths to distract us from our ~~death~~ murder?

The next pile to appear was the size of a small city. An archaeological ~~find~~ cache suddenly exposed because of some don't-ask-why ridiculously specific earthquake caused by the don't-ask-why shifting of the continental plates?

The next appearance of weird stuff contained some stuff that seemed organic. Loosely defined. Or redefined. Biologists rushed to the scene. And what did they discover? They ~~didn't~~ weren't allowed to say.

And then, after the next ~~pile~~ whatever, nearly the size of the Great Pacific Patch, a recently ~~retired~~ fired sanitation engineer figured it out: some other world was getting rid of its ~~garbage~~ waste by tossing it into a wormhole and we happened (?) to be on the other end.


"Pity their garbage isn't our gold. Well, not gold, but … something that ingests plastic and excretes … top soil."

"Actually—"

"Seriously?"

They all nodded.

"Huh. Though what we *really* need is an Earth whose people breathe carbon dioxide and are … suffocating. We could trade planets until …"

"Until we need to trade back."

"Or trade again."

They all sighed.

"Yeah."

"Unless—"

# Alleviation

Of course, one day it got to her. The first-world guilt. Here she was, living during the end of the world, and doing so quite comfortably in her cabin-on-a-lake-in-a-forest. She'd been lucky. Lucky to have been born in Canada. That's pretty much it. She hadn't been lucky in terms of jobs, in terms of income, in terms of friends and family, but even so, she had it good. She had food, water, heat—

Well, that was pretty much all, now, she reflected. Electricity was sporadic, but she had wood for back-up (because whether she heated by oil, propane, thermal heat pump, or baseboard heaters, electricity was needed; switching to solar heating wasn't an option for her because there simply wasn't enough sun unless she cut down all of her trees, and even then, well, half the time, it was cloudy); she also had back-up battery packs (which enabled a few hours of internet access when the power went out), a few solar lights (which meant she could read—and she had hundreds of books, many of which were still unread; she'd stocked up, buying used from online sites when the library's inter-library loan program was cancelled), a couple ipods that she kept fully solar-charged (so she could still listen to music), and a solar-powered laptop (more books and music, and other stuff). Furthermore, she was still fit enough to go kayaking out on the lake and to go walking through the forest. What else did she need?

Flooding wasn't a concern where she lived, in general (three hours north of Toronto) or in particular (her cabin was up a short, but steep, incline). Same for drought. And hurricanes. Tornadoes were occurring more frequently where she lived, but she had a half-basement in which to wait it out, and so far, so good.

Her biggest concern was forest fires. If there was no time to evacuate—or nowhere to evacuate to—she figured she could paddle out to the middle of the lake and be safe until ... well, then, yes, she'd be homeless. And no, her insurance policy probably wouldn't cover building a new house—they'd started adding exclusions for natural disasters years ago. In any case, merely the thought of starting over exhausted her. So she hoped that she had enough in the bank to lease a small piece of land somewhere, hopefully on some other lake, no matter how remote (in fact, the more remote, the better), on which she could put a second-hand trailer and perhaps live out her days happily enough. She had an emergency 'take with' bag down at the water for such an event: face masks and goggles, of course, but also a tent, a sleeping bag, extra clothing, a couple weeks worth of food (most people didn't realize how little one really needed), and a few essentials.

Eventually, she'd have to worry about looters, gangs, from the city. She'd thought about buying a gun, but they'd come in a group and she couldn't kill all of them. Instead, she stocked up on things they might accept as trade for moving on, leaving her alone. Soap, toilet paper, antibiotics, ibuprofen. Initially, she'd thought of stocking up on booze and cigarettes, but the pandemic—one of the pandemics—had been full of lessons:

liquor and beer stores were considered essential services and allowed to stay open, fully supplied, while, for example, libraries had to close. Go figure.

So, she was, yes, quite comfortable. Hence, the guilt. She'd donated to many aid organizations when she was young, but over time, she'd stopped. She'd read about the corruption in some, the money not going where it was supposed to go. And she'd gradually come to understand that the problems were too complex for such organizations to solve. Reading Kim Stanley Robinson's *Ministry for the Future* was incredibly depressing. Because there was no way ...

At some point, she'd wondered *why* the developing countries were, well, *developing* countries. Why hadn't they already achieved a comfortable standard of living? Did the people just sit around all day? Was it too hot to work? She did some online research and discovered that a hundred years ago, Argentina was among the seven richest nations in the world. A mere twenty years ago, Zimbabwe was doing very well. She read about, yes, geographical explanations (coastal areas had better access to trade, for example), but she also read about resource endowment explanations (which would explain Saudi Arabia's richness), economic explanations (applicable to Japan, Taiwan, and South Korea), technological explanations (applicable to the United States), political explanations (elites keep the riches to themselves, by force) ... And of course, one had to consider invasion by other countries and the consequent destruction of natural resources and infrastructure, as well as theft of said natural resources by other countries. She'd already known about the exorbitant interest rates on loans which guaranteed to keep the borrower impoverished ... Then she read that quality of life isn't, need not be, all about the GNP; by other standards, perhaps at least some so-called developing countries weren't so bad off ... Regardless, the older she got, the more she realized she'd have to start saving for her own future. She had no company pension plan and everyone had been saying for years that the Canada Pension Plan itself would soon be completely emptied out by the boomers. So that was another reason to stop making donations here and there.

But now, she probably had enough. At some point, money wouldn't be able to buy what she needed, and before that, well, she probably wouldn't live into her mid-eighties as anticipated. She figured she'd be lucky to make it to her mid-seventies without some fatal injury or illness. And given the now-sporadic health services, not to mention the various pandemics that made it more life-threatening to go to a hospital than not, many more injuries and illnesses would *be* fatal.

So, she had enough. In fact, she probably had more than enough. She figured she probably had at least a thousand dollars more than enough. Which is why the thought occurred to her. She couldn't save the world, she'd never been able to save the world: she'd read that a whopping 71 percent of greenhouse gas emissions were due to just a hundred companies—and the governments that let them be, she'd added to herself—and if the various organizations she'd been giving money to had no power over those companies, or governments, she certainly didn't. She hadn't even been able to convince the local township council to prohibit jetskis (and so they continued racing around, dumping two gallons of uncombusted gas and oil into the lake for every hour of operation).

In fact, she hadn't been able to convince anyone of *anything*. Her neighbours blithely continued their 1960s lifestyle, leaving their thermostats set to 70 even when they weren't home, eating meat every day, taking RV trips every spring, flying to Hawaii, Ireland, France, ticking off their bucket list dreams one by one, when they should've been sobbing with unbearable remorse for all the lives they'd derailed with an endless panorama of forest fires, super storms, heat waves, power outages, food shortages, exorbitant prices, relentless pandemics … And all the lives they'd cut short. When she'd asked a few, point blank, whether they weren't bothered by the global warming consequences of their actions, they'd simply replied 'not really', as if she'd asked whether they liked classical music. It had been truly disconcerting.

But maybe, she thought, maybe she could make the end a bit more comfortable for those would be suffering most the consequences of her lifetime of luxury.

Relative luxury. Because although she hadn't managed to be part of any solution, she had tried to minimize being part of the problem. Unlike her neighbours, she kept her thermostat set to 55, and moved around an electric heater like an IV stand, from couch to desk to couch again; she had one small car and had been rationing trips since the '80s; she'd made only four plane trips, ever; she had a kayak, not a jetski; she didn't own an ATV or a snowmobile; she had a twirly lawn mower instead of a gas-powered one, and a shovel instead a snowblower; she reused and recycled …

She decided that this time she would give the money directly to someone. Or maybe she should use the money to buy something and then send the something directly to someone. Food? Water purifiers? Solar batteries? Mosquito netting? How much does it cost to dig a well? Is there still reachable groundwater … wherever? Maybe rain barrels instead? Then she thought no, surely the someone would know best what they needed. She could attach an offer to help them get whatever it was they needed. Did they want $1,000 worth of mosquito netting? She'd go on eBay and get it for them. A hundred rain barrels? Surely, she could figure out a way.

But then she remembered another reason she'd stopped donating money. Back when everyone was advocating for the starving kids in Biafra or Ethiopia, it had suddenly occurred to her: why should she support other people's kids? *They'd* decided to make them. Their choice, their responsibility. It was, after all, a decision, a choice. Kids didn't just get delivered willy-nilly by the stork. They didn't just appear one morning in your cabbage patch.

Well, maybe not always, for the woman, was it a decision, a choice. Surely rape was as prevalent, probably even more prevalent, in poor countries. Countries full of angry, frustrated men. Who always seemed to feel entitled to take out their anger and frustration on the nearest woman. To *blame* the nearest woman.

Okay, yes, but it was always a decision, a choice, *for the man.* You didn't just accidentally ejaculate your sperm into a woman's vagina. You couldn't just mistake a woman's vagina for—well, for anything other than a woman's vagina.

And then when she found out that the U.S. had been refusing foreign aid to any organization that provided contraception and abortion— Logic would dictate just the opposite. No, logic would dictate tying aid to vasectomies. *That's* what *she* would do!

After all, overpopulation was in large part why the Earth would soon be no longer able to sustain us. There were, currently, worldwide, 7.8 billion people, and that figure was increasing by 385,000 per day. That's like adding a city the size of Beirut. Every day. Earth could comfortably sustain only half that, she recalled.

She herself had not made any new people, so all those who were having ten kids— Hm. She'd had this picture in her head of everyone in developing countries having lots and lots of kids, but a quick online search showed that people in only nine countries were making, on average, more than five kids. The site said 'per woman' but, she wondered angrily, why don't they say 'per man'? Or at least 'per couple'? Even so, someone replicating themselves five times was surely five times more responsible for—

But no, she realized, it's not just about the number of people. The population *density* in Niger, top of the list with 6.9 kids, was 19 people per square meter; in Canada, it was 4 people per square meter. (And in Niger, the median age was 15. That's another issue, she thought.) Granted, much of Canada is pretty inhospitable, but then so is much of Niger. Even so, so what? Yes, Niger had more people than it could support, but Canada couldn't support itself either: didn't we rely on imported food to get us through the winter? (Which begs the question, why haven't we developed extensive greenhouse agriculture?)

So it's not really about population density either. She went back to that 7.8 billion. And back to the internet. At an American standard of living, Earth could sustain about 2 billion. At a European standard of living, 3 billion. People in the U.S.— and let's say people in Canada are about the same—use 5 times the resources as people in Niger. So, she started calculating, let's say I use 500 units; the person in Niger would use 100. But that person would have 7 kids. But we'd have to 'assign' half to the other person, it takes two, so that's 3.5 kids. Assuming each of those 3.5 kids has 3.5 kids (well, also 7, but half …), then during my lifetime, I'd have used only 500 units, but that person in Nigeria, because she'd—he'd—created roughly 15 additional human beings, would use his 100 units plus 1500, for a total of 1600 units. About three times her use. Hm. So … her first-world guilt was unwarranted?

Though perhaps they didn't live to seventy-five …

They didn't, she discovered, but even if they did, her numbers were off: according to Dave Tilford, of the Sierra Club, people in the U.S. cause 13 times as much ecological damage as people in the Brazil, and they use 35 times the resources as those in India. And even though she was surely nowhere near the norm for the U.S, she was also likely nowhere near the norm for Brazil of India.

Furthermore, if that person were in India instead of Niger—India was also suffering consequences of climate change disproportionate to their 'contribution' to said change—if that person were in India, they'd have just 2 kids, split between the mother and father, that's just 1, plus, say, 1 grandkid, so that's 2 additional people, so that's their own 100 units, plus 200, for a total of 300. Compared to her 500.

Regardless, if we'd gone to zero population growth back in the '70s, when we understood exponential growth rate, if *everyone* had, like her, *not* replicated themselves, not even once, until the world was back to 2 billion, from the 4 billion of that decade … So it still made sense to make vasectomy a condition of aid.

But then it made sense to make vasectomy a condition of aid to first world people as well. That would certainly mitigate the feeling of racist eugenics lurking behind her plan. (As consequence, though, not as intent.) But people in the States didn't need the $1,000 to increase their comfort level. They were already comfortable. Like her.

And actually—she'd started searching the net again—the critical thing wasn't so much resource use as carbon footprint. To meet the two degree goal, she read, an individual's annual $CO_2e$ budget must not exceed 2.1 metric tons by 2050. The average in the U.S. was 19.8; in Finland, it was 11.5; in France, 6.6; and in Bangladesh, 0.29.

She also read that 59% of the land capable of growing crops was used for growing food *for livestock*. And that 33% of all the fresh water available was going to livestock. She'd already known that trees provided oxygen and absorbed carbon dioxide, and that when cut down or burned, they released their carbon. But she hadn't known that they were 50% carbon—that forests contained more carbon than fossil-fuel reserves. And she especially hadn't known that *80% of deforestation* occurs to clear land *for livestock*. In Bangladesh, she read, the average person consumed about 9 pounds of meat per year. The average person in Finland consumed that much every eighteen days, for an average of about 180 pounds per year. In Canada, the average was 152 pounds. (Wow. She herself hadn't eaten *any* meat since she'd moved out, into her own home, her own life, but she did consume dairy products.) In India, it was 7.2 pounds. So if she *did* consider giving her $1,000 to someone in the first world, it would make more sense to tie it not to a vasectomy, but to vegetarianism.

Of course, a lot of people would promise to become vegetarians, take the money, and run. With the vasectomy idea, well, she'd imagined that maybe Doctors without Borders would get involved, so that plan was more … viable.

Though, honestly, neither plan made sense. Both would've made sense back in the '70s. But she wasn't doing this to save the world, she reminded herself. They were already past the point of no return, they were already over the cliff and falling. She was doing this purely to make the lives of those who had been pushed over that cliff, through no fault of their own, more comfortable. As they fell. So it made no sense to give it to anyone in the first world. And it made no sense to attach *any* strings.

Though … if people continued to replicate themselves, it would cancel any efforts on her part to mitigate their hardship, because every additional human increased said hardship, reduced the food and water for everyone else, increased the number of environmental refugees …

In the end, she decided to just send the money. No strings attached. It was easier that way. Quicker that way. And they all had so little time left. At that moment, there were severe water shortages, *fatal* water shortages, in Guatemala, Honduras, Eritrea, Somalia, Ethiopia, Sudan, Uganda, Afghanistan, India, Morocco, Syria, and Pakistan ...

She tweeted for suggestions as to how to make it happen. Did people in wherever have PayPal accounts? Could she, should she, instead, send her thousand dollars to someone care of some trustworthy microbank?

Turned out there were several people working in Canadian embassies who were disillusioned with both Canada's foreign aid programs and its role in global warming (for example, instead of ramping down the oil and gas industry, it was ramping up: development of the Teck tar sands mine meant that with only 0.5% of the planet's population, Canada was planning to use up almost a third of the planet's remaining carbon budget). They contacted her. Offered to make it happen.

It also turned out that her tweet had been retweeted.

Soon ten people had sent $1,000, to someone experiencing hardship, via an embassy, because of what we had done. Or not done. Well, she thought, that's pretty good. $10,000 had made its way from—

Then a hundred people. Then a thousand. That was a million dollars. Within a week. There was a lot of first-world guilt.

Within a month, it was ten million dollars.

Within a year, a billion dollars.

She smiled.

Sort of.

# The Women's Party

"So basically, we're all going to die because we can't figure out how to live."

There were five of them. A lawyer, a lobbyist, an activist, a professor, and a journalist. They were having tea at a tea shop, during an international conference.

"Well, more like we can't agree about how to live."

"Every solution—carbon tax, cap-and-trade, capture-and-sequestration, geo engineering, renewables—"

"Population control—"

"Every single proposal has been rejected."

"Well, not by everyone."

"No, just by the U.S., Russia, and China, which together are responsible for 48% of the carbon emissions."

"And what about the methane? Isn't that more of a problem than carbon dioxide?"

"Yes! *Eighty-four times* more of a problem! And 60% of it is due to human activities."

"Eating meat. Clearing for livestock."

"Yes."

"'Live stock'." She emphasized each word separately.

"Kinda like 'human resources'."

They sighed.

"Did any of you see that Baroness Von Sketch piece? I think it was called 'The G4 Summit'?"

They all nodded.

Then sighed again.

And then looked at each other.

And made the decision.

◆

Certainly, there had been women's parties in the past. Though the history books don't mention them. Of course not.

Certainly, there were women's parties at the time. Though the mainstream (malestream) media didn't mention them. Of course not.

Fed up with barriers to participation within existing parties and not seeing women's issues addressed with anything approaching adequacy—so very tired of being sidelined into women's caucuses, because women were, after all, half the population, *fully half* of the *mainstream*—they formed their own parties. As MacKinnon had pointed out, "When men sit in rooms, being states, they are largely being men. They protect each other; they identify with each other; they try not to limit each other in ways they themselves do not want to be limited. In other words, they do not represent women."

Argentina, Australia, Austria, Belarus, Belgium, Cambodia, Chile, Costa Rica, Cuba, Denmark, Egypt, Finland, Germany, Hungary, India, Iran, Israel, Japan, South Korea, Lithuania, the Netherlands, Nigeria, Norway, Poland, Russia, Serbia, South Africa, Spain, Taiwan, Turkey, Ukraine, the UK, even the United States. Every one of these countries had, in the past or at the time, a women's party.

Some of these parties focused on increasing political participation, some focused on achieving equality in the workplace, some focused on reducing violence against women ... Every one of them failed. Failed to obtain the support that would give them power. Or, given the existing system, failed to obtain the power that would give them support.

So why was the Women's Party that was formed in 2025 finally successful? No doubt there were a number of reasons, but perhaps foremost was that it was the first party, the only party, to be a global party. It addressed global issues.

Global warming was, of course, the most visible, most pressing, of these global issues, and identified *as* an important issue more often by women than men. Women have, typically, been more concerned about others; they're not as self-centered and not as selfish. (One could be the former without the latter, but not the latter without the former.) Men seemed to think something like 'Most of the worst climate changes won't occur *here*, so why care?' or 'Most of the worst climate changes won't occur in *my* lifetime, so again, why care?'

Furthermore, men in general accept more risk. Probably because men in general think they're invulnerable. (As if their relatively greater upper body strength will somehow enable them to survive global warming.) (It won't, of course. But their relatively greater wealth might.)

And then there was the attitude, part of the whole masculinity thing, that natural resources were, well, 'natural *resources*', things to be 'used', 'harnessed', 'conquered' (will they *ever* stop competing?), rather than 'just' water, forests, and mountains, let alone 'just' beauty. And so, to accept global warming was to accept a certain impotence, a failure to conquer. (No wonder they increased, rather than decreased, their logging, drilling, mining ...) (Such *manly* things ... )

Further, global warming challenged their belief that they were separate from, and superior to, the environment. It was another element of masculinity, that whole independence thing. Interdependence, let alone dependence, indicated weakness. Go figure.

Not to mention the 'Money is more important than everything else' attitude, an attitude which led to economic growth being more important than everything else. The environment. The planet. Never mind that without a planet that can sustain human life, there will be no economic growth. At all.

One might have hoped that the 'fix it' part of masculinity might have emerged, prevailed, and no doubt it did in some circles. Unfortunately, not the circles with the most power and money. And the status quo advantaged those with power and money. Who were not about to accept blame by changing. (Let alone by giving up their power and money.)

Regardless, global warming seemed to set the stage for successful consolidation. Of which there had been precious little. And consolidation was the key. Not co-operation. Women had always co-operated across national borders. At least, they had done so far more often than men had. But it wasn't enough. A certain co-ordinated critical mass was needed.

In addition to international consolidation among women's groups, it made sense for women to join forces with the ever-increasing young people's lawsuit movement. Suits had been filed in several countries, claiming that their government's actions had caused global warming and so had violated the young people's right to life and property. But, of course, they'd been dismissed. In Canada, because the questions raised were "so political that the courts are incapable or unsuited to deal with them"; in the United States, because "the issue should be raised with the executive and legislative branches of government, not the courts"; ad nauseam. This state of affairs surely garnered the youth vote for the new women's party.

It also made sense to join forces with the many indigenous groups trying to keep the oil and logging industries off their land. Nemonte Nenquimo of the Waorani Nation managed to save 500,000 acres of Amazon rainforest from oil exploration and drilling, and the Sioux in the United States succeeded against the Dakota Access Pipeline, but such successes were rare. The Tsleil-Waututh Nation in Canada, acting against the Trans Mountain expansion, was not successful.

And surely misogyny, increasing in scope and severity, was responsible for much of the support. Domestic violence had started to move out of the home. Even *before* the first pandemic, incidents like the Montreal Massacre had started happening more often, edging slowly but steadily from the fringe to the mainstream. Ironically, although men as a group have since forever proclaimed open season on women, expecting willing sex while simultaneously raping at random, it was the men who 'identified' as 'women' who triggered a sudden increase in violence against women. They took to the streets bearing baseball bats and wearing shirts proclaiming their intent to kill women (or at least a subset thereof: those who dared insist they were *not*, in fact, women and so should *not* be allowed to compete in women's sports, to be at women's shelters, as clients or staff, to access women's health services—dude, you don't have a uterus ...), and that action, along with the media attention and the protection provided to those 'women' by the ill-informed, paved the way for regular men to do the same. To take to the streets bearing baseball bats and wearing shirts proclaiming their intent to kill women. And *that* action changed *a lot* of women's minds.

Prior to that, many women were opposed to a women's party: they didn't see anything sexist in the world as it was, or they didn't see anything wrong with sexism (hard to say which was worse), or they thought a women's party itself was sexist. (Which it was. But there's justified sexism and unjustified sexism. And the women who created the women's party were, for the most part, women who understood and wanted to eliminate unjustified sexism. Among other things.) But ordinary women, hitherto apolitical women, could not ignore parades of ordinary men carrying baseball bats proclaiming—out loud and in public—their intent to kill women.

On top of all that, the religious right gained popularity, at least among men. Men who were no doubt attracted more by the tribalism and conservatism than by Jesus. Acid attacks moved from the Middle East to North America. Legislation permitting stoning was discussed in some states. That changed more minds.

So. Women of the world united. Their concerns crossed borders. Their oppression crossed borders.

Oddly enough (well, odd only to Americans), the initiative to globalize a women's party did not come from the States. Contrary to the delusion held by most Americans that their country was the best, most advanced, country in the world, in 2019, the U.S. ranked 75th in terms of women's representation in government. At the time, only three countries had a female majority in government: Rwanda (where women held 61.4% of parliament seats), Cuba (53.2%), and Bolivia (53.1%). The U.S.? 23.5%. So no, the five women in the tea shop did not include an American or even a Canadian. They were from Sweden, South Korea, Germany, Rwanda, and Cuba.

Most men are, well, stupid. Maybe that's why they so easily, so often, assume women are stupid. Imagine their surprise when we took over. When they realized we'd taken over.

And then, what did we do that was so different? Where do I start?

Perhaps by saying that we filled all positions of responsibility and power with women. We knew that, by and large, women did better: "Women read their briefs, they don't just read the summary of their Cabinet papers, they've actually done the homework, often much more diligently," said Mike Ramm, former premier of South Australia; women-run private tech companies earn a 35% higher return on investment, reported Allyson Kapin in a *Forbes* article; female lawyers are less likely to behave unethically, reported Hatamyar and Simmons in the *Florida State University Law Review*; patients treated by female doctors are less likely to die or be readmitted to the hospital, according to a Harvard study; countries that have more women in power are less likely to go to war and less likely to have a civil war, reported Mary Ann Sieghart in *The Authority Gap* ...

To the objection that there wouldn't be enough qualified women to do this, we simply pointed out that men of mediocre, rather than exceptional, abilities had occupied such positions forever; surely there were enough mediocre women to take their places.

Beyond that ...

+

"I wish you'd get rid of your ATV," Ann said to her teen-aged son one weekend. They were in the hallway. He was on his way out. "And your snowmobile." He ignored her.

"We're supposed to be *reducing* our emissions, and here you are producing them. *For fun.*"

No response.

"Are you not aware at all of global warming, carbon footprints, etc., etc.? You're the one who's going to be still in your twenties when the shit *really* hits the fan."

He shrugged.

Then, since she clearly expected some sort of reply, he said, "You're not the boss of me."

The first time she'd heard that insolence, that condescension, she'd actually gasped. It had started the moment he'd hit puberty, with the first surge of testosterone. But now, she was used to it. And she was tired of it. So very, very tired of it.

"Actually, I am." She leaned against the wall and crossed her arms.

"I'm eighteen."

"Then move out."

He laughed.

"I'm serious. I'm kicking you out."

Separatism begins in the home.

One might think that having to pay himself for his food and shelter, he'd not be able to afford insurance, gas, and maintenance on both his ATV and snowmobile, but he managed. She didn't ask how. Afraid she'd find out that the job he'd gotten paid more than hers.

◆

We prohibited the recreational production of fossil fuel emissions. It was beyond shameful that so many countries had been permitting the production of greenhouse gases *just for the hell of it*. Well into the 2020s. Canada, perhaps the worst on this matter, had established *121,000 kilometres* of trails *just for snowmobiles*. Recreational vehicles accounted for 20% of transportation emissions. Which is a significant chunk when you're struggling to reduce by 50%, the target set for 2030 by the IPCC in order to reach zero emissions by 2050 and thus have *a chance* of avoiding extinction. PWCs (jetskis, seadoos) became completely illegal; ATVs became illegal except when used as an essential, efficient replacement for tractors; snowmobiles were allowed only in certain northern regions for certain purposes.

◆

"But it makes no sense for both of us to have a vehicle," Beth said to her husband. They were in the kitchen. "The insurance. The maintenance." The first, in particular, had just gone up. The opened envelope was still on the table.

"Then sell your car," he said with annoyance.

"Then what'll we use when we have to get groceries?"

"We can put the groceries in the back of the truck!" Duh.

"And if it rains, they'll get wet."

"So we put a tarp over them."

"Well, that's a lot of work for nothing. I mean, with my car, we just put them in the back seat. End of story."

Silence.

"And what'll we use when we have to take the kids somewhere?" she persisted. "Really, don't you see how stupid your truck is? No covered trunk. No back seat. It uses more gas."

"I'm not selling my truck!" He glared at her.

"But you don't *need* a truck!" She was puzzled by his vehemence. (She obviously hadn't seen the 22 *minutes* spoof. Aptly titled "A Man and his Truck.") "Is it peer pressure? All of your friends have trucks?" She knew very well that made him sound like a child, but … if the shoe fits. "Will they make fun of you if you get a car? Because a car is smaller? Is that it?"

It was. She could see it. Oh for fuck's sake.

"You know, in many ways," she said, casually, "I'm bigger than you."

He stared at her.

"My chest measurement is bigger. My waist is bigger. My hips are bigger. My thighs are bigger."

"I'm taller. And I weigh more."

"So I guess it depends on your definition of 'bigger'."

Silence.

"You've been suckered!" she tried again. "All those ads showing tough rugged guys driving their trucks over tough rugged land, doing manual labour, getting muddy, working up a sweat … You've never done *anything* like that! You don't *need* to *do* anything like that! You just think—" He worked in an office.

"I might." He shuffled through the rest of the mail on the table.

She sighed. Men's affection for their trucks was like their affection for sports: vicarious and delusional. When they watched *other* men being athletic, they somehow felt that *they* were being athletic. When they drove *a vehicle* intended, promoted, and sometimes used for hard work, they felt like *they* were doing hard work. An honest look in the mirror would provide conclusive proof to the contrary, since most sports fans and pick-up owners were considerably overweight.

"What if we have to buy a new fridge one day?" he challenged. "Is it gonna fit in your car?"

She looked at him with such incredulity. "We can have it delivered. How can you not know that?"

◆

We legislated, and enforced, a significant increase in the minimum efficiency, kilometres per litre, for fossil fuel engines in cars and trucks.

We also legislated, and enforced, limits on greenhouse gas emissions: a maximum carbon footprint *per person*. Thousands of men found they couldn't have their ATVs, their snowmobiles, and their pick-ups too. Not to mention *also* their jetskis, their gas-powered lawnmowers, and their gas-powered snowblowers. *And* unlimited oil or propane for their furnaces. When individuals exceeded their limit, not only were they fined, their vehicles were impounded, their heating fuel deliveries stopped… Draconian? Not at all. If you can't control yourself, if you can't make the right decisions, we have to make them for you. It's a matter of maturity. And survival.

(Given the obesity of North Americans, it was good for them in particular to walk a little more or ride a bicycle, to cut their grass with manual mowers and to shovel their driveways with actual shovels ...) (It was also good for their country's healthcare costs.)

The footprints of children were calculated and added to the parents' total. Because hey, it was their choice to make those children, and they too would be producing carbon emissions, causing the planet to warm. People without kids had carbon to spare and so could trade, but most of them didn't want any more carbon—that was partly why they didn't have children: they were fully aware of over-population, resource use and abuse. And so they didn't sell; they kept the unused carbon sequestered. (Despite pressure to the contrary.)

At the same time, we redesigned the transportation infrastructure as needed, with on-off streetcars, subways, light rail transit to service urban centers, and train systems modelled after Eurail for cross-country travel.

We set limits for industry and business as well, based on a number of factors. And of course, we repealed subsidies to oil industries and awarded them instead to alternative energy industries.

Atmospheric carbon declined.

◆

They sat down for dinner, and Catja scooped onto her plate some veggie stirfry, salad, and mixed beans from the bowls she'd set onto the table.

"What, you've become a vegetarian?"

She stared at her husband. She'd been a vegetarian for a while. Apparently, he hadn't noticed. She'd become increasingly uncomfortable with the cruelty, in life and in death, suffered by chickens, pigs, cows … Then she'd read Foer's We are the Weather: globally, 59% of all arable land is used to grow food for livestock, 33% of the fresh water goes to livestock, and 80% of all deforestation is done in order to clear land for livestock, which adds more carbon dioxide to the atmosphere than all of the cars and trucks on all of the world's roads.

"Well, where's my supper?" he asked. There was no platter of chicken or pork on the table. No steak. Not even a couple burgers. This was simply the first time she hadn't prepared the usual. For him.

She passed the bowl of veggie stirfry to him.

"Right. Just because you've gone off your rocker doesn't mean I have to."

"If you want to eat dead animals, you buy them and you prepare them. If you were a pedophile, would you expect me to supply you with young girls?"

"I'm not a pedophile!"

"You weren't listening." As usual. "I said 'if'. I was making an argument by analogy."

"Well, it was a stupid argument."

"How so?"

"Because I'm not a pedophile."

"I don't think you understand argument by analogy. Or hypotheticals."

"I understand that a body needs meat. Protein."

"Protein, yes. Dead flesh, no. There was a study done, comparing flesh-eating athletes, vegetarian athletes, and vegetarian non-athletes. Vegetarians, athletes or not, had the greatest endurance. Measured by three strength tests." She'd anticipated his objection. Because oh how men are in love with their physical strength.

Next day, he bought a steak and grilled it on the barbecue. Of course. She'd also read *The Sexual Politics of Meat*. And had started thinking again about why her husband insisted on doing the cooking when the barbecue was involved, but not otherwise. She'd thought at first that it was because the barbecue is *outside*. And the outdoors is the male domain, whereas the indoors is the female domain. Well, except for the basement—the rec room part, not the laundry room part. And the garage. Because tools. And cars.

But then she realized that barbecues also involved, more directly, more visibly, fire. Danger! Manly men face danger.

And, of course, barbecues are typically used to prepare meat. Which means status. Poor people eat rice. And, meat is hard, tough, which somehow implies that those who eat it are hard, tough. Real men don't eat quiche. Or yogurt. But most of all, eating meat required killing. Even if one didn't do the killing oneself.

When the steak was quite done, he brought it inside.

"No." She stared at him.

"What now?"

"You're not eating that in front of me."

"Smells good, doesn't it."

"No, it smells like burnt flesh. Which is exactly what it is. Go eat it somewhere else."

"No."


She made one last attempt. Insisted that he visit a factory farm and a slaughterhouse, getting the full tour of each.

"If, then, you can still eat meat …"

She filed for divorce. It seemed that not only did he enjoy eating flesh, he had no problem with animals being hurt, killed, for him to do so.

◆

We made flesh-eating illegal. (And so, also, livestock farming and deforestation for livestock farming.) Forests recovered. Atmospheric carbon declined even further.

More broadly, we made it illegal not only to hunt animals, but also, in the case of sentience, to hurt them. Killing was allowed only in self-defence or when it was in the animal's best interests, and in those cases, it was done painlessly.

◆

Donna sat down to her bowl of oatmeal. She loved oatmeal for breakfast. She poured some soy 'milk' onto it, then reached for the brown sugar. The little dish was empty. She got up and went to the cupboard.

"We're out of brown sugar," she said with annoyance. "You did the grocery shopping last week."

"Yeah, I must've forgot." He sipped his coffee and continued to read his tablet.

"To do the grocery shopping or to get brown sugar?"

"To get brown sugar."

"How can you forget? It's on your list, you stroke off each item as you put it into your cart— You didn't put it on your list?"

"Guess not."

She persisted. "How could you not put it on your list? You open this cupboard, you see that the brown sugar tub is empty, you look for another bag to refill it, there isn't one, you put it on your list." She paused. "Did you not open this cupboard?"

"Guess I forgot."

She stared at him. "You sound like a child. You're a Project Manager, for godsake. And either not a very good one, in which case you should have been fired years ago, or you just didn't apply your management skills to the task."

"I'll have you know I'm a very good Project Manager," he glared at her for a moment, then turned his attention back to his tablet.

"But you can't handle inventory?"

He ignored her.

"We'll go together after breakfast," she sighed. "I'll inventory the kitchen, you do the bathroom and the laundry room."

"You go, I'm good."

"Well, *I'm* not. *Good.*" She put her hands on her hips and stared at him. "We agreed to split the chores. Last week was your week to do the grocery shopping. You messed up. So you're coming with me. I'll show you how to do it right."

Fuck you. He didn't say it aloud. But definitely wanted to.

Instead he said, "So you're going to cut the grass and shovel the snow every other time it needs doing?" He snorted.

"Of course. Why wouldn't I? I've been cutting my grass and shoveling my snow *every* time it needs doing, for the last ten years."

Moving in together had been a huge mistake. She'd suspected as much the day of the move. She knew it now, just two weeks later.

"And changing your tires and your oil too, I assume," he grumbled.

"No, I hate working on my car and don't know how to do it anyway, so I take it to the garage for that stuff." She looked at him. "But if I *did* do that too, why would that be cause for anger?"

"I'm not angry!"

Right.

"Ready?" She handed him two of the cloth bags hanging by the front door.

"We'll get bags at the store," he opened the door to head out.

"They'll be plastic. Or paper. You *know* plastic doesn't decompose very well. Our dumps are— You *know* about plastic. And paper comes from trees. Alive, they keep their carbon and produce oxygen."

He shrugged. Wouldn't touch the cloth bags.

"What's the problem?" she persisted. "Is it unmanly to hold a cloth bag? Do you need it to be … stiff leather? Perhaps a steel box? Or is the problem that it's a reuseable bag?" Yes. To all of the above. In a 2017 article in *Scientific American*, researchers presented a study that found that men distance themselves from eco-friendly behaviours because they're worried that such behaviours might make them look feminine. A 2019 study showed that people question a man's heterosexuality if he engages in activities such as recycling or shopping with reusable bags. *What* people, she'd wondered, absolutely flabbergasted.

"Is it unmanly to care about the environment?" she asked him. Ah. To be a man is, apparently, to not care. About anyone, any- thing. Men, do you not see that? Do you not see that masculinity is toxic? That it's past time to let it go? To *not* be a man?

"I'm just not a tree hugger," he replied.

"Tree *hugger?*" Right. Dismiss by feminization. That was something else she'd read about: a chief scientist was referred to, in a public discussion, as "this Julia Slingo *woman*" instead of Professor Slingo; Professor Joanna Haigh, Atmospheric Physics at the Imperial College London, was called a "puffed-up *missy*". And it wasn't just feminization, but sexualization: Dr. Emily

Shuckburgh, an experienced climate scientist, was referred to not by her name or job title but as "some *foxy chick* from the British Antarctic Survey."

"Why don't you call us tree *defenders*? Or planet protectors? Hey, I've got it: Soldiers of the Future!"

He stared at her. As if realizing for the first time that—what? Words had meaning? They expressed attitude?

"Caring about the environment," she continued, "just means understanding that we depend on it." Another 'Ah'. Real men deny dependence. "Don't you need oxygen? Water? Food?"

He was silent.

"Please answer me when I ask a question."

"Don't speak to me like I'm a child!"

"Then don't act like one!"

She grabbed all of the bags, then headed out to her car.

He headed out to his car.

"No fucking way," she said. "We are *not* taking separate vehicles."

"Then I'm driving."

"It's my car."

"Then we'll take my car."

Oh for Christ's sake.

She got into her car, started the engine.

"Okay, okay, you win," he grumbled, as if it were a competition. "I'll ride shotgun."

"Shot gun?" She stared at him as he settled into the passenger seat with a great deal of fuss. She'd heard the phrase for years before she'd looked it up. It originally referred to the man with the gun who rode alongside a stagecoach to 'ward off bandits and Indians' or some such.

"You'll ride in the passenger seat. Say it," she challenged.

Silence. Real men were never passengers.

"I'm surprised you don't hijack the bus—" Ah. That's why

men never rode the bus. Or hated doing so. That's why the first thing every male teenager had to have was a car. Of his own.

"I always have to remind you to separate the recyclables too," she circled back, once they were on their way.

"They go the dump same as everything else anyway."

"Do they? How do you know that?"

He shrugged.

"You *don't* know that, do you. You're just *pretending* to know."

"I'm not pretending—"

"Yes, you are. You do that a lot. Pretend to know something when in fact you're just guessing. You should say 'I *think* it all goes to the dump anyway.' Present it as your *opinion*, not a fact."

"What, you want me to say 'I think' every time I open my mouth?"

"If what comes next is an opinion, not a fact, yes!"

"Fuck that."

"You don't think the distinction between facts and guesses is important?"

Silence.

"It's lying. Pretending you know something when you don't. And it's manipulative. It's presenting yourself as an authority when you're not. No wonder male dominance. Well, now that I know that you lie all the time, I just won't believe you anymore."

They walked into the grocery store. She pulled a cart out from the row.

"I've got it," he took it from her.

She didn't let go. "No, obviously *I've* got it."

He stared at her. Fuming.

"*Now what?* Is pushing a shopping cart a *man* thing too?

Funny, I've been pushing my own shopping carts—"

"For ten years. Got it."

"Twenty, actually. I lived in an apartment for ten years before I could afford the house. Didn't have to cut grass and shovel snow. But explain. Why does that also make you angry?"

"It doesn't."

"Clearly it does. Is it a matter of control? You want to control the shopping cart? You don't want me, a woman, to control— Anything?"

"No, it's—"

"It takes strength to push a shopping cart, and you don't want me, a woman, to have that much strength?"

"Oh don't be ridiculous!"

"Well, explain your anger then."

Silence.

She put her bags into the cart, pulled her list out of her pocket, and started down the first aisle. He followed. Morose.


They were at the bathroom/laundry products aisle.

"Go ahead," she urged, when he didn't take the lead.

"Oh, *now* you want me to lead?"

"Yes," she replied. "I said I'd inventory the kitchen, while you did the bathroom and laundry room. So you're the one who knows what we need in this aisle. Go ahead! Get what we need and put it into the cart!"

He wandered slowly up the aisle, looking at one side then the other.

"You didn't make a list?"

"No I didn't make a fucking list!"

"You committed it all to memory?"

"No I didn't commit it all to memory!"

"You didn't inventory." She sighed.

"This is women's stuff!" he shouted angrily, gesturing at—The whole store. Possibly the whole enterprise of shopping. For anything other than tools and cars. "How the hell am I supposed to know what detergent you buy?"

"Well, if you'd looked in the laundry room, you'd know, but no matter, buy what you normally buy."

He stood uncertainly before the laundry detergents.

It finally dawned on her. "You don't do your own laundry?" She hadn't been keeping track of what he did with his dirty clothes; she'd been washing only her own. Of course.

"I had a cleaning lady come in and do all that! Before."

Ah. Then just as she was wondering whether said cleaning *lady* would be coming to her house now instead of his apartment (doing *all* the cleaning or just his half?), it occurred to her that his 'cleaning lady' was his Mom. *She'd* been coming to his apartment every week … What a child. (And what an enabler! Moms like his, coddling their boys, making them feel like they're god's gift to the world and teaching them indirectly that it's a woman's job to look after them.)

How did she not know this? She'd just assumed that … that he was an adult. He *looked* like one.

She stared at the toilet paper selection.

"Did you at least wipe your own ass?"


Turned out she didn't have to ask him to move out.


◆


We mandated the use of customer-provided bags at all stores. We also passed legislation about excessive packaging and mandated that all plastic and paper be recycled and reused. We established 'give away' sheds at every rural dump, encouraging people *not* to *throw out* everything they simply didn't need or want anymore, and we made it easier for urban residents to give away or donate … We encouraged, with subsidies, repair shops. For almost everything.

◆

"Yeah, but she can't get a job if she has to look after her kids," Ekaterina said. "That's the problem."

"No, the problem is we think of them as *her* kids," Fiona replied. "Why aren't they *his* kids? And why does *she* have to look after *his* kids?"

Ekaterina was momentarily stunned. Fiona was absolutely right. The man, the father, is almost always left out of the picture. As soon as he pulls out. How convenient.

That's what made her realize, the next day …

"They really are barking up the wrong tree, aren't they." She tossed the pamphlet onto the table. Once been an avid supporter of sex ed programs for women in developing nations, now— Yes, as Lionel Shriver put it in *Game Control*, "No one has the right to produce ten children for whom there is no food, no room, no water, no topsoil, no fuel, and no future." The way things were going, there would soon be over 10 billion people on a planet that could comfortably sustain 2 billion. The focus on women was understandable: it's the woman's body that hosts the embryos that become those ten children.

But now, after yesterday's conversation, it had suddenly dawned on her that those 'ten children' were probably due to men. (Many of whom seemed to think that babies were delivered willy nilly by the stork. Not *made*. By *them*.) Women weren't the ones doing the raping. They weren't the ones poking holes in their diaphragms or 'stealthing' (taking the condom off part way through). They weren't the ones threatening their spouse with injury if contraception was used.

Yes, in some countries, childless women were stoned, which would certainly explain their 'willingness' but surely women weren't the ones doing the stoning. (And if they were, it was no doubt due to fear of being stoned themselves.) More to the point, why weren't the childless *men* stoned?

The problem was men. Men who measured their manliness by how many children they sired. It was 'just' another instance of their obsession with size, with putting quantity over quality.

Because really, when you think about it, what woman would *want* ten children to look after? Even in developed nations, one study, published in *Macleans*, showed that 70% who'd had children would, if they had a do-over, *not* have children. Not even one.

"Yup," Fiona agreed. "They should be educating the men. And it's really quite simple, isn't it. 'Don't stick your dick into a woman without an enthusiastic invitation.'"

◆

So contraception for women? Yes. Free, available, reliable, and safe. Worldwide. (It turns out it wasn't that difficult to make them safe. When enough funding was provided for the necessary research.)

And for men? Vasectomy after two kids. Mandatory. Worldwide. (Would that reduce rape? 'I fuck, therefore, I am'— How much does it depend on actual replication? Perhaps they'd find out.)

And so, and therefore, mandatory paternity testing.

Ova, sperm, and embryo freezing was encouraged. And free. That increased earlier vasectomies. And tubal cauterizations.

Bottom line, without men and their toxic masculinity dominating everything, half of the women didn't want kids and the other half were quite content just a couple. (There's a reason the word 'screwed' has the doubling meaning it has.)

✦

"But how can you do that?" he asked, staring at the ceiling. They were in bed. She'd just told him of her decision. "How can you kill an innocent unborn baby?" He propped himself onto his elbow and turned to her with horror. Demanding an answer.

"I don't care if it's a guilty born adult," Greta replied, turning to face him. Then decided to sit up so he wouldn't be looking down at her. "*No one* gets to use my body without my permission. Why should I cede my rights to something with a half-formed brain that doesn't even *understand* rights? What kind of doormat would I be if I subordinated myself not just to men, or even dogs, and frogs, but to bits of microscopic goo? You want me to say they're *all* superior to me? That whatever any one of them wants, or in this case needs, since it can't even *have* wants, trumps whatever I want or need?"

✦

So, abortion? Legal. Everywhere. Free. Everywhere. Available. Everywhere. On demand. By the woman. It's her body the fetus uses.

Home pregnancy tests? Free. Available. Reliable. Blood tests? Free. Available. And even more reliable than urine tests—as early as six days after ovulation, nine days after conception. So almost all abortions (and there were fewer and fewer) (of course) occurred well within the first trimester. Within six weeks, actually. When it was easiest. Physically, emotionally, and morally.

✦

They were discussing 3D printing at a party. It was fascinating. Apparently human cornea tissue could already be printed. Hailey wondered if eventually life itself could be printed. "The human genome is completely mapped, isn't it?" she asked. "So all we'd have to do is add the necessary minerals, chemicals, for bone, muscle, blood ..."

"No," her husband shook his head with authority. "Won't work. Probably take months."

All of the women present stared at him.

Nope.

"How many months?" Hailey asked.

"I dunno. Five, maybe six? And whoever's assigned to the task would have to monitor it 24/7, making sure everything's going well ... No one could be expected to do that! It's just not feasible," he concluded.

All of the women present continued to stare at him.

Still no.

"You know that kid you've been wanting?" Hailey asked.

He gave her a blank look. Then an irritated look. Because what a non sequitur.

"It's just not feasible," she said.

"What?" He responded before he'd even thought about what she'd said. As men do.

"Go fuck yourself," she elaborated.

•

We discussed, but decided against, paying women for pregnancy. Although it seemed a blatant and significant instance of unpaid labour, there was something unique about the labour involved in not only pregnancy, but also childbirth, breastfeeding, and parenting. It wasn't the same as being a daycare worker. And most of us weren't comfortable thinking of children as a public good to be funded through taxes.

However, we did require men to provide pregnancy support (in a number of ways) from conception to birth. And, of course, child support. From birth to the age of eighteen. Again, in a number of ways.

And because every child was now a wanted child, there was no need to coerce 'quality control' (as one man put it): parents educated themselves to become qualified to nurture the physical, cognitive, emotional, and social development of a human being for eighteen years.

◆

"Did you know that corporations have a *legal responsibility* to maximize profit?" Ivy looked up from the book she was reading. Horror on her face.

"What? No, that can't be right." Jane was equally horrified. She looked up from her laptop.

"According to Joel Bakan," Ivy held up *The Corporation*, "'The corporation's legally defined mandate is to pursue, relentlessly and without exception, its own self-interest, regardless of the often harmful consequences it might cause to others.'"

"*Regardless* of the harmful consequences?" Surely that couldn't be right.

Ivy nodded. Then continued. "'The corporation can neither recognize nor act upon moral reasons to refrain from harming others. Nothing in its legal makeup limits what it can do to others in pursuit of its selfish ends, and it is compelled to cause harm when the benefits of doing so outweigh the costs.'"

"It actually says that somewhere? I mean, not in that book, but—"

"Probably not. I think his point is that it's implicit in the mess of laws that apply to corporations."

"Just here?" The U.S. was capitalist mecca of the world. Much to her dismay.

"No. The laws are practically identical in every country."

Of course, she'd realized after she'd posed the question. They would've seen to that. "And what laws? Exactly?"

"Well, simply put, corporations have a duty to shareholders."

"Okay, but—"

"And if they fail in that duty, they can be sued by the shareholders."

"But—a duty to make money? You said, before, their mandate is to pursue its 'self-interest'. That doesn't necessarily mean 'make money'. Especially if while doing so, they ignore consequences like destroying the planet they need to *make* that money." Were they really that stupid? Maybe not. Maybe they were just that selfish. Short-term is all they need worry about because hey, they'll be dead before their shit hits the fan. Not always though. And in those cases, they could just claim they didn't know. As if ignorance is a defence. And then they could claim bankruptcy. And let the rest of us pick up the slack. Their slack. "Though that would explain," she said, with a sigh, "why there are so many drugs for erectile dysfunction and baldness and so few for, say, tuberculosis. No profit in the latter."

Ivy nodded.

"And it would explain why they keep drilling for oil …"

She nodded again.

"Size is also a factor," Ivy continued. "They're so big, just one hundred companies are responsible for 71% of greenhouse gas emissions."

"Okay, but if the companies were smaller, that would just mean that a thousand were responsible for 71%. Isn't it easier to deal with a hundred than a thousand?"

"Not if they've got a monopoly."

"I don't—"

"The bigger the company, the bigger their market share, so the fewer their competitors, so the more they can get away with."

"Ah." She didn't think like that. At all.

A few minutes later, Ivy spoke again. "Oh, this is interesting. Bakan consulted a psychologist and found that corporations are, essentially, psychopathic: they're manipulative, grandiose, and asocial; they lack empathy and relate to others only superficially; they often refuse to accept responsibility for their own actions and are unable to feel remorse."

Jane stared at her. Because—yes. And not just the corporations, but those who run them. Who but psychopaths would *become*, would *want* to become, megalomaniacs? That is, CEOs. Though not all CEOs *were* psychopaths ... Surely ...

"Remember that car that exploded on impact?" Ivy asked.

"Yes. I had one." It had been her first car.

"They actually did the math. Bakan mentions that. Each fatality would have cost the company, on average, $200,000 in legal damages, and because there were 41 million of them on the road, that worked out to $2.40 per car. But to fix the fuel tank would have cost $8.59 per car. So they saved $6.19 per car if they just allowed people to die rather than fix the tank. Psychopathic."

"Okay—well, not okay—but not only is 'make money' not the same as 'whatever's in your own best self-interest', 'make' isn't the same as 'maximize'. And if the corporation's decision-makers had actually *consulted* the shareholders, don't you think that at least half of them would've voted to fix the tank?" Ditto to accept, say, a 1% lower return on their investment if that was the price to pay for *not* polluting the water table ...

"Maybe."

And maybe not. Jane didn't have to say it.

"Regardless, all over the world, CEOs think it's okay to allow people to die if that means they make more money. They're allowing us *all* to die, to become extinct, or at best live a very difficult life, just so they can be rich. Rich*er*. Ordinarily, that would be a crime."

So why isn't it?

◆

We changed the legislation regarding corporations. In fact, we banned them. There was nothing good about becoming incorporated. (And, note, they had been banned before. England. 1720.)

◆

"Have you read *Post-Mortem Report*?"

Ivy shook her head.

"It's a story purporting to analyze the end of humanity, in which the author postulates that maleness and/or masculinity enabled a widespread psychopathy characterized by four dominating beliefs ... Hang on ..." A few moments later, Jane carried her laptop over to Ivy, who read the screen:

*1. I must win. (I must conquer.) Therefore, competition.*

*2. Quantity trumps quality. (Without this, we can't conclusively determine who wins.)*

*3. I am independent. (Without this, we can't have individual winners.) That is to say, I do not depend on anyone or anything. Therefore, obsession with self, to the exclusion of others.*

1 and 3 lead to

4. *An obliviousness to consequences unless they are personal and immediate (and, as is the case for even non-psychopaths, visible).*

3 and 4 lead to

5. *A disjunct with reality.*

Ivy had been nodding throughout.
"The author calls capitalism 'masculinity on steroids'," Jane said.
Ivy looked up. "I'd go so far as to call *the world* masculinity on steroids. I mean, this analysis explains *so much* …"

                        ✦

Along with 'corporations' went 'limited liability'. People should be fully liable for the harm they cause.

                        ✦

That night, Kamila went home to, yet again, housework. She'd tried everything. First, they agreed that whoever made the dinner, the other would do the clean-up. But it seemed he always made so much more of a mess than she did. When *he* made the dinner, the kitchen ended up looking like a disaster zone. It was like he *enjoyed* making a mess. It was like he was *proud* of making a mess. Eventually, she realized that the difference was due, at least in part, to the fact that he didn't do any 'as you go' clean-up. As soon as the spaghetti sauce splashed onto the stove, *she* would turn down the heat, put a lid on it, *and swipe the stove.*
So then they agreed to take turns making the dinner *and* cleaning up after. He started preparing something non-messy

whenever it was his turn. Sticking frozen pizza into the microwave, for example. Or just ordering out whenever it was his turn.

As for dusting, vacuuming, cleaning the bathroom, doing the laundry … Whatever it was his turn to do, he did a cursory job or just let it slide, saying he was okay with it as it was, it was clean enough. So the week after, when it was her turn, it took her twice as long to do whatever it was …

Eventually, she didn't do it. And it took months before he— No, he didn't do it. He hired someone to come in. Apparently his fraternity had had a housekeeper. Twenty-four/seven.

"No fair!" she'd cried.

"Why?" he'd responded. "What's not fair about it?"

"I want you to do it yourself. I want you to clean up your own mess."

"Why?"

That he had to ask—

She went to visit her friend for the weekend. She needed a break. She needed to think. Lily had a cabin on a lake in a forest. It was beautiful. Or could have been—

They were walking along the country road that surrounded the lake. It was a gorgeous summer day, sunny, but not too hot, with a nice breeze …

After passing yet another beer can, Kamila expressed her disgust. "Do they just toss their shit out the window as they drive along?"

Lily nodded. "I used to take a big garbage bag with me twice a year and pick it all up. Initially, as a sort of civic duty, but then simply because *I* didn't like seeing garbage all along my walk."

"Yeah, it really wrecks the ambience, doesn't it. I mean, this is, could be, such a pretty road." There was a wall of forest on each side, branches often arching overhead providing shade or dappling the light … "Why'd you stop?"

"Some guy in a pick-up slowed down one day to insult me. Told me it was nice to see that I was good for something."

Kamila came to a dead stop. Shocked. "And why, pray tell," she resumed walking, "had he thought that up to that point, you were *not* good for anything?"

"He thought I was a lesbian."

Again she stopped. It took a few moments to work through the logic. And when she did—

"I found a battery halfway down there once," Lily pointed down the little waterfalls. "Hauled it all the way back up here to the road, then picked it up next time I drove by, and took it to the dump."

"But—that must be a seventy degree incline!"

"Yeah. It wasn't easy."

"So, what, the asshole who dumped it there didn't think that eventually it would leak? And then the acid would be carried *down* by the waterfalls into the *lake*? Where it would, I don't know, kill the frogs and ducks and, well, the lake?"

Lily shrugged. This was all just ... her everyday life. "Maybe he just didn't care."

"And what's up with the fridges? Dare I ask?" They'd just passed the second one, lying in the ditch. "I mean, isn't it as much hassle to put it here as take it to the dump?" "Yeah. But then they'd have to pay, I think. The dump charges extra for the freon to be safely extracted."

"Ah. So they dump it here to save money. And ensure damage to the ozone at the same time."

◆

We made it illegal to externalize costs. To externalize waste disposal. Contamination in all its forms. Of our air, our water, our land, plant life, flora, fauna. Companies had to take responsibility for the damage they'd done. Retroactively. The floating garbage patches in the ocean? The contaminated water tables? The smog? Get to work, men. Clean up the mess you made. Doing so would double the prices of their products, they warned. No, they were told, doing so would halve your profit.

◆

"You know," Kamila said, as they continued their walk, "I used to think that if people had to keep their garbage on their own property, there'd soon be less of it. The whole 'Not in My Back Yard' thing. But …"

"They don't mind," Lily anticipated. "Seeing their garbage whenever, wherever." She thought of the many trailers on the lake. Each with at least one abandoned vehicle nearby. Some guy just up the river from her had two abandoned *trailers* on his lot as well. As soon as one got—dirty? out of date? out of repair?—he'd buy another. Drive it in and just set it up beside the old one.

Sometimes the trailer was actually an RV—she shuddered to think about what happened to the grey and black water, because she'd never seen *anyone* drive an RV off the property to empty the tanks wherever one does that, nor had she anyone cart their tanks away in their pick-up—but most often it was just a camper, so there was an outhouse nearby. Just a few feet from the lake. The lake in which they— Well, actually, no, those people tended *not* to swim or paddle or even fish. They came with their ATVs and their dirt bikes and then spent the day thundering through the forest as if it was their personal racetrack. Why did they even buy waterfront? She had no idea.

"Though when you say 'they'," Kamila said, "I think you mean—"

"Men. Yeah."

Kamila nodded. "I doubt all these beer cans, and car batteries, and fridges are dumped here by women."

"No need for doubt. We've got the data. Men do 72% of the deliberate littering and are responsible for 96% of the accidental littering."

"Well, that's no surprise, is it. I mean 'cleaning up after' is seen as a woman's task." She certainly had the data, albeit anecdotal, for *that*.

Lily nodded. "It was Mom who cleaned up after them when they were kids."

"But 'Mom cleaned up after me, Mom is a woman, so women should clean up after me' is the same as "Princess is a kitten, Princess is white, so white things should be kittens.'"

"And they say men are the logical ones."

They made the last turn, that would take them back to her cabin.

"Of course," Kamila added, "a mistake is made too in thinking that when you're old enough to drink beer and buy your own fast food, you're still a kid who needs Mom, or a woman, to clean up after you. "

"No, you're making the mistake there," Lily said. "Confusing chronological age with developmental age."

Kamila grinned. Then resumed, "And why don't *girls*— Ah. They *become* Mom."

"Or they're just taught that yeah, 'cleaning up after' *is* a woman's task."

"I think, and this is related, it's also a power thing. A status thing. Cleaning up is a menial task."

"Yeah. Mom/women do it, therefore it's menial. Or it's menial, therefore Mom/women do it. Either way."

Unsurprisingly, subsequent to the prohibition of ATVs and snowmobiles for recreational use, roadside littering decreased. Fewer trucks on the road probably also contributed to the decrease. Some suspected that men felt less 'manly' driving a small electric car and so didn't get drawn into the whole toxic masculinity thing, that apparently included tossing your shit just anywhere. Others hypothesized an effect of the distance: just as killing with a gun was easier than doing so up close and personal, littering from four feet up was easier than doing so from just two feet away.

We'd also increased the fine for littering and encouraged people to use their car cameras to record and report violations. You want the right to use the roads? You have a responsibility not to dump your shit along the way. Acting on a right without accepting its attached responsibilities is a sort of theft: responsibilities are the cost, the expense, of rights.

✦

"Oh, listen to this." Ivy was still reading. "Ray Anderson. Founder and chair of the world's largest commercial carpet manufacturer, and yet 'he never gave a thought to what [they] were doing to the earth in the making of [their] products'—in *1994*. Then he began to read a book about ecology."

"Duh."

"I know, right?"

"Though," Jane said, "I suspect that *most* business students have no idea." She recalled her years in university. "And they're the ones who become the CEOs."

"No idea—of what?" Because really, the possibilities were endless.

"Of the consequences of their actions. Environmental conse-quences. Psychological consequences. Aesthetic consequences.

They're *business* students!"

"Hm. Do you think it's because they're business students or because they're male. I read an account of a woman who had 'transitioned', and she said that since she'd been on testosterone, her thinking had changed. She said she became more decisive because she focused on utility. To the exclusion of everything else, apparently."

"Really? That would explain a lot," Jane said. "Men value things only in terms of their use. Natural *resources*. Human *resources*."

"Trees. Women."

"So they don't see any aesthetic value. They don't see any intrinsic value, any autonomy in the other. They see only instrumental value, value only in relation to themselves."

"The woman also said that everything was more black and white. On testosterone."

"Oh god, if that's true— No wonder they're so ethically challenged!"

"Now that I'm remembering the article, it sounds like an alternative version of the *Post-Mortem Report*."

"It does, doesn't it. Or at least an addendum to."

✦

We made Environmental Science courses mandatory. From grade one through to grade twelve. We also made Sexism 101 and Racism 101 mandatory. Because.

And we required every company over a certain size, and every municipal council, to enlist the services of an Ethics Officer. And a Philosopher, a Psychologist, and a Sociologist. All of whom contributed to policy-making and assessed, well, everything the company was doing. They also had to hire a Historian, to manage the information, to develop true, coherent archives, with intelligent analysis, and to liaise with policy departments; they replaced public relations departments. *And* they had to hire two Artists: one for the aural environment, one for the visual environment; companies already had finance departments to look after their money and maintenance departments to keep things clean (according to a very limited definition)—why not art departments to make the place beautiful?

After all, that a humanities degree is useless for the workforce says more about our workforce than the degree. It says that we value, that we'll pay for, someone to provide cars, electric toothbrushes, and running shoes. But not insight and beauty. We thus have so many more jobs for business majors (the managers and the accountants) and non-majors (the clerks and waiters), for people whose raison d'être is to make or serve profit, than we have for people whose raison d'être is to develop insight and understanding, beauty and joy. Not everything has to have a price. Not everything need be, or can be, sold. Or bought. Some things just are. The cultivation of curiosity and interest. The achievement of exhilaration and understanding. The recognition and appreciation of beauty and joy ...

And so we built a world in which knowledge about ourselves was valued as much as knowledge about our money. Not only companies, but individuals started hiring philosophers and psychologists as often as they hired financial advisors.

◆

"Hey, did you read about that woman who's suing the company with that huge advertising billboard on the highway?" Kamila asked. She was still at Lily's cabin. "The one with all the blinking lights and animated bits dancing around? She's blaming it for taking her attention off the road; she rear-ended the car in front of her."

"About time. Those things should have been illegal from the start," Lily replied. "They're *designed* to grab our attention. While we're *driving!* They *know* how we're wired: our attention *is* caught by things that move."

Kamila nodded.

"Allowing them is like allowing people to watch tv while they drive!" Lily continued.

"Hate to break it to you, but a lot of new cars have dashboard tvs."

"What?" She was stunned. "Have we put *no* limits on capitalistic greed? Because that's what it's for. TV. It's just a vehicle for advertising. For 'BUY MY SHIT' messages."

"I think people like them, the dashboard tvs, not the ads— though they probably like them too, go figure … They keep the kids entertained. The dashboard tvs. Not the ads. Though they probably keep them entertained too …" Kamila faded into an abyss.

"They can't entertain themselves? By, I don't know, looking out the window?" Of course not. Compared to the hyper-real neon-colour ever-moving world of tv and video games … Lily joined her in the abyss.

"Some places have put limits," Kamila pointed out. "On capitalistic greed. Places in France, Brazil, even the States. In fact, Hawaii banned billboard advertising way back in 1920. Vermont, 1968."

"Canada's conspicuously absent from that list."

"Yeah."

"We have— We *had* so much natural beauty … And now, it's being ruined, stretch by stretch, day by day …" Lily sighed.

Kamila nodded. "Perhaps not quite as awful, but it was a sad, sad day when advertising was allowed along the perimeter of rinks and even on the ice during figure skating performances. Years to achieve the perfect line, sullied by persisting in-your-face BUY-MY-SHIT signs we can't help but see while we try to focus on the beauty." She sighed. "And it's not like the sign enhances the beauty. It's not like the sign itself is remotely beautiful."

"It really is indefensible, isn't it. You can't even walk through the park or down the street without seeing— Ads cover the walls of buildings, for godsake. I mean, would those of us who can hear allow a deaf person to make a clamour with cymbals all day long? We would not. So why do we allow aesthetically-challenged CEOs to do the same? Why do we allow beauty to be degraded, destroyed, by those who are, obviously, blind to it?"

"Because 'we', the ones in charge, are aesthetically-challenged too."

They both sighed.

"At least it is just a visual assault," Kamila said. "Can you imagine if there *were* people clanging cymbals all day?"

"I can. There are. Sound travels remarkably well across water. So every nail gun, every chain saw, every leaf blower—"

"People use leaf blowers? *Here?*"

"Men *love* their power tools."

"Okay, then ...," she searched for a better comparison, "can you imagine if there were people paid by perfume companies wandering through the streets assaulting us with sample sprays?"

"Yes. It would be horrible. But given men's apparent immunity to gasoline fumes, I suspect it would be legal."

They both sighed again.

"Remember you said that it seemed like 9 out of 10 guys around here drive pick-ups?" Kamila asked a moment later.

"Yeah ..."

"And you noticed—as of, what, a couple years ago?—the appearance of trailers all over the place, along the shoreline, on land you thought was crown? Not as temporary habitat while a house was being built, but as a sort of man cave?"

"Yeah … And every frickin' weekend, a herd of pick-ups with ATVs appears—"

"You don't watch the game, do you."

"What game?"

"*The* game," Kamila smiled. "Hockey, football, doesn't matter."

"No. I don't."

"Well, an average NFL broadcast lasts three hours, and has an hour's worth of commercials."

"Really?"

"Yes. Now, there have been beer ads during the game since forever. And ads for pick-up trucks."

"Ah."

"But what's new—as of two years ago, maybe—are ads showing a bunch of guys hanging out at the lake. Trailers, pick-ups, ATVs. Beer."

Lily just— "So I don't even *watch* tv and my life is being ruined by its ads. Because all these tough, strong guys are empty-headed weaklings who can't resist the mere suggestion …"

"I dare say a lot of the shit that pisses you off is just people doing what they see other people do. In ads. At least, initially."

They thought about that for a while. Social contagion at its worst.

"A whole hour's worth?" Lily was catching up.

Kamila nodded.

"Well, it's one thing to allow ads during 'the game'," Lily grinned, grimaced, actually, "it's quite another to allow it … everywhere. I mean, it has almost single-handedly destroyed the concept of public space, because of its invasion of said public space with constant and loudly-proclaimed messages intended for private gain. We should be able to go about our lives without the constant assault on the senses, on the mind, that is advertising. That's partly why I live here."

"But you're the rare person who *notices* ads, who *pays attention* to her environment, who *thinks about* what she sees. For most people, ads are not such an intrusion, because they're unconsciously perceived. Which makes them even *more* manipulative," Kamila anticipated.

"And even more indefensible."

Kamila sighed. "Advertising has gained so much power, it's allowed pretty much everywhere. And because it's allowed pretty much everywhere, it has gained so much power."

"But," Lily protested, "there's simply no justification for the desire of one person, let alone the desire of one person *for money*, to be imposed on everyone. I mean, on what basis do they figure they have a right to do that? Even if there's no physical harm, even if there's no psychological harm, what right do they have to grab our attention like that?"

"They're men," Kamila shrugged. "They grab at our clothing. They grab at our bodies. No wonder they think they have the right to grab at our attention."

"It's such a lack of respect for other people's autonomy, isn't it. No one has a right to another's attention except infants."

"Speaking of which," Kamila grinned, "so much of men's behavior is 'Look at me!', isn't it? It's like they can't do anything without their own private audience."

"Their own private cheerleaders. Wife and kids. No wonder divorced men suffer serious mental health issues."

"And why are they like that? I mean, is it just their socialization? Is it habit? Or do they seriously think that what they do is *worth* attention, worth *applause*? All the time. *More* attention and applause than what others do."

"It reminds me of a mob of reporters, every one of them shouting out their questions, not only *demanding* the person's attention, but acting as if *their* question is the one most worth answering. That has always seemed to me to be the epitome of arrogance!"

They sighed again.

"And who is it who creates all these ads?" Lily asked. "Who is it who decides which words and which images the rest of us will be forcibly exposed to day and night for most of our lives? Predominantly, male business students. Predominantly *B* students."

"Because they're the ones who major in Business," Kamila got it.

"Actually, it's predominantly *C* students. Because *among* Business students, it's the *poor* ones who major in Marketing. The good ones choose Finance or Administration. Regardless, that is to say, it is largely uneducated young men. Who decide which words and images the rest of us will be forcibly exposed to day and night for most of our lives."

Again Kamila got it. "Because business students don't take any courses in the sciences or the humanities after high school. And they probably didn't do very well in those courses back *in* high school.

"And," she continued, "business students don't take any sociology or psychology courses either, except for the one focusing on manipulating human behaviour."

Lily nodded. "And they probably haven't read a book, not one, since they graduated."

"Well, they probably didn't read a book, not a *whole* one, before they graduated either."

"All of which is to say," Lily sighed, "that they probably have very little comprehension of sexism, racism, environmental responsibility, ethics … I mean, most ads are outright *lies*, aren't they!"

"I remember reading the words of one young man who'd said that he was studying political science at the time 'and so had never thought about social processes like misogyny and sexism'. I was appalled. Now that I think about it," Kamila said, "I suspect business students are even less aware, less informed, than poli-sci students."

Lily nodded. Then spelled it out. "So they have no clue as to the consequences, for both men and women, of seeing images of subordinated and/or sexualized women every day all day. Of seeing images of only attractive people. Only young people. Only gendered people, who've bought into feminine and masculine."

"The rest of us begin to feel … invisible. Best case scenario," Kamila added.

Lily nodded again. "They are similarly clueless about the consequences of showing pick-up trucks and ATVs driving through pristine forests. They know that attention is grabbed by flashing lights, and they surely know that driving a car requires one's full attention, but apparently they can't put two and two together in an ethical way, and so continue to put huge billboards with flashing lights along highways."

Kamila nodded.

"And here's the thing: people should understand the consequences of their actions before they're granted unsupervised freedom to act. Certainly before they're granted the power to bombard people with words and images. With power should come responsibility. Especially in the case of *harmful* words and images."

They thought about that for a while.

"You know," Lily said angrily, "we don't even *need* ads. We can become informed about available products with a simple and comprehensive online directory."

"Even by their own logic, ads are unnecessary," Kamila added.

"What do you mean?"

"Well, on the one hand, they tell us they're just supplying what people demand, but then they turn around and spend billions on advertising. They can't have it both ways. If people genuinely *wanted* their products, *demanded* their products, as they say, they wouldn't have to try to manipulate them into buying them."

"Oh, good point!"

"Did you know that the pharmaceutical industry spends twice as much on advertising as it does on research?"

"Seriously? That's fucked up."

"It is."

"I'd like to see all advertising banned," Lily stated. "Not just *in* public spaces, but also where it can be seen or heard *while in* public spaces. *And* in private spaces except for residences. So arenas, stores, office buildings, hotels … It's intrusive, coercive, manipulative, and harmful, physically and psychologically."

"But what about free speech? Freedom of expression?"

"Neither is, or at least should not be, *unlimited*. Both are justifiably constrained when they violate others' rights. Their right to autonomy. To be free from intrusion, coercion, and manipulation. Their right to safety. To be free from harm, both physical and psychological."

"Yeah."

They were silent for a while.

Then, "Can you imagine?" Kamila asked. "A world without any advertising whatsoever? Most television shows would go belly up. We'd have to subscribe to television programs. We'd have to pay to watch a movie. Or borrow from the library."

"Which just means we have to really want them. No more casual exposure to all sorts of shit. After all, you become what you're exposed to."

Kamila nodded.

"And without that steady diet of stupid and immature men-with-guns being forced into people's minds—"

"Well, not exactly forced—"

"No," Lily said, "but if you want to watch television *without* seeing stupid and immature men-with-guns, you have to work very hard at being selective."

"Agreed. I think the current stat is that over 90% of the movies on tv have violence. One begins to think it's inevitable. Violence."

"Yes!"

"In fact," Kamila continued, "if I recall correctly, by the time a person is 18, he or she has seen some 200,000 acts of violence. And that's with just an hour and a half tv exposure a day. The average child—and this I *do* recall correctly—will have seen 8,000 murders before they reach elementary school."

"No wonder. Our world."

◆

We banned advertising. Everywhere.

Worldwide, $1.4 trillion (total global advertising and marketing industry revenue) became available. Instead of spending billions to make their products *look* good, companies used it to make products that actually *were* good.

People quickly realized how much of their attention had been stolen by advertising. They discovered beauty.

And if they were at all introspective, they realized how much ads had influenced what they wanted to have, what they wanted to do … Without that relentless onslaught, they discovered what they *really* wanted to have, what they *really* wanted to do. Simply put, their values changed.

◆

"Did you know that the Global Climate Coalition spent millions lobbying against the Kyoto protocol?" Mei said, looking up from her magazine.

"*Against?* That can't be right." Nayra figured that someone had gotten it backwards.

"It's a coalition led by oil companies."

"Ah. The fuckers. There oughtta be some laws about how we use language."

"There are," Mei replied. "Slander, libel, fraud—"

"Well, such a misleading name is surely fraudulent."

"Actually … that's a really good point."

They thought about it for a while. How could— Could just anyone press charges of fraud when names were so misleading? How expensive would that be? And what were the chances of success?

Eventually, Mei circled back. "But my point was that lobby groups subvert democracy."

"Oh." Nayra grinned. "*That* was your point?"

"Well, you had to … make a bit of a leap." She grinned back.

"Yeah, no, I'm with you. I agree. I was just thinking … I've written letters to my city council, my MPP, my MP, even the Prime Minister. All to no avail. All I get is a form letter that all but shouts they didn't even *read* what I'd said. Often, I don't even get that."

Mei nodded.

"I even went to a town hall meeting once, when they were preparing a five-year plan and they'd asked—they'd actually *asked*—for input. So I prepared a list of recommendations. More parks, *safer* parks, stricter noise bylaws, no smokepits or meat smokers allowed in residential areas, bicycle lanes, areas of downtown closed to traffic altogether so people could walk, and talk, and visit the art galleries, the libraries, and yes, the stores … For each recommendation, I provided links to supporting data—evidence for my claims about the current harms done, precedents in other places for the suggested changes, proof of benefits … I had sixteen recommendations in all. Eight pages—"

"And they ignored it."

Nayra nodded. "Didn't even acknowledge receipt."

"Maybe—"

"I'd delivered it in person. So," she nodded at Mei's magazine, "maybe it's become the case that unless you're a lobby group with a lot of money— Maybe it's lobby groups that make it impossible for ordinary individuals to advocate any change."

Mei nodded. "A negative effect in addition to their direct efforts, their smear campaigns …"

"So why don't *you* run for council?" Mei asked a few moments later.

"Because I've read Elizabeth May. And others. It's a sham all the way up."

◆

We outlawed lobbying. Reinstituted democracy at the individual level. Established a truly world-wide web online at which people could see what legislation was in place (in non-legal language, with implications made explicit) and what legislative changes were being considered, with neutrally-presented arguments for and against. They could then cast a vote, if they so wished. They could also propose legislative changes. Themselves.

We took politics out of government as much as possible. No campaigning. No political contributions. By anyone. (Because, really, contributions weren't given, or accepted, as anything but promises.) One vote per person, accompanied by a 500-word essay as to why the person was voting for the person they were voting for. (That in itself had a *huge* effect.) Each person who sought a position, who sought votes, could put their views online. Their background, their qualifications, their record (if they'd previously had a position of responsibility, of power), was also online.

◆

"So … it didn't go well?" Patrice asked. Olanda had had dinner with a new guy the night before.

She shook her head. "He's a day trader."

"What's that?"

"Someone who makes money from money," she said, with disgust. Then added, "He plays the stock market like it's a casino. Only he's not gambling with his own money; he's gambling with other people's lives."

"So, not a keeper," Patrice smiled at the understatement.

"No. Not a keeper," Olanda smiled back. "The stock market used to be … like crowd funding. A way to raise money for some worthy enterprise. But now … People trade stocks like … baseball cards. No, actually, baseball cards are valued, as far as I can tell. Stocks— Apparently people hold stocks, on average, for only five days. They have no *real* interest in investing in the companies they choose. Used to be eight years."

"So if a company is driven by the stock market," Patrice had read that that was the case, "in that when their stock goes down, that means there's a problem, they have only five days to respond? To fix the problem?"

"Well, that's the thing. The price of a stock doesn't indicate value anymore. A decline doesn't mean there's a problem. The stock prices, the swings up and down—they have no basis in reality. And we're not talking up or down by ten or twenty bucks, though that would be dramatic enough, we're talking about swings of one or two *hundred* bucks."

Patrice stared at her. That was nuts.

"High-frequency traders—he's one of those—he actually *bragged* about it—hold stocks for no more than 16 seconds."

"What the fuck—"

"He showed me a subreddit called 'Wall Street Bets.' *Bets.* And a twitter feed. It's like a huge cheering stadium, 'BUY THIS!' 'SELL THAT!' It's so easy to be caught up in it."

"If you like that sort of thing." Which men do. It has the appeal of 'going to the game', being in a huge crowd, losing yourself to the mania … "Let me guess. Most day traders are men."

Olanda nodded.

"No surprise. That psychopathic disjunct between reality and whatever the hell they're doing, with no ethics in their way, just make as much money as possible, as quickly as possible, and the speed, the risk …"

She nodded. "One article—I left before dessert and went online as soon as I got home—one article compared day traders to both drug addicts and rutting stags. There are measurable spikes in testosterone, which are both cause and effect of day of trading."

Patrice nodded. "High levels of testosterone correlate with confidence, a tolerance of risk, quick reaction times … No doubt these guys think they're some sort of athlete."

"Instead of some fat guy sitting at his computer all day eating Doritos."

"Affecting people's lives."

◆

The stock market was dismantled. The enterprise of investment was restructured.

◆

"I read today that CEOs now make almost 300 times what the average person makes," Quinn said.

"Yeah, I've heard something like that," Rose replied.

"It's impossible."

"No, it's—"

"I mean it's impossible to work 300 times as many hours. There's not that many hours in a day. It's impossible to work 300 times as hard. Consider the high risk of fire fighters. The back-breaking work of fruit and vegetable pickers. The emotional work of nurses. And I don't for a minute believe their work is 300 times as important or valuable. Forementioned fire fighters and nurses."

"Agreed." After a moment, Rose said, "Imagine a world-wide strike by all the *minimum* wage workers."

"We'd have no clothing under $100. No shoes under $100. No smartphones, period."

◆

We increased the minimum wage. To a living wage. Worldwide.

It was easy. Because we also implemented a maximum wage. It *was* impossible to work 300 times as long or as hard.

In the process, we closed all the sweatshops. Studies had shown for quite some time that doubling the salary of sweatshop workers would increase the price of the items made by only 2%. *And* that most people would be willing to pay *15%* more. To stop sweatshops.

◆

"And you know," Quinn continued, "equal pay for work of equal value is fine in theory, but as long as male values continue to dominate— Even something as obvious as daycare teachers versus university professors. We *know* that the first six years are critical. And yet we pay those who teach 18- to 22-year-olds far more than we pay those responsible for the 0- to 6-year-olds."

"You're absolutely right." Rose couldn't believe she hadn't thought about it that way before.

"Even people who deal with inanimate objects—I'm thinking construction workers—are paid more than childcare workers."

"I wonder if part of the problem is the whole 'development' scam."

Quinn looked at her, eyebrows raised.

"Say 'development' and people automatically think it's good. Like 'progress'. It's whitewash. Not all development is good. Development, which always involves construction, often means ruining the natural environment."

"Ah. Agreed. I think it goes back to toxic masculinity. Development is conquering nature."

"*Mother* nature, note."

Quinn nodded.

"And it's *using* resources. It's an instrumental, active, do-ing, kind of mentality."

"Nothing wrong with that mentality," Quinn said, "*when appropriate*. Doing for the sake of doing, no. You have to consider the *reason*."

"Agreed."

"The language doesn't help," Quinn came back to her initial example. "'Teachers' versus 'professors'."

"And 'assistants' versus 'supervisors'. 'Support workers'. That's one I've always hated. If women go on strike and the world falls apart—and people *die*—how can what they do be called 'support'? And 'subordinate'?"

"I think men created the words," Quinn said, "introduced them into the workplace, to designate women *as* support, subordinate. What was wrong with 'secretary'?"

"Well, it became a job ghetto," Rose suggested.

"Yeah, well, now 'assistant' and 'support worker' are job ghettos."

"Yeah."

"Despite their importance."

"Did you see the old movie *Nine to Five*?"

✦

Many countries already had equal pay for work of equal value legislation. It was enforced. And the values used were reconsidered. Jobs involving caring for other human beings were valued over jobs whose sole purpose was to make money (of which there were a surprising number). Teachers, daycare workers, eldercare workers, nurses ... Overnight, they were making six figures. We started paying *actual* doctors more than we paid people who *pretended* to be doctors. (Hollywood ... changed. It became clear that there was something very wrong about spending billions filming make-believe while in the real world people were dying of droughts and floods, hunger and thirst ...)

Development became judicious. Unnecessary construction work was prohibited. We needed the trees alive. And concrete was even worse, environmentally speaking.

And 'assistant' and 'support staff'? Replaced with 'partner'—administrative partner, care partner, etc. It helped.

✦

"So I was looking into the algorithms used by search engines—"

Rose groaned. "Popularity begets popularity."

"Yeah. But what I found out was they're often used in the hiring process. Rather cluelessly, I might add. One company coded, for shortlisting applicants, a rule whereby if the applicant had graduated from a university that current employees had graduated from, they made the cut. Well, the company had never hired someone who had graduated from a women-only university, so all applicants with degrees from Bryn Mawr, Wellesley, Smith were rejected out of hand."

Rose stared. Momentarily stunned. She thought about it. "You don't think that was intentional?"

"Could've been," Quinn said. "I also read that study about men and women with identical CVs. 'John' gets the job as lab manager, 'John' gets mentoring, and 'John' gets $4,000/year more pay. Than 'Jennifer'."

Rose nodded. "Yeah, that study has been done almost half a dozen times now. I think the first time was in the 70s. Always the same result."

"Ah. No surprise then that women are starting to put male names on their CVs."

"Really? I hadn't heard about *that*! Good one!" She'd been using only her initial, but that doesn't work when it's only women who do it.

"'Erin' went from a zero response rate to, as 'Mack', a 70% response rate."

"Wow. That's disgusting. Okay, so," Rose said with some excitement, "everyone should be doing that. Starting right now. Might—"

"Or they should do what symphonies do."

She waited.

"Blind auditions," Quinn said. "They walk on stage from behind a curtain, then sit behind a screen, and play. The adjudicators have no idea whether they're hearing a man or a woman. The percentage of female musicians in the five highest-ranking orchestras *tripled*."

"Yeah, but how would that work, exactly, for job interviews?"

"Remember that 'cat lawyer'?"

She giggled. Then laughed. "Wouldn't that be *wonderful?* Women could interview as—"

"Isaac Newton. Abraham Lincoln."

"Yeah. Try paying *them* $4,000 less."

✦

We implemented a number of policies to ensure equal opportunity. It really wasn't that hard. Algorithms were revised. By women who knew what to watch for. New protocols were established that ensured the removal of all sex-indicators in the CVs and letters of recommendation; voice modulation tech was used for all phone calls and online interviews; video filters were used for all online interviews. (And all interviews were done online.)

+

"Yeah, but once we *get* the job," Rose said, "there's still all that sexism to deal with."

"True." Quinn sighed. "Though ... did you read about that guy who accidentally started sending out emails under his female colleague's name? Martin? He finally got it. Having experienced it himself. People were rude and dismissive and condescending. They ignored his questions. Everything he did or said was challenged. He said 'It fucking sucked.'"

"An understatement."

"It reminded me of those two women who started an art marketplace, and they invented a third co-founder, a man. They named him Keith. Hang on ..." she poked at her tablet. "Here it is. 'It would take me days to get a response, but Keith could not only get a response and a status update, he'd be asked if he wanted anything else or if there was anything else that Keith needed help with.'"

"Wouldn't that be nice."

"Back in 1994, Kristen Schilt—read her book, *Just One of the Guys*—did a study about post-transition 'men' and found, no surprise, that once the women appeared as men, they gained authority, respect, status, recognition for hard work, pay increases, promotions ... Some respondents said that as men they got away with more, were given the benefit of the doubt more."

"You're kidding." Because if that was all it took—

"I'm not. I also read an article in *The Guardian* written by a transitioned sociology professor. One thing he noted was that as a man, he didn't get any push-back when he said 'no'. 'The first time I say "no",', he reported, 'it is heard.'"

Rose sighed. As did Quinn. To get support, rather than challenge. To say 'no' and be heard. It was a dream come true.

"You know what?" Rose finally spoke. "We should make it mandatory. That men use female names."

"And female avatars with voice modulation for all virtual interactions."

She grinned. "For a whole fucking year."

▫

So that's what we did first. For *five* years. And then we phased out altogether sex-identifying names and pronouns. And, where applicable, color-indicators and class-identifiers.

▫

It was Saturday night. His friends had come over to watch the game. The women were in the kitchen.

"Why do they like it so much?" Siku asked, setting various drinks and snacks onto the table. "I simply cannot see the attraction."

"It's like a booster shot of masculinity," Teagan replied, pouring some pretzels into a bowl, then starting to nibble. "Reinforcing tribalism and competition as the primary values of life itself."

"She's got it," Ulrike agreed, as she opened a package of cookies. "My team and your team. Winners and losers. *The Stronger Women Get, the More Men Love Football*. Mariah Burton Nelson. 1994. You should read it."

"It's also a *badge* of masculinity," Teagan added. "It *proves* their manliness."

"Again, she's got it. Haven't you noticed that 'the game' is always on in men's spaces?"

"They tolerate female fans," Teagan said, "but really, we're trespassers."

Siku saw that. "Like female scientists, surgeons, mathematicians, engineers, architects—"

"Construction workers, miners—"

"Warehouse forklift operators—"

"Some of whom were killed for their audacity," Ulrike noted, raising a glass in a memorial toast. The others followed.

"And, they're addicted," Teagan summarized. "To masculinity, and therefore, to football, baseball, hockey ..."

"Still," Siku said after a moment. "It's hard to see the appeal. In a three-hour broadcast, take away the ads and the commentary, there's only 18 minutes of play!"

"And most of that is men running into each other."

◆

We discussed banning professional sports. There was something very wrong about adults engrossed in playing games while all around them ... But once we'd banned advertising, well, professional sports leagues couldn't survive on ticket sales. The salaries, the equipment, the arenas ... It was a very expensive enterprise. Over $600 billion. (Meanwhile, pandemics raged and there weren't enough vaccinations.) And of course there was no way the new governments were going to subsidize men's addiction to masculinity.

Slowly, neighborhood leagues developed. After-hours and weekends, on school fields and in school gyms. Mostly for soccer and basketball, though there were some baseball leagues, and in places with rinks, some hockey leagues. Football fell into obscurity: without all the hoopla, very few men chose to risk the brain injury of repeated concussion.

✦

We'd intended to address the media, starting with mainstream newspapers and broadcasts, but most people were personalizing their newsfeeds. And, without advertising, as noted, professional sports fell apart, so there was no longer a need for a (whole) Sports section. The (whole) section on Homes consisted largely of real estate ads, so that disappeared on its own as well. And since we'd dismantled the stock market, there was no need for a (whole) section dedicated to that.

We did mandate that the Auto section be replaced with an Environment section.

Otherwise, all we did was prohibit gender stereotypes. That in itself would have leaned heavily to no more Sports, Stocks, or Auto sections, but as it was, it meant no more Fashion section.

✦

"So I visited PornHub the other day," Vic said. "And I cannot believe it's not hate speech. A directory listing images of women being 'destroyed' by men?"

"Not hate speech," Waseme said.

"Images of women being raped by men?"

"Not hate speech."

"So badly that tissues are bruised, muscles torn, bones broken?"

"Not hate speech."

"Images of women being urinated on by men?"

"Not hate speech."

"Images of women being defecated on by men?"

"Not hate speech."

"Images of women being gagged by men?"

"Not hate speech."

"Images of women being strangled by men?"

"Not hate speech."

"Images of women being dismembered by men?"

"Not hate speech."

They were silent.

"Even though we have *proof* that watching porn changes men's attitudes toward women: they become unable to see us as equals, they start to see *all* women as things for their sexual use, they become *sexually aroused by violence toward women.*"

"Not hate speech."

"That it thus changes their *behavior* toward women: they—"

"Not hate speech."

◆

Pornography was declared hate speech. A hate crime. Its production, its sale, its purchase.

(Men spent over $97 billion watching porn. Watching women be humiliated, hurt. Which was more than they spent on the NFL, the NBA, and major league baseball. Combined. More than they spent on NBC, CBS, and ABC. Combined. More than they spent on Microsoft, Google, Amazon, eBay, Yahoo, and Apple. Combined.)

We'd read MacKinnon (*Only Words*). "Some consumers [of porn] write on bathroom walls. Some undoubtedly write judicial opinions."

We'd read Dines (*Pornland*). And so knew that most first exposure to porn happens *before* real sexual experiences, at ages 11-12. That is to say, porn is males' sex ed.

And we'd read Reist and Bray (*Big Porn Inc.*). We'd read the about the porn-soaked man describing with delight the crack he heard when he fully penetrated a two-year-old.

And so we decreed that men had to have *not* watched *any* porn for three years before even *applying* for a position as a teacher, doctor, counsellor, member of or advisor to parliament (at any level), juror, judge … Basically before applying for any position in which they would have any power over women. Almost overnight, all of the forementioned sectors had an overwhelming majority of women. Thus, we finally achieved the critical mass required for so many changes …

Further, and not at all unrelated, street harassment, verbal and physical, became offences, the penalty for which included (but was not limited to) a 7pm curfew and a daytime prohibition against associating in public with other men. After all, women had long known, even if men denied it, that its purpose was not to compliment or even solicit, but to remind women that they were subordinate, and very much so, by sex. It was amazing how well that new legislation worked. (And it was so nice. To be able to move freely in public without being a target … )

But it should have been no surprise. Most male misogyny—indeed most male violence—occurs when there are two or more of them together. And with the new fashion of remote-controlled cameras sewn into women's clothing and jewellry, offenders could easily be charged and convicted. (Many women used these cameras during sexual encounters as well, in the event of rape. When charged with rape, men had to prove enthusiastic consent. This standard alone changed things. Considerably.)

We also banned marriage to children. For obvious reasons. Well, not so obvious to the men who insisted they had a right to buy girls and rape them. But there were fewer and fewer such men … (Many suggested that the absence of pedophilia porn was a factor.)

Then we decided to just ban marriage altogether: sever the connection between love and law, between love and money. It turned out that many men were happy with that. Alimony had always been unjustified sexism. Child support, on the other hand, which is why women had endorsed the institution for so long, was perfectly justified, but could be ensured without the need for marriage.

We also banned genital mutilation and breast ironing and foot binding ...

We ensured that all women could vote, drive, go to school, get bank loans on their own merits, buy, own, and sell property... Basically anything indicative of a second-class standard for women was abolished.

✦

"Men are responsible for well over 90% of the violence," Xanthe stated. "It's as simple as that. Whether with guns, knives, fists; whether for money, revenge, fun—"

"And yet," Yoon noted, "it's always reported as sex-neutral. No one ever says '*Men* beat up ...' or 'A *man* raped...'"

"You're right. It's always 'A woman was raped ...' as if men don't have any agency."

"And given that statistic, you have to wonder: is it something in their wiring or in the way we raise them?"

"Either way ..."

"Yeah."

"We should just exile them," Yoon said, after a moment. "I mean, there aren't enough prisons. And even if there were, why should we support violent men? Why should *we* house them, clothe them, feed them?"

Xanthe was inclined to agree. It's not as if they didn't know that what they did was wrong, harmful, hurtful. And if they genuinely *didn't* know, then all the more reason. To remove them from society.

♦

Given men's propensity for violence, it became illegal for them to have guns and other weapons. Of course, they could, and did, from infancy, make a weapon out of anything. A bat. A pencil. Or nothing at all. Torture. Cruelty. For offences prior to puberty, the parents were penalized. For offences after puberty, the penalty was exile.

Testosterone inhibitors became publicized and freely available.

(And tranquilizer guns replaced bullet guns. And so police forces continued to be effective.) (When needed.)

We'd consulted men. Point blank. In public. "What penalty do *you* think you deserve? For making the groundwater undrinkable? For making the air unbreathable? For knowingly selling cars that explode on impact? For shooting someone in order to steal their shoes? For sexually humiliating and ripping apart a woman the way you did? For forcing her to be pregnant?"

Because we were curious. We genuinely wanted to know what men thought was a fair consequence for the many things they'd done. Most refused to answer.

We designated Australia as the place for exile, as it once had been. It had become, or was soon to be, so ravaged by global warming (primarily forest fires and drought, then rising sea levels) that most of its residents were eager to re-locate. The materials for boat building were still there, but sufficient fuel to make it to Asia or Africa were not. And the nearby islands wouldn't be any better off than Australia.

Of course it wasn't big enough. For all the violent men in the world. But over time, that problem solved itself.

And of course, we stopped the arms trade. Made the manufacture of weapons of mass destruction illegal. Of course, none of the women wanted to make bombs and machine guns anyway. Nor did the men who were left.

◆

"Did you know that churches receive $136 million a day from their members?" Zoe stared at Andrea.

"$136 million *a day?*"

She nodded. "And yet because of their status, they don't pay taxes. So they don't contribute to roads, schools, hospitals …"

"Well that's not very Christian."

◆

We discontinued all subsidies of religion, faith-based groups.

◆

And we put a hold on space exploration: when we get our own house in order, we said, we can go looking for neighbours. Not to colonize, but to contact.

◆

Anyone who wanted to leave the planet (and could afford it) left. The second half of "One giant leap for mankind" turned out to be as literal as many of us thought. (The first half turned out to be false.) (As the same many of us thought.) Those who left were overwhelmingly male. And rich. The ones who had caused most of the problems. (Good riddance.) But, so, their departure didn't decrease the population by very much.

However, with all of the new laws about reproductive rights and responsibilities? Zero population growth was achieved within one generation.

And since we'd started with a mere 4 billion—of the original 8 billion, 4 billion had died of thirst, hunger, bad air, flooding, extreme heat, wildfires, hurricanes, pandemics of one kind or another … and, of course, direct interpersonal (overwhelmingly male) violence—within four generations, we had a sustainable population: we had enough of everything for everyone.

Especially since the required resources per person had decreased. Women were far less … greedy. We didn't need big cars. We didn't need thick steaks. We didn't need large houses. In a word, we didn't need trophies. Because we weren't competing all the time.

And then, along with the billions previously spent on oil industry subsidies, advertising, professional sports, porn, the arms trade, religion subsidies, the space industry, some of which was now available for other endeavours, it was relatively easy to make sure that everyone had access to clean water and nutritious food. Decent housing. Medical care. Education. Sanitation infrastructure. Energy infrastructure. Worldwide.

And all of that was just the beginning.

# My Last Year

Kazzi heard them first. Of course. Compared to her, I'm deaf. I peeked out through the tiny hole I'd cut into the blind.

"Hide. Quiet. Stay." I reinforced the commands with gestures.

She scooted behind the blanket hanging in front of the alcove beside the door.

"Good dog." We'd practised for weeks and weeks. It was a hard lesson for a watchdog. Especially a 25-pound watchdog who had to make up for her size. And her cuteness.

The alcove was actually the entrance to her doggy door. From the outside, it looked like a little dog house had been built against the wall of the cabin. From the inside, it looked like a small storage space. (I reinforced that misinterpretation now by setting the nearby pail full of cleaning products in front of the blanket.) But the back of the alcove opened to the back of the dog house. I could squat down, reach in, and close the opening, and I used to do that at night, but now, I left it open. Always. Just in case. If something should happen to me, Kazzi could escape, run away—for help, I used to think, though I'm not sure there's anyone left here who would, or could, help.

Perhaps she'd just stay here, with me. At least, then, she'd have access to the outside to do her business and access to the lake for water. Hopefully, she could gnaw her way into one of the many bags of kibble in the other room. Or maybe she'd just lay down beside me and die too.

"Hello," I opened the door. And smiled. So not like me. But. My hope was that the smile would surprise them. I was trying to defuse aggression with niceness. And, I'd thought, it wouldn't hurt to make them think I was too much of an idiot to be a worthwhile conquest. Though I hoped that my being over forty and without a shred of femininity would do that.

"You got any food?" the one in front asked. The alphas were always the most rude. That's how they became alphas. No consideration of others. It cleared the way to the satisfaction of self-interest.

"I do have a bit to spare, yes," I smiled again. "Hang on—" I closed the door most of the way and got the small bag of rice I kept on the counter for just this reason. Not too quickly or they'd suspect it was decoy food. But not so slowly they'd get impatient and barge in.

"Here you go," I opened the door again and handed it to him. "It's not much, I'm afraid. As for water," I tried to distract him from demanding more, "the lake's right here, but it's a pretty steep climb down and back up. If you go over to Brant Road, there's a public access, you can back your car right up to the shore. Easier that way." I smiled again.

"Thanks," one of the beta males behind him said.

"There are a few houses on Brant Road," I said then, as an afterthought. (Right.) "They might have some food to spare too. Though, come to think of it, most are seasonals or rentals, so there may not be anyone there now ..." Code for *Empty houses you can move into and/or ransack'*. I was pretending I didn't know why they were there. At my door. At my house.

"Where is this Brant Road?" another one of the beta males called out.

"Well, you have to drive around the lake a ways ..." I gave clear directions. Very clear directions.

"You got any gas?" The alpha spoke again.

"Oh, well—" I hesitated. Convincingly, I thought. "I guess we could spare one ..." I nodded to the two containers sitting by the shed. Also for this reason. "My husband will be furious when he finds out that I gave one to you, but, as I keep telling him, we have to help each other out as much as we can now ..." Did you see that? How easily I slipped in mention of a husband? I'd rehearsed it, of course. Had to. It was so hard to concede to, and perpetuate, the sexism. Yes, there is a man of the house, I have a protector, a defender, an owner, I can't possibly be living on my own, a woman, alone. But. As I'd explained to the principal who'd fired me when I'd screamed at an asshole-of-a-seventeen-year-old to 'Sit down and shut the fuck up!', you have to use the language they understand. I'd mention a couple twenty-five-year-old-sons too if need be.

I repeated the directions, then turned and closed the door. So they wouldn't see me see them take both containers. So I wouldn't have to noticeably put my tail between my legs. Or worse, object, challenge, then pay the price. Neither container was completely full. And of course I had several others. Hidden in the forest.

I bent down and pulled aside the blanket. "Good dog!" I reached for her. She'd want to chase them. Bark at them. "Good Kazzi! What a good little dog you are! Yes!" I made a huge fuss over her. She *was* a good dog. That was hard, and she'd done it perfectly. I gave her a treat and lots of snuggles. Another treat. And more snuggles.


She'd known about global warming for years. Decades, actually. Who didn't? Pollution (air and water) had made it to the mainstream media in the '60s. She'd been minimizing her use of fossil fuels since then, running or biking whenever her destination was less than ten miles away and being frugal with heat. Then acid rain and the ozone layer, in the '70s. She stopped using aerosol deodorants at that point. Then global warming, in the '80s. She didn't have an RV and wasn't about to fly anywhere. She tried to buy local produce, but discovered that the grocery stores were actually prohibited from carrying it. She stopped once at a 'Farmers' Market' on the highway, only to discover that it was some schmuck who'd just bought stuff from the grocery store and was reselling it, pretending it was local when in fact it was from California and Chile. She'd stopped eating meat as soon as she'd moved out. And she'd never planned to add to the population.

She was vaguely aware of the IPCC (1988), the Kyoto Protocol (1997), the Paris Agreement (2015), and various international summits. Truthfully, she'd never gotten into the habit of 'watching the news' and once she'd bought her cabin-on-a-lake-in-a-forest, she could no longer afford the alternative newspapers she'd been subscribing to. When she read Naomi Klein's *This Changes Everything*, she knew there was no way they would stay under 400ppm, the maximum for keeping the global temperature rise under a 'manageable' 2 degrees. And when she found out that the Greenland ice melt that happened in 2019 wasn't 'supposed to' happen until 2070, shocking even the scientists, the so-called *alarmists*— Well, she wasn't surprised, a couple years later, to read that they'd passed the point—several points, in fact—of no return.

Most people thought it was just a phrase. 'The point of no return.' They didn't take it literally. But now it was inevitable: even if they stopped—immediately, that very day—all of the emissions that were turning the planet into a greenhouse, there would be, by the end of the century, an increase in global temperature of at least 3 degrees. By 2050, they'd probably reach 2 degrees. By 2030, quite possibly sooner, 1.5 degrees.

White surfaces reflect heat; dark surfaces absorb it. Polar ice is white; melted, it's dark ocean. Ergo. Yes, in theory, they could engage in carbon capture and sequestration, but— Not gonna happen. On the scale required. Certainly not soon enough. Not while Brazil bulldozes ahead with its psychopathic plan to clear previously protected swaths of the Amazon for livestock, thereby releasing more than twice the annual emissions of the entire United States. Not while China, single-handedly responsible for one-quarter of global emissions, continues to increase, not decrease, their emissions. Not while Canada approves development of the Teck Tar Sands, essentially planning to use up one-third of the entire planet's remaining carbon budget. And so. The sea level would rise, the hurricanes, wildfires, droughts, floods, and heat waves would increase, houses would be destroyed, food supplies would be gone, mass migrations would occur, livelihoods and lifestyles would be changed overnight, most to nomadic subsistence ...

Once the anger was gone, she was left with overwhelming sadness. Now that it was final. Now that these few years ahead of her were going to be her last. She decided to become a total hedonist. She stopped tutoring for the LSAT, because what would be the point? She couldn't bear to tell her students that they'd never be able to practice law: by the time they'd written the LSAT, gotten accepted into law school, completed the three years of study, and passed the bar, the world would look very different, priorities would have radically changed, and it would be unlikely they'd be hired by a law firm. It would be unlikely there'd even *be* any law firms hiring. And she didn't need the money: she'd planned for another twenty years, but now, she doubted she'd survive another ten. And, so, like the musicians on the sinking Titanic, playing to the very end, she wanted to spend every last minute enjoying, basking, in the beauty ... snuggled comfortably on her second-hand couch, reading, listening to music, and staring out the huge window to the nothing-but-trees-and-water until the sun hit the dock, then—at least, in the summer and fall (in winter the lake froze, and in spring it was too buggy to be outside)—sitting down at the water, watching the sparkles, then heading out with Tassi, now Kazzi, for an afternoon of kayaking, to the end of the lake then up the little river, or if it was too windy, an afternoon of walking through the forest ...

The infrastructure was already becoming unreliable. Power outages were becoming more frequent and lasting longer. So she filled her lean-to with wood and bought a lifetime supply of matches. She kept her propane tank topped up, fearing the day there would simply be no more available, but the furnace needed electricity to run, hence the wood. Given the price of propane, she'd been using electric heaters for warmth beyond what was necessary to keep the pipes from freezing, but when the power went out ... She'd thought about going off-grid, but her property simply didn't get enough sun for solar heating. (And no way would she cut down any of the trees.) Even solar charging was iffy. She could close off most of the cabin and just live in the room with the woodstove and the bathroom next to it. She already had lots of books to read and a few ipods full of music (her stereo system needed electricity too, of course), but she bought a few more solar lights she could clip onto her visor for reading (and just getting around in the dark) and a few more solar chargers for her ipods. She had several battery power packs for her laptop and her wifi router, but unless she could plug them in to recharge, they'd be useless after a week or so. She had a battery-powered radio for emergency news and lots of batteries.

She stocked up on food that didn't need to be refrigerated or cooked. She stocked up on kibble. She had a virtually unlimited supply of water, the lake, though she'd get her drinking water from the nearby spring (because the pump—she had a drilled well that was unlikely to go dry—also needed electricity); she had a little saucepan, several small propane tanks, and a screw-on burner, so she could boil water if need be. She stocked up on some medical supplies—antibiotics, mostly, and painkillers. As long as she didn't get seriously ill or seriously injured—emergency medical assistance would surely become unreliable, hospitals themselves would become overburdened and understaffed—she figured she'd be okay. For several years.

She thought long and hard about what else to do …

The second group came a few weeks later. They came in two vehicles, both cars, which made me think they weren't local. Most guys around here have pick-ups. So, I thought with a sigh, the migration has started in earnest. Or maybe it had already started, last spring, but only now was Muskoka, with its surfeit of summer homes, full. (And wherever people had ended up last summer, they'd decided to stay put for the winter.)

Although protected by the oceans from the wandering masses in Europe, Africa, and Asia, I figured Canada would still suffer an influx. Central Americans would migrate north to Mexico, Mexicans would migrate north to the U.S., and Americans north to Canada, misbelieving it was some sort of wilderness paradise. Immune to climate change. In fact, the warming was happening twice as fast in Canada as in the rest of the world.

I turned to Kazzi, but she'd already gone into her hiding spot. Since that last time, every single time we heard a vehicle, I'd been telling her to hide.

"Good dog," I said. "Quiet. Stay."

I opened the door. "Hello," I smiled.

"This your house?"

"Yes, my husband and—"

"Liar." He pushed his way in. Five or six men followed. Suddenly the room was too small. Much too small.

"I have food—" I offered the bag of rice that had been sitting on the counter. He looked at it with disdain, then spat on it. I wiped my hand on my pants. What had he expected? A freezer full of steaks? Apparently.

"Sorry, I'm a vegetarian," I explained. Besides, the power has been out for weeks, you fucking moron. I would have gladly given him spoiled meat. Let him die of food poisoning. Hm.

"I can offer you some canned beans, if you like." Somewhat past their expiration date. "And I've still got some juice left." Fearing that Kazzi would respond to his aggression with some of her own, I bent down, and moved the cleaning supplies in front of the blanket, as if making room to open a lower cupboard. I hoped she'd snuck out and run away. We should've practised *that*.

As I straightened up, he shoved me aside, then proceeded to open all of the cupboards, pulling stuff out at random, with increasing anger. Nothing I had was good enough. For him.

"There's nothing here," one of his men said to him. Then looked at me with such disgust. He'd already taken in the large open-concept room and seen that the tv in the corner was an old one. And huge. It would take two of them to get it out of the house. Not worth it. There were LPs in crates against the wall, CDs in racks above. They'd have to take the whole stereo system. Again, not worth it. I guess they'd been hoping for a large-screen tv and a state-of-the-art mp3 player. Not that either would work without electricity. Did they miss tv that much? Perhaps. Perhaps they wanted to watch the game—as if the NFL or NHL were still— Well, maybe they were. Priorities. Men. Teams. Competition. I sighed.

The alpha strode into the next room, his men following him like a phalanx. I almost laughed when they hit the doorway en masse. There was a lot of swearing and shoving as they had to let each other pass, one at a time. And all for— books. Three walls of books and my desk. Well, they had to do something about that. They started pulling my books off the shelves and throwing them onto the floor. I let them. Of course I did. I protested, weakly, for show. I knew to not even try to engage them in rational discussion. Most men had no idea why they did what they did. They were simply not that aware, not that introspective. And, so, any inquiry as to their reasons would send them into a rage. Because they could not, *would* not, admit they didn't know why— Why anything, actually.

As I'd hoped, they didn't go into the next room. The curtain I'd put across that doorway must've deterred them. It was pink. I almost laughed again. Men would rather die than touch anything pink. It was a lesson learned from the pandemic, the first pandemic, when for a while the only masks available were for nursing staff, and so in pastels, florals, or pinks. (Go figure.) It took a while for black, grey, and navy masks to show up on the market. And so, a while for *men* to start wearing masks. When the ones in camouflage print appeared, they sold out almost overnight. (Pathetic, that.)

Perhaps they hadn't noticed the propane tank when they'd approached the house. Perhaps they hadn't connected it with having a furnace. And so they hadn't wondered where the furnace was. On the other side of the curtain was, yes, my bedroom, such as it was—a mattress on the floor so Tassi, then Kazzi, could get into bed with me, right below a lakeside window that I opened to feel the breeze and hear the loons— Oh, the loons. Such a beautiful call, so rich and sonorous— Gone now for years.

But also, on the other side of the curtain, were the stairs

down to the semi-basement. I'd added both, the extra room and the semi-basement, twenty years after I'd bought the cabin. Which was when I could finally afford a furnace (instead of just baseboard heaters) and a well (until then, I'd drawn from the lake—not recommended, the intake valve kept getting clogged and I'd have to dive down, often in too-cold water … ). And in addition to the furnace, and the pump and the hot water tank, the semi-basement contained my freezer and several shelves of food.

I'd considered putting up a fake wall in front of the freezer and shelves, but it would be a lot of work, and I thought the power would probably have been out for some time before the gangs showed up, so I would have eaten all of the food in the freezer by then. It turns out I was correct. I'd had the last of my ice cream, my last ice cream ever, shortly after the first gang had come. Then I thought about hiding the rest of my food behind my old speakers and a stack of boxes. But then I came up with a better idea.

When they tired of throwing books onto the floor—short attention spans, every one of them—the herd moved back into the main room. I followed.

"I'll take those canned goods now," the alpha turned and stared at me.

I was surprised. They were in one of the still opened cupboards. Fully visible. Ah.

"Okay," I said, then walked past him, reached into the cupboard, and handed one to him.

He turned and whipped it through the window. I gasped. Too startled to scream 'Why the fuck did you do that?!' (Probably a good thing.) It had been a completely gratuitous act of destruction. And he had no idea— That window— For me— And who did he think was going to clean up all that broken glass? And then repair the damage he'd done? And with what?

I waited until they'd driven away, then looked in the alcove. No Kazzi. Okay, good. Maybe. No need to get frantic just yet.

I went outside, crouched down, and spread my arms wide. Tassi would've come running in an instant, with such joy— It still put a smile on my face. Once she leapt into my arms so enthusiastically, she knocked me over. Kazzi was a little less— less affectionate, less close. She'd been six months old by the time I'd found her, adopted her, whereas I'd had Tassi since she'd been a baby, ten weeks old. It had made a difference. Kazzi and I were making up for it, but …

I walked around. Hoped she'd see me from wherever she was and come running— No.

I called her name, softly. And then saw her squirm out from under the shed, a tentative smile on her face.

"Good dog! Oh, sweetheart—" I fell to my knees and again opened my arms. She came to me then. Let me hold her. She was shaking. Although it made me sad to see her so afraid, I knew it was good that she was. I'd worried that her watchdog bravado would get her killed.

"Good dog!" I repeated, comforting her and just happy to have found her, safe and sound. She'd crawled under the shed on the side facing the forest, where no one, from the cabin or from the road, would see her go in, or come out. And once in, I suspected no one could get to her. It was a brilliant hiding place.

We went back into the cabin, and I put her on her comfy chair, told her to stay. She was happy to. She curled up with her little white half-unstuffed stuffed rabbit. Then I put on a pair of gloves and carefully picked up as many shards of broken window as I could, putting them into an empty cardboard box I hadn't yet been desperate enough to use as fire-starter. But no electricity meant no vacuum cleaner, and Kazzi would surely cut her paws on the small slivers I couldn't even see. And a cut paw could become critical. I thought for a minute, then decided to just lay a tarp over the area. Anticipating that she'd want to come with me when I went out to the shed, I lifted her off the chair, carried her across the carpet, then set her down once we were outside. I chose the heaviest tarp I had, wiped it down, threw Kazzi's ball for her while it dried, then went back in and spread it out, double. I started to nail it in place, but quickly realized that it would soon tear off the nails, so I went back out to the shed for a couple of the boards left over from the last dock repair, lay them along the edge, and weighted them down with rocks I gathered from the shoreline. Then, with one of my reading lights, I examined the uncovered carpet along the edge very carefully for tell-tale glints of glass.

Then I went outside and around to the front of the cabin—Kazzi followed and sat at a distance where I told her to—good dog—and again I picked up all the shards I could see. I had a few sheets of plywood I could put over top, because again, Kazzi, but I'd need them to repair the window, come winter. Again, I thought for a minute, then went back around to the lean-to and carried out, one at a time, four now-empty skids—I stacked my firewood on skids to keep it off the ground, and, so, dry—and set them onto the ground under the window. Then again I made a microscopic examination, this time of the exposed dirt and scruffy grass along the edges of the skids.

As for the window, I super-glued a sheet of heavy plastic onto the remaining window from the inside, working ever so gently, then did the same on the outside. It occurred to me that I probably should have broken out all of the glass—perhaps what remained would fall out of the frame on its own accord, and I'd have to start all over—but I didn't have enough plastic for that much open space. As it was, since it had been a double-paned thermal window, it wouldn't be nearly as warm come winter, even with the sheets of plywood … But at least for now, it would keep out the black flies and mosquitoes, and I could see through to the lake.

Three seconds to smash the window. Three hours to deal with the consequences. No, more than three hours. For the rest of my life, I'd have to look through crappy plastic instead of clear glass. And during the winter, I wouldn't be able to look out at all. *And* I'd be cold.


The first pandemic brought inconvenience, but no real hardship. Even so, it was difficult. More difficult than it should have been.

Men, more than women, denied the danger. Hell no, they weren't going to get sick, they were tough. (As if toughness, rather than, say, a diet high in fruits and vegetables, and low in beer and cigarettes, has anything to do with resistance to viral infections.) Never mind that the stats show not only that men die sooner than women, but also that they're more likely to get sick: generally speaking, women have stronger immune systems.

Men didn't keep their distance. It suddenly became very clear that they were pack animals; they naturally herd together. So they found the whole do-not-congregate thing difficult. In the city, young men continued to hang out together during the day and go on the prowl together at night. Apparently, they simply couldn't stand being alone.

When she had occasion to engage with a man, she noticed that she had to keep stepping back, to maintain the recommended six feet of distance, and every time she took a step back, the man took a step closer. It was as if they defined masculinity as proximity to women. Or maybe it was that being close to a woman, any woman, was sexually arousing, and men simply *had* to be horny. Proof of manhood.

It didn't help that they'd called it 'social' distancing instead of 'physical' distancing, 'social' being associated with the feminine, and 'physical' being associated with the masculine. And it didn't help that many of the public health officials issuing the recommendations were women. Real men don't listen to women. They certainly don't accept their advice. (And—use hand sanitizer? Cleanliness was, had long been, a girl thing. Real men don't wash their hands. Certainly not several times a day.)

Men more often than women violated the stay-at-home recommendation. Because, for the most part, the home was the woman's domain. After all, she was the one who put curtains on the windows, carpets on the floor, blankets on the beds; she was the one who spent hours in the kitchen, in the laundry room; she was the one who knew where everything was; she was the one who kept everything clean. So unless that home came with an attached garage, a man cave, real men weren't going to stay there all day. (Certainly not all week, let alone all month ...)

Even so, even with the intermittent relief that such violations provided, being ordered to stay home and inside for days, weeks, at a time took its toll. On the women and children who became punching bags for frustrated and angry men. (Because, you know, it's their fault.) (Men. Irrational to the core.) Of course, many such women and children had always *been* punching bags, but now they couldn't escape to a shelter or a relative's home. They'd been ordered to stay home, inside, with their assaulter. For days, weeks, at a time. Who came up with that bright idea? Male policymakers who hadn't thought about all those women and children locked up with the husband/father who had little enough patience when he was there for only a few hours in the evenings. Seriously, did they not foresee that so-called 'domestic violence' would skyrocket?

No. Because when had women's realities, women's lives, ever been important enough to be considered when making policy? (Why weren't hotels appropriated for the quarantined women and children when the shelters became full? No wait, why weren't the hotels appropriated for the men? Why should the women and children have to leave their homes? When the men were to blame?) It was always *men's* needs, *men's* wants, that were considered. First. Foremost.

It didn't help that beer and liquor stores remained open. They were considered essential services. While libraries, for instance, were closed. (Even though said libraries could have provided a steady supply of books and DVDs for the kids forced to stay home and inside, for days, weeks at a time. Books and DVDs that would become especially important when the wifi infrastructure started to deteriorate, reducing access to the internet, with its social media and streaming amusements …) Of course, the beer and liquor stores provided a steady stream of tax revenue, whereas the libraries did not, but if that was the reason, it just showed that money trumped well-being. Surprise.

Women's work continued to be invisible and therefore considered less important. Or, more likely, considered less important and therefore invisible. Either way, therefore under-funded. And therefore under-resourced. And therefore unable to deal effectively with even the first pandemic. Schools became infection centers. Thirty kids in a single room all day long? They should have been closed on day one. Care homes became hazmat depots. Even hospitals, critically dependent on nursing staff, which was overwhelmingly female, became epic failures. If health services had been dominated by men, you can bet that every single country would have managed the pandemics better. Much better.

But attention, money, resources kept getting poured into

men's endeavours. Construction companies survived. Land-scaping companies survived. Hardware stores remained open, and because they were considerably larger than pharmacies, considerably more people were allowed inside at any one time. You didn't have to line up to get your new power drill. But contraceptives? Diaper cream?

The second pandemic coincided with a marked increase in both the frequency and severity of storms. That's when the infrastructure really started falling apart. Quite simply, there weren't enough people to fix things. Imagine the Montreal ice storm of '98 or the Northeast blackout of '03 happening every week in ten different places. As it was, after the ice storm, it had taken two weeks before the downed power line on her property was attended to. If something like that happened now, it would take months. Though now, well, the line would be dead, so ... she'd just move it out of her way, perhaps carry one of her summer tires out of the shed (she'd decided to leave her winter tires on year-round) and stick the end into it, just in case.

The last time she made the trip into town, the way was still unobstructed, but she regretted not having a gas-powered chainsaw. (The price of gas had not gone up very much; in fact, it continued to be subsidized. Men and cars.) (She'd only recently noticed that when they absolutely *had* to ride in the passenger seat, which was to be avoided at all costs, notably at the cost of having *their own cars*, they had to call it 'riding shotgun'. So pathetic.) Just in case, she hauled out her old, very old, ten-speed. Filled the tires. Lubricated the chain.

It was during the third pandemic that the media started reporting stories about global warming again—actually calling it 'global warming' rather than the less upsetting 'climate change'—this time mentioning the various turning points. That had, by then, long been passed. Perhaps pandemics had become old news. Perhaps they realized it didn't matter anymore if they defied their advertisers' instructions to censor anti-BigWhatever stories or their governments' instructions to censor anything that would create panic. Whatever, that's when the shit really hit the fan.

Up to that point, had any of the millionaires (for the most part, men) contributed any of their millions to providing more health services? Had any of the drug companies (for the most part, owned and run by men) provided any of their vaccines free of charge? Of course not. They chose private wealth over communal well-being. They put themselves first. Front and center. Same old, same old. It's what got us where we were. Men didn't become multi-millionaires for the public good. (They were men. They needed to have more, to be bigger, to compete, to win—) They didn't overdevelop natural resources because we needed them, because it was in our best interests. No. It was all in *their* best interests.

But even then, when the rich had more than they would ever need, 'ever' now being in sight, did they give it to those who, through no fault of their own, had less than they needed? Of course not.

All of which suggested that the main lesson from the pandemics was that in a state of emergency, nothing would change. It would all just get worse. So when it became mainstream knowledge that we'd passed several points of no return and the world as we knew it would end within ten or twenty years, everything just ... intensified. In particular, male dominance intensified. The more men lost control over their lives, the more they insisted on having control over other people's lives.

And given the male propensity to avoid introspection, denial was to be expected. Along the way, and even now. Even when the flames of forest fires and the winds of cyclones—'No, we *aren't* ruining the planet for human habitation. There will *always* be a way to fix things ...' Right. Most people, which included most men, hadn't studied science beyond high school. And they certainly weren't going to listen to a bunch of nerds tell them—well, anything. So, okay, ice *doesn't* melt at 32 degrees. White *doesn't* reflect more heat than dark. Trees *don't* absorb carbon dioxide. (She recalled with horror a billboard that had appeared on the highway one day: "Wood products help fight climate change." What? *What?* Cutting down trees, to make wood products, will *increase* our atmospheric carbon, because as long as they're alive, they *do* absorb carbon dioxide. And once they're down, all the leftover of the cut decomposes, *releasing* carbon.) (Okay, yes, using wood is better than using concrete, steel, and plastic/oil-based products, and okay, yes, it's better to turn already-down or about-to-fall trees into wood products, sequestering the carbon, than to let them decompose. But she doubted that *that* would be the take-away message of the billboard.)

So it was unsurprising that even before the third pandemic, hell even before the first pandemic, *way* before, when it would've made a difference, when everyone should have been doing everything they could to *reduce* carbon emissions, so many men kept racing around on their jetskis, their ATVs, and their snowmobiles (in the first case, spewing two gallons of uncombusted oil and gas for every hour of operation; in the last case, spewing as much hydrocarbon in one hour as a car does in two years)—*producing* carbon emissions. For *fun.*


I knew that the next group would be even worse. The last time I'd paddled around the lake, I'd noticed that every seasonal house and every rental was occupied. And most likely, not in every case by their owners or official renters. So even without a large-screen tv or a fully-stocked kitchen (and even with that damn broken window), my property had become prime real estate: it was on a lake, it had a woodstove, and, with restrained use, still one or two winters' worth of wood. And it was occupied by a woman. A lone woman.

When the next group came, they'd move in. They'd kill Kazzi. For food. They'd keep me. For fun.

We both heard them coming down the hill around the cove. It sounded like two or three vehicles and a few ATVs, men carousing as if having a party. (As if?)

"Quick."

She followed me into the study. I knelt down, pulled back the carpet under the desk, lifted the trap door, and dropped into the crawlspace the two kayak bags I kept there, along with my snowsuit. I put Kazzi's harness and muzzle on her, both also at the ready, then leashed her and carefully lowered her. I followed, closing the door behind me, making sure the carpet settled back on top.

I'd prepared the crawlspace long ago. And we'd rehearsed our escape. She didn't like the muzzle, but I think she realized it was sort of like being leashed: it relieved her of some responsibility. It reminded me of the time Tassi, a hunter, not a watchdog, had found a nest of baby grouse. I'd gotten her away before she'd killed them all, carrying her well past, then setting her down so we could carry on. She froze. It took a few moments to figure out that the scent was still strong to her and she wanted to run back, but she also wanted to be a good dog—she was paralyzed with indecision. After a moment, she put her paws up, asking me to carry her again. So I did. I made the decision for her.

I felt around in one of my kayak bags for my visor, with its clip-on light. I hoped not to have to turn it on, but I wanted the option. Then I unfolded the tarp I'd put near the lakeside entrance to the crawlspace, and we settled in. Kazzi could still growl, but unable to open her mouth, it was a quiet rumbling. Even so, when the yelling, the laughter, and the stomping around began, I stroked her throat to calm her, and hopefully keep her from growling even a little bit.

And now. Certainly we wait until dark, but do we make our run for it while they're having a loud time or do we wait until they're all asleep? I decided on the latter in case one of them wandered down to the water. Once asleep, I hoped they'd be in a deep drunk passed out kind of sleep.

Finally, after a simultaneously boring and anxious six hours, there was silence. Had been silence for maybe half an hour. I put on my snowsuit—nights could be chilly, and there was only so much storage room in the kayak. As it was, I was leaving behind a good stash of canned food I'd hidden in the crawlspace. Next, I put on Kazzi's life jacket. Tassi had been a good swimmer; Kazzi was not. Happily, that hadn't stopped her from wanting to go kayaking with me, often standing on the prow like a little hood ornament, exactly as Tassi had done. Then I unscrewed the piece of plywood that led into the crawlspace (with the screwdriver exactly where I'd put it) and set it aside.

I took a firm grip of both kayak bags with my left hand (they were bulky and heavy, but I needed them both), and a firm hold of Kazzi's leash with my right. Carefully, quietly, I crawled out, Kazzi at my side. I took a deep breath, glad to be out into the fresh night air. No matter how much I'd cleaned it up, the crawlspace was still stuffy, dusty, dirty, and fibreglass insulation fibrey. There was just enough moonlight, I noted with relief. We made our way down the steep hill to the dock. Carefully, quietly, I put one bag behind the seat of the kayak, the other under the prow. Kazzi jumped in. I smiled. Tassi had always waited for me to get in first. I unclipped the rope that tied the kayak to the dock, then, a little awkwardly, got in behind her. I reached for the paddle, lying on the dock, then pushed away. And started paddling. Carefully, quietly.

Plan A had been the plan for winter. They'd get out of the cabin and circle around to her fully-packed, fully-prepped car, parked out by the road so as not to get blocked in and so as to say 'This house is *not* empty.' She'd hidden her spare key in the remains of a fallen tree. She kept the tank full. The problem was she wasn't sure there'd be anywhere to drive to. She'd be in the same situation as these guys, escaping god-knows-what, looking for a place to hang out.

But it was May. She'd always liked Plan B better anyway.

She paddled past the several cottages and summer homes. She was a familiar sight to the permanent residents and the regular summer people, heading out in the early afternoon to paddle into the sparkles, often not returning until dark, Tassi still, or again, on the prow, but with her night collar on, the little red lights a beacon ... But she was paddling out now. Not back. And two o'clock in the morning was significantly different than nine o'clock at night. No matter. If anyone saw her, so what? Even so, she didn't relax until she turned to head up the river, out of sight, with no more cottages to paddle past.

She continued paddling in the dark, mindful of the whirlpools, the rocky outcrops, the barely submerged fallen trees, all of which, if not negotiated well, could send Kazzi overboard ... She knew the river well; indeed she knew the whole lake well. She'd paddled both with Tassi almost every day for fourteen years, as soon as they were able in April or May until they could no longer do so in November or December. Along many stretches, she'd let Tassi out to run or splish splash along the shoreline, perchance to chase some geese ... She'd pull up beside many a muskrat lodge if Tassi indicated that it was at the moment occupied, then sit back and watch as she dug with great enthusiasm (the muskrat escaped underwater as soon she started digging, so there was no danger, for either one of them), basking in the sun, the breeze, the sparkling water ...

They'd seen moose grazing in the shallow marsh just past the river, once with two little mooselets, so sweet, the smooth turtles and the dinosaur turtles sunning on fallen trees, the iridescent emerald of the mallards and the bad-hair-day ducks, a catfish laying on the ice, the otters chittering at them to leave it there, the little mink making its way across the stony section where, she was sure, it lived, a bear, first mistaken for a large black dog, swimming across the lake ahead of them then, no doubt catching their scent, changing its mind and turning back, and in the evenings on their way back, beaver surrounding them like furred crocodiles before slapping the water and disappearing ... Paddling with Tassi had been her greatest joy.

She was ever so glad that Kazzi also enjoyed kayaking, but it was quite a different experience with a dog who insisted on trying to catch the dragonflies ...

After about half an hour, she reached the fork. She paddled to the left, around a bend and onto a small weedy patch at the base of the rapids. Barely rapids, but still. The fork on the right circled back, far behind her place, and was eventually joined by the stream that came down, down, carrying winter run-off that created genuine rapids. Impassable rapids. She took off Kazzi's muzzle, then unclipped her leash. The little dog jumped out, happy to be able to run around a bit. After a short rest, she took off her snowsuit, bundled it onto the kayak seat, then put on the hipwaders she'd hidden there. Kazzi jumped back in. She knew what was coming and, oddly enough, was happier in the kayak than running along shore. After clipping on her leash again and fastening it to the seat of the kayak, she tied the rope still attached to the front handle of the kayak around her waist. This was the hard part. A hundred metres of walking on slimy stones and rocks, against the current, the kayak tugging at her as it trailed behind. The good news was that she was now beyond road access. Beyond even motorboat and jetski access. And anyone else who paddled to this point, now or later, was unlikely to go any further. And there was no rush. In fact, the slower she went, the better. She'd fallen many times before, the water was cold, and if it got inside her waders, it made for a very unpleasant trek. And now, more than ever, she did not want to twist an ankle or dislocate a knee …

A painstaking two hours later, she hauled the kayak onto the shore, unclipped Kazzi for a well-deserved run-around (she'd been so good, not fussing, not whining), took off her hipwaders, put her snowsuit back on, and sat. Just sat. She hadn't planned on doing what she'd just done in the dark. And she had indeed fallen. Several times. Even though this early in the season meant there was less algae on the rocks. Nevertheless, she'd made it. The worst was over. Yay. After a while, she carried her hipwaders inland a bit, out of sight, and hung them upside down from a low branch. Then carried on.

Notwithstanding the current, the next two hours were lovely. Why hadn't she done more kayaking in the middle of the night? It was absolutely quiet, the moonlight glimmered on the water … Kazzi sat in the cockpit, ever-vigilant, listening, scenting …

And then she was there. At her chosen spot. About halfway to Algonquin Park. In the faint light of pre-dawn, she pulled her kayak onto the shore, set up the tent she'd stashed there, moved her kayak bags inside, called to Kazzi, zipped the door closed after her, unrolled the sleeping bag, and crawled inside. After a moment, Kazzi crawled in after her. They both fell asleep almost immediately.


Mornings would be chilly. She knew that. And so, as was her plan, she slept until the sun reached the tent. And then some. Kazzi didn't complain. Eventually, she got up. And out. While Kazzi did some exploring, no doubt establishing a perimeter, she began setting up the rest of her stuff. Their temporary home. Over the course of the previous summer, they'd made this trip once a week, each time bringing stuff she then stashed in various places. She'd brought, in addition to the tent and sleeping bag, six little propane tanks, a screw-on burner, a little saucepan, and a cup. Tea. Must have tea. While the water was boiling, she opened the first of her food stashes. She'd packed—in tins and, when she ran out of tins, plastic containers, spraying the latter with Kazzi's 'no-chew' for added protection against squirrels and raccoons—and then transported over a hundred pounds of food: a six-month supply of kibble and a six-month supply of everything-granola. She'd also packed a six-month supply of one-a-day vitamins. She gave Kazzi a third of her cup for the day. She'd do without. Could afford to. For quite a while. She'd regained the twenty-five pounds that she'd lost during the months up to and after Tassi's death, having eaten everything that was still in her freezer when the power went out for good. She'd become a walking freezer.

She'd also stashed some first aid supplies. An ipod and a solar charger. Books and spare glasses and clip-on solar lights. Spare clothes. Spare shoes. Waterproof matches. A hand saw and a hatchet. Several of Kazzi's favourite balls. She'd have to clear a runway for chasing said balls …

May was colder than she would've liked. So she spent an hour every morning gathering kindling and sawing fallen branches, clearing that runway. Kazzi was delighted, racing after her ball again and again.

And then, while the happy little dog napped, she listened to music from her life with Tassi. And lost herself in the memories ... (Music was like scent for her, triggering images so vivid, she was sure her body experienced a biochemical change, a surge of dopamine or serotonin perhaps.) One day, she'd choose one of the albums she'd listened to when they stayed in a cottage over on the Bruce Peninsula (every spring for five years, to escape the black flies), kayaking on the amazing teal and turquoise water ... On their last ever kayak there, Tassi had stood on the prow the whole way back, and the light, on her, on the water, against the cliffs ... Another day, she'd choose an album from their too-few winters in Georgia during which they'd stayed in a house on Lake Lanier, paddling to and around the several islands (because yes, the lake was liquid, all winter long, and hardly anyone was out on it), Tassi gleefully running along the shorelines, stopping at will to smell, investigate, and track the occasional deer or fox ... It was sheer bliss, for both of them. They'd had fourteen years of joy ...

Once Kazzi was refreshed, they'd go kayaking, sometimes back the way they came, but usually further up the little river—not too far, as the current was still pretty strong from the winter run-off, and not too fast... Along the few sunny stretches, she saw the impossible green of spring gradually emerge ...

Every night she sat near a small fire at the water's edge, in her snowsuit. Good idea to bring that. Kazzi would not crawl onto her lap, despite several encouragements, because that was too close to the fire, but she did sit near her, behind her. Insisted on doing so, actually.

At the end of the month, she located, with Kazzi's help, the second of her stashes. Intact.

June was nice. Buggy, of course. (Pity there were no more bats; years ago, whenever she'd gone for a night walk, she'd see them dip and dive around her, feeding on the mosquitos … .) But she'd brought her bug jacket and bug pants. And a mosquito net bed canopy she'd purchased on eBay. She hung it from a tree near the river, where it would catch the breeze. It created a bug-free zone, and she often sat inside, reading, Kazzi by her side. The black flies in particular bothered the little dog, their bites leaving marks like cigarette burns, so she spent time every day picking them off her belly, Kazzi willingly rolling over for her to do so. She thought, belatedly, that she should have purchased, and brought, some bug spray with DEET: it was apparently pretty effective, and now she wouldn't live long enough for its carcinogenic side-effects to matter. But then she remembered that the smell gave her a headache, so … just as well.

One day, partly because the bugs were 'better' out on the water, she decided to paddle further up the river than usual. She was curious. So, apparently, was Kazzi. The little dog jumped up onto the prow now that the current wasn't as strong, and stood, attentive … While making their way along a side stream she remembered as being eventually blocked by a fallen tree, she discovered that it was no longer blocked. So she kept going, losing herself in the way the sun lit the weeds, creating an ever-changing array of a multitude of greens, a stark contrast to the dark depth of the forest … and suddenly came to a small lake, its entire surface sparkling. She actually gasped, it was so beautiful. And as far as she could see, the lake was completely secluded. There were a few sandy spots, but she couldn't see any gaps in the forest that would indicate a road or even an ATV trail. She paddled around its perimeter, slowly, cautiously, examining the shoreline carefully. No signs of human presence whatsoever. So the next day, she moved. It took all morning and most of the afternoon, but it was worth it.

She spent much of July playing with Kazzi in the morning (a new runway had to be cleared), staring out at the sparkles in the afternoon, from shore or from the water, depending on the wind, then at the sun rippling through the shoreline trees in the late afternoon, and then, oh joy, watching the sunsets in the evening. (Back at her cabin, she'd have to paddle out around the point to see the sunset.)

And listening to the loons! She'd thought they'd gone extinct. She listened eagerly for the tell-tale toot-toot of a baby loon, but neither heard nor saw evidence of such, despite paddling around the lake almost every day. They did discover the loons' nest, by accident (and from that point on, avoided it), but it was empty. Occasionally, some ducks and geese flew in, landed, paddled about, then left. Kazzi watched them with interest but, unlike Tassi, showed no desire to chase them. Odd, since she was so addicted to chasing her ball.

Early on, when she'd first bought her cabin, a heron would come to her end of the lake, to the cove, every day, but she suspected it had followed the frogs ... There'd been doves too, but it was years since she heard their coo. And the fat little squirrels she first saw in winter at the squirrel tree shelf she kept stocked with birdseed— Eventually, she realized that the zzzt she'd been hearing— They were flying squirrels! A few winters later, she was delighted to see two adults with four little ones huddled on the shelf ... But they had disappeared too ...

She continued to read (Jodi Taylor, Janet Evanovich, Terry Fallis, Tim Dorsey, Lionel Shriver, Robert J. Sawyer, Kim Stanley Robinson, Nancy Kress ... brilliant, every one of them ...) and listen to music (Pachelbel, Bach, Vangelis, Bjornstad, Malmquist, Richter, Darling, Deuter, Parijat, Caufield, and *all* of Gibson's *Solitudes* albums ... all so ... enthralling ...), but more often she just stared out across the water. And listened to the silence. She thought a lot, about a lot of things, as she sat staring at the lake …

August was simply, wonderfully, more of the same (with fewer bugs). Some days, they paddled back out along the stream and further up the river. On one occasion, they saw a deer standing at the edge of the river. It looked thin. And so would be any wolves that were left. (She remembered that bright day when, rounding a bend in the trail, she came face to face with a young wolf, as surprised to see her as she was to see it—and it was gorgeous, red and cream, fit and confident …)

Speaking of which, part of their September stash was gone. Something had chewed through the plastic and then through one of the foil-wrapped pouches of kibble. Red squirrels, she thought. Raccoons would have just opened the container and taken the pouch. Well, she didn't begrudge them the food. Though she was surprised it happened in August rather than May or November. Of course, it could have happened in May, she belatedly realized. No matter. She could share her granola with Kazzi if it came to that.

September was warmer than expected. She often wore shorts and a t-shirt, and Kazzi continued to seek shade for her post-ball-chase naps. Sunsets had become barely visible from her spot, so in addition to their afternoon paddle, they often went out in the evenings to see the clouds slowly colour, into pastel pink or fiery orange …

October. For two weeks, the lake was circled with splendour, the birch becoming golden, the maples scarlet, some of the conifers amber … On one of their paddles, they discovered a pair of otters. And spent a delightful hour watching them.

November. The silver month. All of the leaves had fallen, leaving skeletons, grey and black against the pewter sky. The water gleamed like mercury. The loons were gone. As were the ducks and geese. So too, the otters. It was cold. And they were on their last food stash. Decision time.

She couldn't survive the winter in her tent. And she'd be out of food in a few weeks. Actually, that wasn't quite true. She'd cleaned out and hidden two trash cans in the forest behind her cabin. Out of sight from the road, and accessible only through rough bush, not from the trail. Then she'd made several trips over the course of a week to fill them with her stockpiled bags of rice, pasta, dried beans, lentils, chickpeas, nuts, seeds, and dried fruit. And kibble. She'd put a cinder block on top of each to make them impossible for raccoons to open. She'd wondered whether bears would raid them in the spring, but then she figured no, the road was too close. Then she figured no, there weren't any bears left.

Even so, it was too cold to stay in her tent. Yes, the winters had become warmer, but there were still a couple weeks of minus 15 or 20. And even if she could survive the winter, she didn't really want to spend six months shivering in a tent. No kayaking. Only difficult walking.

She knew of several hunt camps in the area. She'd discovered them while hiking through the forest. Unfortunately, all but one was accessible by the old logging road, which meant they were probably occupied, if not by their owners, or their owners' friends, then by the same kind of men who'd come to her cabin. The remaining camp, Foster's cabin, was past the creek, up a trail that branched off the logging road. But *really* up. ATVs could manage it (unless they got stuck in the mud in spring) and people like her. Although she'd done it a few times, years ago, she thought she could still do it. It was tempting. His cabin was on a small lake. He had an off-grid set-up, a bit of solar, a bit of propane, a bit of firewood. But if it was occupied, the hard trek would be for nothing. And then what? And if it was empty, she'd have to break a window to get in. Which would reduce its warmth, considerably. Besides which, she had no idea whether there was enough firewood in his lean-to for the winter. And she'd have to climb down and back up several times for food …

What she really wanted to do was paddle back and reclaim her own cabin. Maybe the men who'd come had gotten bored and moved on. Though if they *had* moved on, they may have trashed it first. Either intentionally or just out of carelessness. Perhaps *all* of her windows would be broken.

More likely, all of her firewood would be gone. She couldn't imagine they would have replenished the supply; it would have been a lot of work, going into the forest, sawing downed trees into manageable pieces, carrying them back … And it would have required forethought. A consideration of the consequences of their actions. Which, no doubt, had included huge drunken bonfires every night. She suspected it hadn't even occurred to them to wonder how they'd stay warm all winter long. (And they say men are the logical ones.) Let alone wonder whether there was a fire ban …

No, their modus operandi was probably 'use it and move on'. After all, they were no different than the men who ran the hundred companies that had destroyed Earth. More to the point, the men who ran those companies were no different than the men who'd taken over her cabin. Why should she have expected otherwise? The gratuitous damage. (No, not completely gratuitous. They *enjoyed* wrecking things. Blowing things up.) The expectation that someone else would clean it up. (They 'externalized' their waste disposal costs.) The failure to comprehend the losses that were due to their actions. Which was perhaps due to their inability to perceive beauty, to experience joy independent of conquest …

She could perhaps scavenge in the forest for— No, she couldn't. There wouldn't be enough time. The snow would soon cover it all

And even if she *could* move back in, who's to say *another* gang wouldn't come the next month, the next week, the next *day* …

Maybe things had gotten better over the last six months. Then again, although 'better' might mean vaccinations for the pandemics, what could it possibly mean for the environment? The global warming would continue. The effects would worsen. 'Better' might mean that the government had gotten back on its feet, declared the province, the country, a state of emergency (again)—and instituted martial law. 'Better' might mean that her cabin was still appropriated, but *officially* now, rather than unofficially. Because over 1,000 square feet of living space on a whole acre of land for one person? She may be required to house additional people. No, more likely, all of the crown land around her would be cleared for temporary housing, a trailer park for refugees, evacuees… She didn't want to live like that. Maybe for a few months, but not for the rest of her life. Which would be the case. Because it would never be like it was. 'Temporary' would be 'permanent'. Well, until— She sighed. Deeply.

Maybe she could implement Plan A. There was a lot of food in her car. A lot of everything in her car. But if *her* cabin was unavailable, what were the odds some other cabin would be available? And even if she could find something, she'd have all the same problems. Warmth, food, security.

And even if she had that— It wasn't enough. Life was, could be, should be, so much more than that. She missed her bed, she missed her couch, she missed her window—funny how no one had invented a see-through tent—but she also missed her stereo system, her laptop, electricity and indoor plumbing, hot showers …

She decided to make the trip. Partly out of curiosity, partly because if there was even a slight chance she could regain her cabin-on-a-lake-in-the-forest— It would be a long trip. Three hours to get to the rapids, two hours to get through them, then another— No, wait. It occurred to her that she could leave her kayak at the top of the rapids and make her way from that point on foot, coming out behind her cabin. It would be a hard trek, because she'd have to go through what she called Canadian jungle, but it wouldn't take as long as negotiating that difficult stretch of slimy rocks in her hipwaders. If she could reclaim her cabin, she could come back for her kayak the next day. If not, well, yeah. Long trip.

About an hour before the rapids, Kazzi could smell it. Half an hour later, so could she. There had been a fire. Probably caused by one of the forementioned huge drunken bonfires. Or maybe by some guy who'd just tossed his cigarette. Because that's what real men do. (She recalled that when she'd had the extra room and semi-basement added to her cabin, she'd had to spend hours afterwards, picking up every single cigarette butt tossed by the construction crew, as well as every piece of discarded packaging and what have you. If a woman had been on the crew, and a smoker, she would've asked for a can or something to use as an ashtray. She was sure of it.)

She didn't have a map of where exactly the river ran, but the part she was on and the fork to the right, to the greater rapids, must have stopped the fire from reaching her spot. And, typically, the wind blew down the river, not up. She didn't see any smoke, so perhaps it was done, burned out, and she was smelling just the charred wood. All that carbon, she thought ... And her cabin.

So. It was over. She'd come to the end.

She rested a bit, then turned around, and slowly headed back, cursing the stupidity of—well, men, mostly. They'd had the power. So they'd had the responsibility. And they'd acted like children. No, worse than children. Most children care about others. And about right and wrong, about what's fair and what's not.

The loss. She sighed at the magnitude of the loss. The beauty, the joy, the utter delight— Life on earth was, could be, exquisite. Yes, she'd had it better, much better, than most, but with thoughtful management of population and resources, there was no reason why, after a certain point in time, everyone couldn't've had the same quality of life.

And it was utterly unnecessary. The loss. All this, she looked out across the ever-stunningly-beautiful water and forest, would be gone because of men who wanted more, who wanted to be bigger, men who valued power, who valued victory over everything else. Men who dismissed caring about beauty and joy as wimpy. She recalled a poem she'd read a while ago, titled "Masculinity Kills." It had been an understatement.

She also recalled a line from some tv show: one of the aliens taking over had said to a protesting human, *You don't deserve this planet.* The alien was absolutely right. We didn't—

Well, right except for the over-inclusivity.

Then again, maybe it wasn't over-inclusive. Because how is it that the rest of us *let* such men *have* power, *take* power? Well, easy. Though it was a lesson she herself had learned quite late, when one of her neighbours, angry at her for calling the township to ask about bylaws concerning cutting down trees along the shoreline, had kicked Tassi. Hard. She'd wanted to protest, to retaliate— But she knew that that would just make it worse, would 'make' him do something worse. Because the truth of the matter is that the person with the least ethics wins.

So if we'd tried, if we'd tried *harder*, done *more*, to stop them, to prevent the dumping, the drilling, the clearcutting ... they would've killed us.

So what should, what *could*, we have done? Euthanize, or at least exile, at the first sign of—what? Gross inconsideration of others? Willingness to hurt others? Perhaps.

Because, she thought, as she stared at the river ahead of her, they killed us anyway.

And now— It wasn't going to get any better. It was going to get worse. She didn't want to live as a survivalist. That was regression. For someone to whom beauty, and thought, were paramount, having to spend most of one 's time and energy on food, water, and warmth was ... frustrating. It suddenly occurred to her that that's why so many people, perhaps mostly men, were enjoying these last years. It favoured them. It favoured the bully with the muscle and the guns who would just *take* food, water, warmth. No matter that in the long-term, they couldn't produce any *more* food, water, warmth. There would *be* no long term.

And so on the next warm, sunny day, after a vigorous ball-throw-chase with Kazzi, she spent the rest of the morning sitting down by the water, staring at the sparkles, the little dog napping by her side. She listened to one more album, remembering Tassi and the truly good life they'd had together. That afternoon, she went for one last, slow, kayak around the lake, Kazzi, so like Tassi, perched on the prow ... After, she threw Kazzi's ball for her again until she was ready to stop. Then one last treat, one last snoogle, and then as she lay beside her, tired, happy, she took the prepared syringe from the small black bag she'd packed and injected the sedative. Kazzi gave a short yelp at the prick. "I'm sorry, sweetheart," she said, then watched as she quickly, too quickly, fell asleep. Then she took the other prepared syringe, carefully felt for the vein, then injected the phenobarbitol. She gathered Kazzi in her arms then, feeling her weight, her soft fur, and just sat. Too sad to cry.

After a long while, when she was sure that Kazzi was indeed dead—the thought of her *not* being dead, but regaining consciousness to find that she herself— She bundled her up and set her gently into the kayak, set the black bag beside her, picked up her paddle, then pushed off. She headed to just the right spot, then put on her headphones and selected one last memory of exquisite joy. Then she took the razor blade from the bag, made one long careful slice, and swallowed as many sleeping pills as she could. And then she settled back, cradling Kazzi in her right arm, dangling her left in the water, to remember—everything, to lament        everything,
and                        to watch                        the sun